SUPERNOVA

ERICKA WALLER

GW00902041

CONTENTS

APRIL

*S*he took a deep breath and pushed open the door leading into the maths corridor.

The second it closed behind her, she felt the first wave coming on. Her legs suddenly felt too weak to support her, her heart raced, and her palms became sweaty. Then it got worse...

Her vision blurred, making objects around her swim and swirl. She went into a dream mode, as if the world was moving in slow motion. Each sound became a drawn-out roar, every movement a graceful dance – all enveloped in a sickening soft focus that April knew all too well. Waves of fear were crashing over her, drowning her.

On unsteady feet, she pressed a hand to the cool wall tiles, running the fingertips along the grooves of the grouting as she walked. It grounded her a little and she managed to stay upright. All April wanted to do was to run. She had no idea where she'd go, but it was what her gut was telling her to do. She pressed herself into the wall a little harder.

Approaching full-blown panic, April felt as if she was going crazy. Nobody else appeared to be struggling with walking down the corridor. Everyone around her was laughing, or pushing and shoving, bending heads close to bitch and gossip. Boys bounced footballs off the walls, and the squeak of rubber trainers screeched in her ears.

The bell rang, making her jump and clutch her hand to her chest. Class was about to start. She took the excuse to run, and bolted down the corridor.

April found that it helped to break her school day down into manageable units. Most classes were sixty minutes long. Sixty minutes of not leaping from her seat and racing out the door. Sixty minutes of keeping herself from falling apart, whilst pretending that she was just fine, and listening to the teacher. Sixty minutes that would feel like an eternity.

Checking the exits and calculating the quickest exit route from any room she was in had become second nature to April. It was one of her many coping mechanisms. She already knew the fastest way of getting out of any classroom and corridor in the school, but she habitually worked them out again each time she sat down for a lesson. By the end of morning classes each day, April would already be exhausted.

Lunchtime brought its own set of horrors, of course. How far from the door would she have to sit today? How many staring faces would she have to run past if something happened? What if all the stalls in the girls' toilets (her most reliable refuge) were locked? What if she choked on one of her chips?

It's best not to eat at all, she thought. *Best to skip lunch altogether.*

Her best friend Jamie was waiting for her outside the main entrance to the dining hall. Jamie always skipped lunch, spending the money on cigarettes instead. She was wearing her trademark scowl; her arms were crossed, and she glared at anyone who came too close. She was tall, with black hair and a pale face. She looked pretty scary, until you got to know her and then realised she wasn't scary at all.

Well, not that scary.

Jamie spotted April coming her way and gave a half smile, then pushed herself off the wall and headed down the corridor next to the dining hall, which led to an exit to the top playground. She was on her way to the bike sheds at the back of the playground, her favourite place to smoke. Jamie needed her smoke breaks like April needed her fresh air ones.

As Jamie lit up a Silk Cut, April took in a lungful of crisp September air... and then another.

"What's the point of Religious Education?" Jamie said, sucking on the end of her cigarette angrily. "It's an utter waste of time. Thirty-five minutes of my life I can't ever get back." April knew this was a rhetorical question and that she wasn't supposed to answer. Jamie wanted to rant, which suited April fine; she just wanted to breathe.

"We don't even learn anything useful - just a bunch of religious bollocks, a load of rules to live by. Religion is just a list of stuff you can't do. Where's the fun in that?"

The end of Jamie's cigarette glowed redly in the gloom of the shed as she puffed away. "We could be learning about stuff that might actually be of benefit."

Pause...inhale...exhale...

"Even bloody PE is better than RE and I bloody hate PE. Gym knickers, really? What is this, the 1940s?"

April breathed in and out in time with Jamie's smoking and felt her body relaxing.

Jamie was too lost in her angry tirade to notice April's silence. "And why do boys get to wear shorts and we have

3

to wear knickers? Why do boys get to do basketball and we go on trampolines? I'm fifteen, not five."

April hated the gym knickers too. The girls' changing rooms were at the end of the English block, two long corridors away from the sports hall. She imagined everyone could see her skinny knees knocking together as she walked. She also hated the trampoline. She felt untethered enough to reality as it was. Trying to turn *pikes* into *front flips* - which turned her world upside down - only made her feel worse. There was only one trampoline too, so everyone else had to stand in line watching.

April hated people watching her.

"Plus, I had to partner with Claire," Jamie seethed. Claire was the most popular girl in school and Jamie's nemesis. They'd been friends once at primary school, but when got to high school, everything had changed overnight. Claire arrived on the first day in a short skirt, with a new haircut and a brand-new attitude. The new attitude went especially well with the brand-new group of girls she had suddenly found to hang out with. Claire blew Jamie out, right in front of everyone. Jamie had never got over it.

April was secretly grateful to Claire for dropping Jamie; it meant she could have her for herself. April was quiet, and tended (if not preferred) to blend into the background. She hated drawing attention to herself and found it hard to speak up. This made it hard to make friends.

Jamie had walked into their first maths lesson, thrown herself down into the empty chair next to April and thrust out her hand: "My name is Jamie, ignore what the teachers call me. I hate the Spice Girls, any kind of segregation and Claire Wilks. Especially Claire Wilks. I'm an A student in all subjects and I don't care if you copy my homework. Wanna be friends?"

April had been stunned by Jamie's forthrightness; so

confident and self-assured. She was everything April wasn't. Jamie seemed so much older than everyone else, like she'd already done this growing up stuff before and had had it all worked out. Jamie knew exactly who she was. All April knew was who she wasn't. April felt like she was full of holes.

Her brain had scrambled for a response. Back then, even on that first day, she'd been frantically trying to work out her exit route when Jamie had interrupted. It was almost impossible, because this new school was ten times bigger than her old school had been and she had no idea where she was, or where the door to the playground was.

Jamie took April's silence as agreement, and that had been that. She dug into April's bag, pulled out her schedule, and ran her black painted nail down it. "We have maths together, science together, history, French…" she broke off and said, "Cool. You're in all the top sets too. Maybe I can copy *your* homework?" she grinned at April and it made her whole face soften. The frown line faded from between her eyes, showing how young she really was. Maybe they were the same age after all.

Jamie wore a lot of black mascara, which made her lashes look like spider legs, complemented with a dark plum lipstick. By the end of the day, she'd have been made to wash it off three times, by three different teachers. Jamie would wipe it off as instructed, before reapplying it all over again for the next class. Maybe Jamie's make-up was her war armour, April wondered, as she watched Jamie deftly remove any trace of her actual features with charcoal eyeliner. Maybe Jamie needed to hide her face to feel safe, while April needed to know how to get out. They were both war strategies she supposed.

They worked well together. Jamie was loud and liked talking fast. She was quick, sarcastic and frighteningly bright. She challenged all her teachers on everything, and never made any notes.

In contrast, April would write everything down and never participate in class discussions unless she absolutely *had* to. They were both at the top of the 'top' sets. Both were big readers, and, like April, Jamie had usually read the books assigned to them in English class already, although they tended to have very different views on them.

Jamie forced opinions out of April. She'd tap her on the head and say: "Hello? I know this head works, tell me what you think" and slowly April would put across her interpretation of a poem, or novel.

Being such opposites, they were perfect partners. In science class, Jamie would throw herself into the experiments, casually tossing in more of all the chemicals whenever the teacher wasn't looking. She was obsessed with trying to blow things up. April would hastily make notes of all the reactions and try to keep Jamie from setting fire to herself.

Jamie was a *supernova* - a catastrophic explosion that ejected mass. She was a star that dazzled with brightness - her words, her energy, her adamant determination to do things her way. She was powerful, and she used that power in everything she did.

April tried to do whatever felt easiest, or whatever might make her disappear. She was a black hole, with a gravitational field so intense that neither matter nor radiation could escape its pull. The worst part for April was that she couldn't escape from herself.

They became the perfect team: Jamie lit up April's darkness and, somehow, April stopped Jamie from burning out.

"Claire spent the whole lesson talking about how she got it on with Alex at the weekend" Jamie said, stubbing her cigarette out on the wall before flicking it into a corner, where a tiny ember still glowed.

"Like anyone cares. Like she's the first person to have been there. Sheesh, who hasn't?"

"I haven't" April said. She hadn't been anywhere. She didn't go to parties and she'd never snogged a boy. She wasn't sure Jamie had either, but she never asked. Jamie would just scoff at her and say something about how she refused to mould herself into a typical teenage girl, who only cared about boys and fashion and what was expected of her by her 'peers'.

"Why would you want to? An utter waste of time" Jamie said, fishing around in her bag for a mirror to reapply her lipstick. "It's your choice that you haven't had a tongue-sandwich yet anyway" she added, rubbing her finger over her teeth to check for lipstick marks. "You could always ask Tom to make an honest woman of you" she said this with her trademark sneer.

April blushed slightly and looked at the cigarette ends and Golden Wonder crisp packets littering the floor. She decided to turn the conversation back to Claire Wilks and what she said she'd been doing with Alex at the weekend.

Jamie filled her in on the details of some great party they'd both missed (she made quote marks with her fingers as she said the word 'great'), while she inhaled another cigarette. As she finished smoking it down to the butt, the bell rang, signalling the end of lunch. Jamie was already marching back into school, muttering something about 'local bikes'.

April squared her shoulders and prepared herself for a double science class. This was a little easier to do than usual as science was one of her favourite subject: physics particularly. She could spend the next two hours experimenting and theorising about the possibilities of the universe, rather than fighting off ever-worsening bouts of anxiety. It was so difficult to comprehend, she had something to blame the light-headedness on.

As she made her way back into the building a few steps behind her best friend, her mind strayed to thoughts of her other friend, Tom, and then she thought of kissing.

April had been so busy convincing Jamie that they were only friends (and that was all that she wanted), she'd almost managed to convince herself. She had to. There was no way she could be anything more than friends with Tom, even if *he* wanted to be (which she doubted). If she let him get too close, he would start to see that she was not quite normal. Like in *The Terminator* – Arnold Schwarzenegger's murderous robot assassin appeared to be 100% human, until you got a look under his skin. April was not a murderous robot, obviously, but she was a very faulty version of a human.

She could never let Tom see her crazy side; she needed him too much. Being with Tom was the only time her life didn't feel surreal. Mostly she felt as if she was floating above everyone else, detached and alone. Tom was her ladder, helping her climb back down to earth.

She thought back to their walk to school that morning. They'd huddled together to share Tom's tinny headphones, so they could both listen to Beck's *Odelay*. Tom loved music and was always raving about some cool new band he'd discovered. When he'd realised April's music collection was non-existent and that she didn't know a thing about Britpop, or about any music at all, he'd taken it upon himself to educate her.

Each day he'd have a different cassette in his Walkman for her to listen to. Tom's enthusiasm for music was infectious. She fell in love with his tapes as hard as she was falling for him; Blur, Suede, Menswear, Sleeper, Ash: so many new names that it made her head spin.

She loved the older stuff he made her listen to as well. The Pixies, The Beatles, The Doors, The Jesus and Mary Chain. He often let her take the tapes home for the night and April would play them over and over. She'd written out the lyrics to her favourite songs and pinned them next to her bed, so she could trace her fingers over them at night and remember Tom singing them quietly under his breath.

"How do you get crazy with a cheese whiz, Tom?" she'd asked him that morning as they listened to Beck croon through the headphones at them.

"Lord knows, but I want to. I don't even know what a cheese whiz is, and I still want to."

"What if it's a person who knows loads about cheese? Someone who just bores other people by telling them blue cheese and gorgonzola and brie are exposed to mould to help them age properly. I don't know how crazy I'd want to get with him."

"God April, you are *so* hot when you talk about cheese. Would you *brie* mine?" Tom turned to look at her as he asked. She noticed, as usual, how greenie-blue his eyes were. They had yellow flecks at the centre. She'd read once that yellow flecks were a sign of a deformed gene. Before that, deformed genes always seemed like a bad thing.

His gaze was intent, and it almost felt like he was being serious, until he cocked up his left eyebrow and waggled it.

"That depends, can you promise me a *gouda* time?" she quipped back.

"You'd be amazed at my *maturity*" he replied.

When she looked up at him he was grinning at her. That lopsided grin which she would often conjure up to stop herself from running out of class screaming *Get me away from my broken mind! Run, don't walk, from my mind!* That grin always made her stomach flip. She desperately tried to think of a quip, anything - anything to stop the images of him amazing her with his maturity. She might be in a permanent battle not to bail on school to race home and hide under her covers, but she was still a 15-year old girl. He'd be very welcome to hide under the covers with her.

"Cheesus, that was lame" she said eventually and put her headphone back in.

When she was with Tom, teenage banter came easily to her (except when it got flirty and her heart beat so erratically she thought she might have a seizure). Talking to Tom was like reading her favourite book. She would lose herself in him, and everything else would fade away. It was just her, Tom, and nothing else. He was like a bubble around her. She knew, if she tripped, Tom would be there to catch her. If her legs gave way, he would break her fall.

Jamie always ribbed April about Tom, even though he and Jamie were great mates. They were April's pillars, and between the two of them she felt almost invincible. April had worried herself sick they wouldn't get on. She and Tom had been friends for a while before Jamie had come on the scene. She didn't ever want to have to swap one for the other. When would April learn how often she worried about stuff that didn't happen?

Tom and April both lived in a tiny village that hung off the end of the town "like a third nipple" as Tom had succinctly described it. They'd seen one another around the local shops and post office a million times growing up but had never spoken. He was good-looking, and he played football all the time. She was quiet and read books. Sometimes she'd see him and his dad in the park kicking a ball around and laughing together, while his mum and little sister watched from the swings.

When April's mum heard that Tom's dad had died, she sent April round to his house with a homemade moussaka, some flowers from the garden, and their address and phone number scrawled on a piece of ripped-out notepaper, with the words *call me anytime* underlined twice in black marker. The gesture was very 'her mum', but April really hadn't wanted to go. It had felt awkward and she'd felt nosy and intrusive standing on his doorstep, massive casserole dish in hand.

Tom took ages to come to the door. April was about to give up, leave it by a plant pot and slip away, but then she heard the lock opening.

"Hi," she said awkwardly, when Tom appeared in the doorway. He looked tired and years older than when she'd last seen him. He'd stared at her, looking slightly surprised, but didn't say anything.

"My mum sent you this. It's moussaka." Her voice was uneven when she spoke.

"Mousse-what-a?" Tom said, frowning at her as he ran his hand through his hair and sniffed in the direction of the pot.

"Um, moussaka" she said again. "It's Greek. It has aubergines in it."

At that moment, she remembered a line from *Dirty Dancing* where Baby says: "I carried a watermelon" and decided that was a far better line than "It has aubergines in it" and wanted to curl up on the floor with embarrassment.

"Okay…" he said slowly. When he reached to take it out of her hands, and couldn't right away, she realised that she was clutching it tightly to her chest. "You seem unwilling to part with it" he said, smiling slightly. "Is it your favourite? I wouldn't want to deprive you of it. You can keep it if you want, go take it down the park and eat it all with your hands. I won't tell. In fact, I'll lend you a fork if you like," he was teasing her, and she felt her cheeks heat up.

"NO!" she said in protest, "it's for you!" She thrust it into his arms roughly and the flowers that had been balanced on top began sliding off. She made a move to grab them and shoved them back on top of the dish. Inwardly she'd cursed her mum again. What fifteen-year-old girl gave a boy flowers?

"I'm sorry" she said, "Mum made me bring it. I was just going to leave the stuff on the doorstep, but her cooking sometimes needs an explanation." God, why had she said that? She couldn't seem to help herself. Instead of stopping she said: "Not that you have to eat it, you can just give it to the dog or whatever." In her head, she was telling herself to shut up, but when she looked at Tom again he was still smiling slightly.

"We don't have a dog," he said to her. "I'll eat it though, if you've finished cuddling it?" He was smiling widely now.

He had a great smile and April felt her face soften in return. She gave him a small grin: "Ha ha" Her arms didn't know what to do now they no longer had the pot to hold - they hung limply at her sides and felt too big for her body. She tried crossing them over her chest, but then worried she looked defensive, so she dropped them back down to her sides again, swinging them slightly. *Who invented arms*, she wondered, *and why make them so long*?

Tom lifted the casserole lid and peered inside, a waft of garlic and onion filling the air. "Smells good" he said, "seriously good." He seemed to mean it and April relaxed, her arms shrinking back to their normal length all of a sudden. They stood there staring at one another for a few seconds before she heard Tom's sister calling him from inside the house. He stopped grinning abruptly.

"I'd better go," he said. "Thanks, for coming over and the Mouss... um, dinner."

"Of course!" she said hurriedly, embarrassed she'd kept him when he obviously needed to get back indoors. She turned and walked away quickly, her cheeks flaming, again.

A week later he appeared at her door with the empty casserole dish. April was so shocked to see him she dropped the book she'd been holding. He passed her the pot, which she put on the hall table, then bent down to pick the book up for her. He looked briefly at the front cover before handing it over.

"Just bringing your dish back," he said, shoving his now empty hands in his back pockets. "You were right, it was delicious. Even Em ate some and she normally only eats yellow food." April laughed lightly, and fiddled with the book. Tom seemed relaxed enough, leaning against the doorframe. He had longish hair that poked out all over his head. He wore faded blue jeans, a stripy red, white and blue t-shirt and scuffed old trainers.

He was tall, so that April had to tilt her head up to look at him. "Hey, we go to the same school, right?" he asked her suddenly. April nodded, surprised he'd noticed her. They didn't have any classes together and rarely passed one another in the hallways. He was normally surrounded by his friends, a group of loud and brash boys that April tended to shrink away from.

"I think so," April said.

"Which way do you walk?" Tom asked her suddenly.

"I, um, I go along the canal and then cut up through Bucks Meadow," she said.

"Do you walk on your own?" he frowned. "The canal is a bit bleak."

"I don't mind it." She quite liked it. It was much quieter than walking on the main road into town, where vans beeped at her, buses rushed by and the road ahead stretched out with nowhere to slip away and hide. The canal path was narrow, but usually empty of other people. She would watch the ducks and peer into portholes of the barges moored up in the reeds.

Tom didn't say much else after that, he just asked her to thank her mum for him, and told her he would see her later.

The next Monday he was stood by the first lock on the canal. It was right next to the hole in the hedge that had been well trodden over the years, as a shortcut off the main road.

"Morning!" he was smoking a cigarette which he flicked into the bush as she neared.

"Hi?" she said questioningly, wondering what he was doing there. Had he been waiting for her? Should she stop or carry on walking? Her arms did their growing-long thing again. She hoisted up her backpack to give them something to do, and decided to keep going. When he fell into step beside her, she supposed he had in fact been waiting for her, and the thought made her stomach do a small flip.

She had no idea what to say to him. They were in completely different leagues at school, and though neither of them had a dad anymore, their circumstances were very different. April thought they had nothing in common at all.

Tom didn't seem to notice April's awkwardness, he simply pulled out his cassette player and offered her an earphone. "Ever heard of The Charlatans?" he asked. When April shook her head, he thrust the speaker into her hand and said: "You're going to love them, they're like the Moussaka of music."

"Are they Greek then?" April asked.

Tom roared with laughter "No, they're from Cheshire, but I'm sure they like aubergines."

She blushed, as she seemed to do all the time around him, and put the tiny speaker to her ear.

He'd appeared by the lock every day since then, and he would always wait outside the chapel for her at the end of school. She never asked him why he walked with her, or why he never hung around with his old football friends anymore and he never told her. He was just there every morning and every afternoon with his trademark cigarette hanging from his lips, and his messy hair all over the place.

He always smiled when he saw her, and asked her about her day. In turn, April started to become less shy and awkward around him. He seemed to find her funny, and would throw his head back and laugh when she told him stories about Jamie. "I've got to meet this chick," he said. "I just can't imagine the two of you together."

A couple of weeks later, April asked Jamie if she wanted to stay at hers for a sleepover. "Finally," Jamie said good-naturedly "I thought you'd never bloody ask."

The following Friday afternoon April, Jamie and Tom all walked home together - Jamie firing questions at Tom the whole time. He batted questions back at her with a speed that made April feel dizzy. She flicked her gaze from Tom to Jamie as they had a furious row about Courtney Love, who Jamie thought was the best female singer in the world and Tom thought was responsible for Kurt Cobain's death.

April had no idea who Courtney Love was, but sensed she was going to be crucial to their friendship. Jamie and Tom squabbled over the location of a gun, the position Kurt was found in, the last gig he'd played and his last public appearance with Courtney. Jamie seemed to have done more homework on the subject than Tom and so of course was winning the argument. Tom seemed to realise this and changed tactics to try to find some more common ground.

They both agreed Dave Grohl was *amazing* and the Foo Fighters were *awesome*.

When Jamie asked Tom if he could score her some weed, their friendship was sealed, and they became a trio.

A couple of weeks later, Tom met them by the village shop and introduced them to Yuki and that was that, the group was complete.

2

—————————————————————————

TOM

"*H*ello? Mum, I'm home," Tom called out, throwing his record bag on the porch floor and pushing open the door into the tiny kitchen.

He sighed at the sight before him. The breakfast bowls he hadn't had time to wash up before he left for school were still on the table. Spilt milk had seeped into a bundle of unopened post next to them. *Bugger*. His mum hadn't moved at all today then. Again.

The red light on the washing machine flashed frantically at him; it had stopped halfway through a cycle. The spin function must have packed up again. Emily's ballet kit was in there, and she'd need it that afternoon. They didn't have a tumble dryer, but he couldn't let her go to class in wet clothes.

He dumped the dirty bowls in the sink on his way to the machine, where he pulled out the soaking wet washing. He'd have to look at the machine later to see if he could fix it again. Right now, he had twenty minutes to get Emily's snack and kit ready and get to her primary school, which was a ten-minute walk away.

The hairdryer was still on the armrest of the sofa, where he'd left it after Emily's Sunday hair wash. He turned it on to the warm setting and, with some difficulty, positioned it in front of the ballet kit, which he'd hastily hung as flat as possible on the clothes-horse.

While frantically hanging the rest of the clothes, he heard a *thump* from upstairs. He paused to see if footsteps would follow.

After he'd heard nothing more he raced back into the kitchen and hunted through the cupboards for something to feed Emily. She was always hungry after school, yet fussy in her food requirements. At the back of the cupboard he found a pack of raisins. He picked an apple from the fruit bowl and polished it on his sleeve, then hastily made a peanut butter sandwich. He cut the crusts off, and used a pastry cutter to make it into a star shape, before squashing it flat under his hand.

He wrapped the sandwich in some second-hand cling film, and scarfed down the dry crusts. The peanut butter clung to the roof of his mouth and he ducked his head under the kitchen sink to gulp at the lukewarm water.

Tom looked at his watch - he had three minutes before he had to leave. He started running water over the dirty dishes in the sink, then remembered the hairdryer was still on. "Bugger" he swore again quietly and raced back into the living room. The suit wasn't completely dry, but it wasn't as wet as it had been either. If he flapped it in the breeze all the way to school, maybe it would be okay.

Tom tossed the suit, some battered pink ballet shoes, and the snacks into a bag, then cast a final look at his watch. He had one minute before he had to leave. What could he do in one minute to make it nicer for Em when she got home? Returning to the kitchen, he rummaged in the vegetable basket for some potatoes. He had to dig out a few green shoots, but they were still good. He pricked them with a fork, rolled them in salt and put them in the oven for dinner.

Tom had once told Emily that the green shoots that grew out of older potatoes were called 'eyes'. Ever since then, she couldn't bear to watch him remove them. "Don't cut their eyes out, Tommy!" she begged him. "They won't be able to see". He'd tried to explain that potatoes didn't need to see - that it was actually better that they couldn't, being as they were about to be eaten - but that only upset her more. And that was before she saw him stab holes in them. After that she had called him *Potato Killer* for weeks. He'd even found drawings she'd made of potatoes with big black holes for eyes, topped with long eyelashes.

It had taken weeks for her to eat a potato again, and he *really* needed her to eat them. Potatoes were filling and easy to cook, but more importantly, they were cheap.

He paused at the bottom of the stairs to see if any of the movement had woken his mother. He could see the upstairs hall light was still on, and her bedroom door was closed. That would be a *no* then.

Sighing, he heaved his bag back on his shoulder and let himself out of the front door. He jogged down the hill and through the park to Em's school, the same primary school he'd gone to. As he ran, the ballet suit flapped in the wind.

Emily was her usual hyper self, pirouetting all the way home (well, her version of). She wasn't pleased about her dinner, but Tom managed to persuade her no potatoes had been blinded in the making of them.

He'd finally got her down to sleep, after three stories and three choruses of 'She'll be coming round the mountain when she comes', which was Em's current favourite song. She loved it when he made up new verses, but tonight he'd been tired, and eager for some time alone. He stroked her hair instead, trying to gently free the knots with his fingers.

When her eyelids finally gave up their battle to stay open, he crept downstairs, slipped out the back door and made his way down the garden. He paused at the bottom to pull a loose plank aside and squeezed though the gap.

"Hey man," said Yuki as Tom opened his shed door and walked in.

Yuki's was the first Chinese family Tom had ever seen. When they'd moved into the house behind Tom's ten years ago, Tom had watched them through the cracks in their shared fence. He marvelled at the exotic carpets and ornate lamps they laid out to air on the lawn. The smell of their cooking wafted across the fence towards him, spicy and fragrant. It was nothing like the food his mum made. His dad liked *traditional English grub* so that was what they had. Shepherd's pie, sausage and mash, fish and chips, or maybe a good old fry-up.

Tom would take his cheese sandwich outside at lunch and watch as Yuki sat cross-legged on the lawn eating rice with long wooden sticks. His fingers moved so fast they blurred. Yuki fascinated Tom. Everything about him seemed exciting and different. One day, after his family had lived next door for a couple of months, Yuki had walked over to the fence, pressed his eye up to a hole in the slats (the exact one Tom used to spy on him) and said "Stop staring and come over to climb the tree."

Yuki had no trace of a Chinese accent, which disappointed Tom, but Yuki's mum did. She came out while they were up the tree and called out: "Yuki, you come in now. Too much time in tree. No time unpacking room still."

The boys had stopped climbing the tree after a couple of years and started reading comics, then riding bikes, and then smoking – cigarettes first, followed by weed.

Yuki was two years older than Tom and his mum never bothered coming to the shed to check on him. His dad had gone back to China a couple of months after they'd moved. He imported antiques and spent most of his time away at markets and fairs, finding stock to sell.

Tom was pretty sure that Yuki's mum knew he sat around getting stoned in the shed, but as long as he drove her to work each morning and helped her with the shopping, she didn't seem to care.

"Hey man," Tom replied. "Christ…" he plucked the lit joint from between Yuki's fingers and inhaled deeply "…what a day" he sighed as he exhaled.

Yuki cleared a space for him on the mouldy old futon and Tom sank down gratefully.

"I can't be long, dude. I've got stuff to do before morning."

Yuki nodded, "All good, man."

Yuki never asked much about what was going on at home, but Tom knew he must see the bedroom curtains – that once opened at the crack of dawn every day, were now almost permanently closed. He'd never see Tom's mum hanging out the washing, it was always Tom, and he knew that Tom never came over in the evenings until Emily was asleep. Tom guessed Yuki knew it was him that put her to bed each evening.

Tom felt a little better after a few tokes - calmer, steadier. He never smoked more than one on a school night, (he had to get Em ready every morning) but he'd *needed* this. By the time he'd made breakfast, got them both to school and back, made dinner, helped Em with her homework (at the expense of his own) and finally got her down to sleep – he'd be exhausted, and his mind would buzz with all the things he hadn't done. The weed silenced the buzzing.

Yuki had his leather trousers on, as usual. He was obsessed

with Jim Morrison and, whenever possible, he would proffer one of his quotes or some sage lyrics that he felt applied to the situation at hand. They rarely did. A collection of The Doors posters adorned the back wall of the shed and a giant confederate flag was pinned up on the opposite.

There were windows cut into the side of the shed which Yuki used to spy on the neighbours. Sometimes he became paranoid that they were onto him: "Drugs are a bet with your mind…" he'd whispered to Tom more than once - proving to Tom just how true that particular Jim Morrison quote was - as he peered out from behind the corner of the sheet he'd draped over the window.

"Man, you need to get out more," Tom had laughed.

Yuki wasn't paranoid tonight. He was calm, sitting cross-legged on the futon, shirt open to the waist, nodding along to 'This is the End' playing on a little boombox on the floor.

Beautiful friend… Tom said the line in his head as he tipped his head back and smoked the rest of the joint.

He stayed until the end of the song, before standing up to bump fists with Yuki.

"Ride the snake, man," Yuki told him as he headed out the door.

"All the way to the river," Tom replied as he shut the door behind him and walked home.

APRIL

"*R*ight, you know the drill," Jamie said, taking a last drag of her cigarette before stubbing it out and beginning the ritual of 'walking-into-the-house.'

Jamie pulled a pack of wet wipes from her bag and used one all over her fingers to get rid of the smell of smoke and nicotine. Then she unwrapped two sticks of Wrigley's Juicy Fruit and stuffed them into her mouth, before finally scooping out a dollop of Vick's Vapour Rub with her finger and wiping it over her chest and then lightly around the cuffs of her sleeves.

"Why Vicks?" April asked, "You don't have a cold - won't your mum just be suspicious?"

"No," said Jamie, screwing the lid back on the pot and putting it in her bag. She'd spent a few days one summer slowly and sneakily digging out a hole at the bottom of her garden wall, where she'd loosened a brick. It was her secret place to hide her cigarettes and lighter and she did so now.

Once Jamie had made sure her brick was back in place, she shoved her face in April's and asked: "Do I smell?"

"Yes" April said. "Of Vicks, when you don't have a cold."

"Noooo…" said Jamie slowly, using another wet wipe to remove her eye make-up. "I don't have a cold, but Mum thinks I have allergies, and she thinks the menthol helps my permanently blocked airwaves." She pulled the wipe away and studied it, then went back to scrubbing it over her eyes.

April waited patiently while Jamie removed the last traces of her mascara and lipstick. She balled up the used wet wipes and passed them to April, who already had her hand stretched out. She stuffed them in the pocket of her own rucksack, just in case Jamie's mum did a random bag search, which was pretty often. April put her hand back out for Jamie's make-up bag, which always followed the wet wipes.

Finally, Jamie pulled out her school tie and re-fastened it, grimacing. School ties were optional, but her mum always insisted she wear one. She normally had to wear the optional school blazer too, but even Jamie's mum had admitted it was a bit too hot for that right now.

Jamie peered in her compact mirror one last time, then declared she was "Ready for the Gestapo! Oh, actually – hang on…" She stopped again and reached deep into her bag to retrieve a small crackling bundle.

"Bloody hell, almost forgot." She opened her hand to show she was clutching a brand-new mascara and a compact of black eye-shadow, still in their plastic wrapping with security tags attached. She promptly passed them to April.

"Come on, take them," she said, when April hesitated.

"Jamie, you know I don't like carrying your stolen stuff for you."

"Stop being such a sissy," Jamie said, thrusting them into her hand. "And I haven't stolen them, I've merely borrowed them. When I'm rich and famous, I'll buy shares in Boots and give them a load of cash back."

"I'm not sure you can buy shares in Boots," April said dubiously.

"Whatever. I'll start up a company that doesn't test make-up products on animals and give something back that way."

"There's one already. It's called The Body Shop and you nick stuff from there too."

"Not as much stuff though," Jamie said, as if that was enough for her conscience. She brushed her hair and secured it with a large green scrunchie (which her mum had made for her) to match her uniform.

"No, but it's still... *stealing*," said April, dropping her voice on the last word.

Jamie sighed impatiently. "Look, April - do you want to spend the evening discussing the morals of *'borrowing'* (finger quote marks) from corporate giants, who pay their staff less than the minimum wage and keep all their profits in off-shore accounts, so they don't have to pay any tax on their billions?" She tugged the scrunchie tighter. "Or do you want to get into my house, do what we need to do and go out to the camp?"

"Point taken," April said, and shoved the stuff in her bag. They both took a deep breath and walked around the side of the house to knock on the front door.

Jamie wasn't allowed a key to her house. Her mum thought that if she had one she'd come home from school early and go back to bed. She was right.

"Jemima, you're five minutes late," her mum said when she opened the door. She did this surprisingly quickly, as if she'd been standing behind it, which April had no doubt was true.

"Sorry Mummy," Jamie said, dropping seamlessly into her posh voice and trying to look contrite.

"We stopped on the way home to help an elderly man off the bus and home with his shopping, didn't we April?"

April was even more scared of Jamie's mum than she was of Jamie, and didn't trust herself to speak. She nodded vigorously instead.

Jamie's mum sniffed and began again: "Why have you got Vicks on again, Jemima? Are your allergies playing up? Let me see you. Oh, your eyes are so red! I'll have to take you down to the doctor's. I'm not sure you can stay at April's tonight; I think you might be coming down with something. How inconvenient of you, this is all I need! I have a very important weekend ahead. I'm hosting a charity auction for the church, your father is away, and now this too."

She huffed and glared at April.

"NO Mum, please, I'm fine. FINE!" Jamie shouted in protest, adding in a quieter voice: "We played rounders outside this afternoon and I had to fetch the ball from the weeds at the back of the field. The pollen made my eyes a bit itchy, but I took one of the antihistamine pills you bought me. Thank you again for that, Mummy," she added, trying to smile sweetly.

April was overcome with a sudden urge to giggle and coughed into her hand.

Jamie was still trying to convince her mum that the strong fragrance of menthol was justified: "…and now I feel fine." She breathed in and out deeply in an exaggerated fashion. "See? No problem." Then she expertly changed tactic and started to suck up to her mother a little: "I know how important this weekend is for you, Mummy. When I get back from April's tomorrow, I can come and help you out if you like? I don't mind! Maybe I could clean the tables, or serve tea and cake. Did you make your yummy lemon sponge? You know how much Mr. Stephens likes your lemon sponge."

Jamie was really laying it on thick now. April wanted to dig her in the ribs to shut her up, but she was still too scared to move, too scared to even blink.

Jamie's mum looked at them both for a long minute before speaking. "While I would appreciate your help tomorrow, Jemima, you have coursework to do and violin practise in the afternoon."

"I'm up to date on my coursework - aren't I, April? We stayed in at lunch and did some extra work, you know, to um, help my allergies calm down and make up for the time we wasted playing silly rounders."

Jamie's mum seemed to approve of this. She thought sport and PE were a waste of time and was constantly going to the school to complain that they should be struck from the curriculum, so the children could focus more on their other studies. If April hadn't been a fellow A-grade student, there would have been no way Jamie would have been allowed to be friends with her. Anything less than excellence was considered a terrible influence on her daughter and Jamie's mother had insisted on seeing April's report cards and meeting her mother, before she'd allowed the friendship.

"Okay, Jemima. You can go. I'll drive you both there though. No arguments," she said, holding up a hand before Jamie could speak. "I'm not having you walking around outside with all this pollen. Now go upstairs to wash and get changed. I'd like to see your homework before we go. Yours too, April," she added, casting another look at her.

"Of course, Mrs. Fenton-Jones," said April hastily, reaching to retrieve her homework from her bag before Jamie's mum could get to it.

As April's homework diary (and corresponding work) was thoroughly inspected, Jamie went upstairs to wash-up and put on her *mufti*, as her mother called it.

April had to stifle another laugh when Jamie came back downstairs. Jamie still wasn't allowed to shop for her own clothes and was now (very reluctantly) clad in a cream blouse with shoulder pads and ruched sleeves. A pair of dark-pink cords - that stopped a couple of inches shy of her ankles, where they kicked out into a flare – finished the ensemble.

"Don't slouch, Jemima!" her mother snapped. Jamie straightened up and April saw that she was also wearing a dark-pink padded Alice-band. It made her ears stick out.

Jamie shot April a death-stare. "I'm ready Mummy, shall we go now?"

"Did you wash thoroughly with a flannel? Everywhere?" asked Mrs. Fenton-Jones briskly. "You know how you sweat in this heat."

"Yes, Mum." Jamie's smile was starting to look very strained.

"And have you packed your pyjamas and your retainer?"

"Yes, Mum," Jamie repeated, now robotically, making her way to the door with her bulging backpack.

"Why is that bag so full, Jemima?" She was suspicious now. "What on earth have you got in there?"

"All my school work," Jamie replied, not missing a beat. "April and I wanted to get a head-start on our English coursework, so I brought my whole folder home with me."

"Hmm…" Jamie's mum didn't sound entirely convinced. "That reminds me, April - I want to talk to your mother about your new *foreign* English teacher. I'm not sure about

28

her; she seems a bit wishy-washy to me. Too young, and too modern in her taste of dress.'

April stiffened and clenched her fists by her side. Miss Khan was one of her favourite teachers.

"They should have an *English* teacher teaching English." Mrs. Fenton-Jones continued, oblivious to April's increasing discomfort with this new subject.

Jamie sensed April was struggling with a desire to verbally unload on her mother and intervened: "Miss Khan follows the curriculum very strictly, Mum. Oh gosh! I forgot to tell you, she's looking for helpers to go along on the theatre trip for *An Inspector Calls* next month. Maybe you could come along and spend some time with her?"

"Is your mother going, April?" Jamie's mum demanded, turning to look at her again.

April forced herself to relax a little: "I don't think so, she's working on a big case at the moment, Mrs. Fenton-Jones."

"Yes, I'm not sure she'll be in when you drop us off tonight," Jamie said. "You mentioned she might be back late, didn't you April?"

April nodded. "Yes, she might be, um, a bit late. But not too late, of course." She knew she sounded nervous. She had no idea how Jamie managed all the lies and the secrecy. But with the way her mother treated her, Jamie didn't have a choice.

"Well, who will be looking after you then?" Jamie's mum sniffed. "I don't like the sound of this at all."

Jamie turned from the door. "Mum! We'll be fine. Please. Please let me go. April has a key and we'll let ourselves in and get on with our homework straight away."

"I don't know, maybe you should stay here…" said Mrs.

Fenton-Jones, narrowing her eyes, "…where I can keep my eye on you."

Jamie shot April a look of desperate panic.

"Please don't worry, Mrs. Fenton-Jones." April tried to speak steadily, if not confidently. "My mother is often home a little late. She will have left out some… um… cold snacks for us, so we don't need to use the oven and she'll be back well before it gets dark. We'll keep the doors locked and we can call you if we have any, um… problems."

Jamie's mum still looked unsure, so April (quite daringly for her, she thought almost proudly) pulled opened the front door. Jamie rushed out onto the drive, backpack bouncing in time to her sandal clad feet.

Mrs. Fenton-Jones made to follow them, but stopped at the door. She called out quickly: "Not so fast, Jemima! I haven't made my mind up. I am going to call your father and ask him." then hurried back inside the house. Jamie sighed, as they returned to the hallway to watch her mum dial the number for her husband's office from their old rotary-dial phone.

April could imagine her checking every number three times before dialling it. To dial a wrong number on a rotary-dial phone is quite a commitment, and surely the woman knew the number by now anyway. She seemed to dial it every five minutes.

Every time Jamie wanted to leave the house for anything other than school, her mum would dial her husband to 'run it past him'. Every time Mrs Fenton-Jones needed to make a decision about anything; what to cook for dinner, what shoes to wear, she'd ring her husband to ask.

"Hello?" Now Jamie's mum was using her *posh* voice (which was extra *extra* posh to everybody else). April could see where Jamie had picked up the habit. "Hello. Yes, is

Mr. Fenton-Jones there? It's Felicity Fenton-Jones - his wife."

Jamie sighed and sent April a look of utter anguish. She hated how her mum patronised everyone, and always spoke loudly on the phone to her husband's secretary, as if she was deaf. She wasn't deaf. She was only fifty-four. April knew this because Jamie was forced to make the woman a birthday card every year, with crayons.

Jamie's dad finally picked up the line: "Anthony Dear? It's Felicity. Yes, again. All's well, but I'm a bit worried about Jamie staying at April's tonight. Her mother is not there, working late apparently. Again." She added the last word in a voice that suggested April's mum Kate worked far too late, far too often.

The initial meeting of mothers hadn't gone very well. Jamie's mum had introduced herself as 'Felicity Fenton-Jones – of the Fentons' then added "Nice to meet you" after a slightly too long pause. She'd finally offered her hand to Kate, April's mother, rather primly, expecting a gentle handshake and a little polite conversation about their daughters' friendship.

Kate had thrust out an arm and pumped her hand heartily. "Felicity, a pleasure! Lovely to meet you too. Please excuse me a moment however, I just want to catch that dishy drama teacher before he heads off. I think we have a mutual friend…" Kate had dashed off across the hall, leaving Felicity's nose out of joint and her hand still swinging in the air.

April saw the look of horror on Jamie's mum's face and, fearing the loss of a newfound friendship almost before it had begun, had raced off after her mother to beg her to come back and talk a bit longer with Jamie's.

"She's really strict, Mum." April had said. "And she insists on meeting you before Jamie is allowed around for tea, or I'm allowed to go 'round there."

April's mum loved Jamie. She'd spoken with her on the phone many times when Jamie had rung to chat to April (which was only permitted after Jamie had done all her homework and her chores and practised the violin until her fingers almost bled), and they'd become quite friendly.

"Oh, fine," Kate had sighed. "But I'm not chatting for long. I remember that woman from the PTA. She irritates me, and her husband is a sexist pig."

Kate worked in law and so did Jamie's dad. Although they worked in different fields, their paths had crossed once at a large client function. Jamie's dad had confused Kate with the event organiser and asked her for a cup of tea. It didn't go down well. "He knew who I was." Kate had insisted. "He just thinks a woman's place is at home in the kitchen. Idiot."

Now Jamie and April stood in the hallway waiting while their Friday night fate was decided by said idiot. He said something down the phone that was almost loud enough for the girls to hear, followed by Jamie's mum's reply: "Oh dear. I see. Yes, not a problem – I'll come and collect you. 6pm then outside the taxi rank. I'll be there. Yes, goodbye darling."

She put the phone down and came back into the hall. "Well Jamie, your father needs me to go and collect him from the station. He's had to lend his car to a colleague and he's frightfully cross about it. I won't be able to wait for your mother, April, but I shall call her tomorrow to catch-up with her then." She moved over to the hallway mirror and opened her purse. She then applied some blusher and pale pink lipstick before patting her coiffured hair back into place with her fingers.

Jamie and April ran out to the car and sank into the back

seats with relief. But there was still the question of how April was going to avoid the phone call between Mrs. Fenton-Jones and her mother. April's mum thought she was sleeping at Jamie's. The parental double-bluff was always a risky move. The truth was April's mum would probably allow April to go camping, but April didn't want to ask her. It was almost embarrassing how cool her mum was compared to Jamie's. She feared her mum would turn up and want to join in.

Jamie's mum drove ten miles below the speed limit all the way there, and spent the whole journey telling the girls not to answer the door to strangers, or to try to use the toaster. Jamie nodded and said, 'Yes Mummy' so many times, that at one point, her nails dug into April's palm so hard April thought that she might have drawn blood.

When the car finally pulled away - after Jamie's mum had been inside to have a look and a not very subtle nose-around - Jamie shrieked with joy and ripped off her ridiculous frilly blouse. She threw it on the floor and stamped on the "Bloody itchy, poxy thing," then scratched herself all over before reaching for her bag to pull out her latest outfit. She'd stolen it from New Look at lunchtime.

April got changed into some loose jeans and brushed her long hair, while Jamie wrestled into skin-tight ones and a skin-tight denim shirt, before applying three times more make-up than she wore to school. While she smoked a cigarette in the garden, April put on a Jane's Addiction album and raced around packing food and candles into the bag they were taking with them.

"Hurry up!" Jamie called from the garden. "We're gonna be late and the boys will have drunk all the alcohol. I need alcohol – badly!"

"Coming!" April shouted, shoving one last packet of crisps into her bag and forcing the zip closed. She ran down the stairs, locked the back door behind her and hid the key in the heating shed under a bag of wild bird feed. She pulled the shed door closed and had one last look around anxiously, before racing to catch up with Jamie who was already marching off down the hill.

April began to relax as she got further from her house and found herself grinning as she caught up with her friend. "Phew, we made it."

"Only just, no thanks to you." Jamie said, lighting up another cigarette and puffing on it deeply. "Um, y-y-y-ess, Mr....um Mrs. F-fen-Fenton-Jones." She stuttered out an impression of April and April elbowed her good-naturedly.

"We can't all be as good at lying as you," April said as they made their way past the shops and onto the road backing on to the camp.

"Just as well, I like you the way you are anyway," Jamie declared loyally, linking her arm through April's, then forcing her to burst into a run.

TOM

*Y*uki and Tom got to the camp first.

They'd dropped Em off at their Nan's for her Friday night sleepover on the way. Em had shot straight upstairs to go and find Brian, the ancient ginger cat. He was the only reason Em agreed to the weekly sleepover. Brian slept on her bed and was too old to object to the petting and dragging that Em would subject him to. She lovingly (and rather naughtily) fed him the ginger snap biscuits their nan would serve with tea (every half hour) and played vets with him, which involved wrapping him in bandages and carrying him around in an old washing basket urging the rest of them to "pray he'd make it through the night."

It had taken a long time for Tom to talk his Nan into letting him leave after dinner and not sleep over too. "Your bed is all made up," she'd say every week, "and you can help me with the crossword."

"No, Nan. I'm okay, thanks. I need some err, man time, you know?" he'd said, trying to sound manly.

"So much like your father," she'd replied the first time he'd said it, and her eyes had filled with tears. *Crap*, Tom had thought, worrying that he'd upset her.

He never knew what to say when she talked about his dad, when anyone talked about his dad. He dreaded people bringing him up. He couldn't handle his Nan's grief; his life was already dictated enough by his mum's.

People always asked him if he missed his dad, which Tom thought was quite a stupid question. Of *course*, he missed his dad. He missed him so much that some days he couldn't even hold his head up straight. Sometimes the pain inside him was so intense he had to bend over and wrap his hands over his chest to hold himself together. Other times though, despite being appalled at himself for it, he sort of hated him too, hated him for dying and leaving them. Hated him for what his death had done to them all.

If there was anything harder to handle than missing his dad – it was hating him for dying. It was all too much to handle – especially while he had to keep his head straight for Em, so he just tried not to think about it. The weed helped.

He wouldn't look at any of the photos of his dad that were still all over the house. He wouldn't wear any of his dad's clothes, even though his mum had kept them all and they'd probably fit him now. He didn't even watch football anymore, because it might remind him of afternoons playing in the park before watching *Match of the Day*.

Tom had shouted his goodbye to Em up the stairs, kissed his Nan on her papery cheek and headed for the door. "Gotta go, Nan. Yuki's waiting for me outside." He opened the door and was halfway to freedom before she stopped him.

"Tsk, why didn't you say? Young lad must be freezing; *they're* not used to this cold weather."

Tom had tried to protest that it was only September and

Yuki had acclimatised to the weather many years before, but it was too late. She had marched to the door and shouted to Yuki, demanding he come in for dinner. Yuki was too smart to argue.

She led him into the living room and patted the armchair, "You sit there and warm up, Yuki," (she pronounced it "Yucky") then bent down and switched on the electric fire. "That will thaw you out in no time. Now then, I'll go make you something hot. Won't be long."

She came back fifteen minutes later with a plate of sausage and mash for Tom and a bowl of rice with some suspicious looking brown powder on top. The powder turned out to be ancient All Spice.

"I don't know what you people eat," she explained as she handed it to him "but I know you like your erotic tastes" she nodded knowingly.

Tom swallowed a laugh and dug into his dinner.

Luckily the boys had shared a joint on the way round, and they both had the munchies. Yuki (or Yucky as he would now be known by Tom) managed to scoff most of his rice down and Tom threw the rest onto the conservatory roof for him while his Nan went and got the dessert.

"I'll always remember your favourite pud, Tom," she said as she presented him with a bowl of steaming sponge and custard. "It was your father's favourite too." She dabbed her eyes with a hankie she'd pulled out of her sleeve.

"Mmmmm, looks delicious," Yuki said, his voice sounding slightly croaky, probably from all the cinnamon on his dinner. "What is it?"

Tom's Nan smiled proudly. "That there is a good old *spotted dick*. Would you like some, Yoko?"

Being stoned had allowed them to get through the

mountains of questionable cuisine that Tom's Nan had served-up, but it had also given the boys a savage case of the giggles.

Tears streamed down Yuki's face as he writhed in silent mirth, clutching at his sides. Tom's Nan was worried that he was choking and so smacked him on the back a couple of times. Yuki spluttered his thanks and mumbled "Sounds delicious." He paused to wheeze in a breath and added "But I'm so full from all the delicious rice, I don't think I could manage it" His face twitched and Tom kicked his leg under the table. "You eat your dick though, Tom. Go on, get it down you," Yuki demanded, grinning widely from behind Tom's grandmother's turned back.

Tom choked on the spoonful he had in his mouth and his Nan rushed out to get him a glass of water. Tom shot Yuki a look of loathing which only made him grin more.

They finally escaped half an hour later, with a box of flapjacks (another name for a British pudding that Yuki, quite rightly, found hilarious), some cherry scones and the rest of the all-spice rice.

Tom was in a hurry to get everything set up before April and Jamie arrived.

"Chill out, dude," Yuki said, plopping down on the old crate they kept behind a tree in the spinney. He started rolling a joint, sticking two regular papers together expertly to make a bigger skin.

They'd camped-out here every summer ever since Tom was eleven. It was only a five- minute walk from their houses, but no one ever used it. Yuki liked getting out of his shed and 'being at one with nature'. Tom used to love being able to smoke without worrying he would get caught. Now he loved the freedom of not being a big brother/dad to his little sister.

The spinney was a tiny wood at the back of the field. It consisted of no more than a couple of trees, some scraggly bushes and some broken fences. When they'd been younger, Tom and Yuki had spent every day of the summer holidays making dens down there. Now they just used it to hide the camping stuff.

He hadn't felt like camping for a long time after the funeral. For the first two weeks, Em hadn't let him out of her sight anyway. She wouldn't eat or sleep without him and even now, he couldn't leave her alone.

Not when his mum was still acting the way she was.

When their mum had taken to bed a couple of days after the funeral, Em had gone and crawled up next to her. She'd curled around her mother's leg, looking for comfort and finally cried herself to sleep. Their mum hadn't appeared to notice. The next night, Emily had sought Tom out instead.

To start with, she'd talked a lot about Dad and how he was in heaven. Tom had let her ramble on, not knowing what to say to her. He didn't even really know her back then. All he knew was that they lived in the same house and she was noisy. She was six years younger than him and cared about flowers and animals.

Tom had cared about football, music and girls. That had all changed overnight. Now he knew the names of all the kids in his sister's class and watched *The Shoe People* instead of *The A-Team*. Now he read *Care Bear* stories instead of comics and plaited Em's hair instead of lacing his football boots.

When they'd first begun spending every Friday night at their Nan's house, Em would fall asleep by the fire with the cat while Tom watched the news and longed for a cigarette. His Nan would sit in her armchair looking at baby photos of his dad, crying quietly. The heat from the electric fire would stifle the room as Tom sat grinding his teeth, trying not to scream.

Eventually, his Nan had put the photos away and hoisted herself out of her chair to return to the land of the living. Friday nights were still boring, but they had become tolerable.

These days Tom would just drop Em off on a Friday evening, collect her on Saturday around lunchtime, and they'd go back the next day for Sunday lunch. Still a lot of Nan-time as far as he was concerned, but her Yorkshire puddings made it worthwhile. Their mum was always invited too but she never came.

Tom's dad had been his grandmother's only child and the apple of her eye. She'd only been sixteen when he'd been born, a fact she loved to tell anybody who'd listen. "More like best friends, we were," she'd say. His dad had told him that she'd cried the day he'd moved out of home. She hadn't even come to the door to see him off, she'd been so distraught.

His Nan always seemed a little resentful of Tom's mum for snatching *her boy* away. That was before life had snatched him away for good. She still talked about how awful it was to bury a child, and what his dad had been like as a boy, before he'd met and married Mum.

It was like she wanted to own all the grief. No one else was allowed a piece of it.

Tom thought people got too possessive about death and grief. As far as his Nan was concerned, no one missed or loved her son more than she did. She never asked how their mum was coping or visited the house, and Tom never told her what she'd find if she did.

Even when Mum had been okay, before all of this, when she'd used to get up at the crack of dawn to make his dad breakfast and wave him off to work – even then Nan didn't think she was good enough for her blue-eyed boy. That was when his mum would polish his dad's steel toe-capped boots each Sunday and made dinner from scratch each night. She had made her family her job: filled every second of her day doing stuff for them, but his Nan would still find something to criticise her for.

The happier Mum made Dad, the more annoyed Nan seemed to get. When she'd come for dinner, which wasn't very often (she liked to have them come to her house. "He misses his mum's cooking," she'd declare, "and needs a proper meal"), she'd complain that the meat was dry, or the gravy was too thin. She'd wander around the house until she found a houseplant that hadn't been watered, or a smear on the window - anything to pick on Mum about.

She'd barely been civil to her when his dad had been around, and would have been even ruder if she thought she could have got away with it. Now that she didn't *have* to spend time with her daughter-in-law to see her son, she had no interest in doing so.

What would she say if she knew that Mum didn't even bother getting dressed anymore, and never left the house? What would she do if she knew Tom was being Mum *and* Dad to Em all on his own? Would she rush in and help, or would she report Tom's mum to the authorities?

Tom decided that telling his Nan was a risk he couldn't afford to take. They'd already lost their dad and Tom was determined to keep the rest of his family together. Their mum might be useless at the minute, but she'd get better with time. She had to.

She hadn't got any better by the time he'd started camping with Yuki again late that summer, when Em was settled enough to leave his side – but Nan had at least stopped crying every ten minutes, so she could babysit. Tom left his mum with food, water, the phone and her beloved pills, Em with his nan, and sprinted away to temporary freedom with his friends.

41

Tom and April had already been friends for a while when he and Yuki had started camping again. By then Yuki had also become Jamie's weed dealer, so everybody was now well-acquainted. Tom had casually told the girls about the camp and asked if they wanted to come along sometime.

He didn't think they'd say yes; he thought that girls wouldn't like sleeping in tents and weeing in bushes, but he was wrong. They both took to it like pros, and just like Tom and Yuki, they seemed to relish the freedom that the camp brought.

The first couple of trips had been spent working on *home improvements* as Jamie had called them. She'd demanded more comfortable seating for April, who she knew would sit around reading for so long that her bum would get cold and numb. She'd happily helped Tom dig up some huge stones to put around the fire and he'd taught her how to chop wood.

Over time, the camp had undergone various improvements. Tom and Yuki had dragged one of the fallen trees from the spinney and Tom had cut deep groves into it for them to sit on and rest beers in. Jamie had stolen various supplies from the camping shop, which had been gratefully received by everyone (except April, who would scold her friend every time she stole something). Yuki had created an elaborate system that was supposed to collect rain water. It didn't really work, but he was proud of it anyway.

But April was the one who'd really made it into a home. Each week she would drag along more and more gear: pillows, candles, incense, blankets and books. So many books. Tom had then made a crude storage box out of some old wooden pallets they'd found and covered it in a tarpaulin to store everything in.

They used his old family tent and one that Jamie had 'borrowed' from her next-door-neighbour's garden shed.

"They'll never even notice, and they don't need it. They bought a caravan last year," she said, as if that settled the issue.

"Don't you ever worry you'll get caught?" April had asked her.

"Caught doing what?" Jamie replied acting confused, and no more was said.

Tom knew April didn't agree with Jamie stealing, but he also knew how happy she was when she was at the camp. The stuff Jamie nicked made that camping experience even more fun, and they all sort of accepted it.

During the previous camping trip (a couple of weeks before), they'd designated *Ladies* and *Gents* areas, which really pissed Jamie off. She hated any kind of segregation, no matter how innocent the intentions.

"Hey, you wanna piss in front of me? Go ahead, Princess," Yuki had said, trying (and failing) to look suggestive.

"It's not about that, arsehole," Jamie had ranted. "Why do we have to have separate areas? Are we all going to need the toilet at the same time? Why don't you two stand guard while we shake the lettuce, in case the fucking bogeyman gets us?"

"Shake the lettuce?" Yuki had asked, perplexed.

"It's what girls do when we don't have toilet paper," April had explained helpfully. "You shake your um, lettuce," she said as delicately as possible, considering the subject matter.

"What, like Chubby Checker and the Fat Boys?" Tom had asked, sounding genuinely interested.

"No, he did the *twist*," April said. She pointed at her bare big toe, wiggling it and twisting her foot to show him. "A *shake* is more like this" She stood, held her arms out in front of herself and did a shimmy/squat kind of movement – April

43

wasn't a great dancer. Yuki started laughing like it was the funniest thing he'd ever seen. Jamie punched him till he shut up.

But Tom was transfixed. April was swaying her boyish hips and wiggling her torso, in a combination of *The Twist* and *The Shake*. She was twist/shimmying so low to the ground that her bottom almost touched it. From where Tom was standing he could see right down the top of her shirt. Suddenly, she looked up and caught him looking. When he realised he was staring at her with his mouth open, he tried to laugh, but it came out more like a squeak, so he coughed to cover it up.

April had suddenly looked embarrassed and stopped dancing.

"Poor girls," Yuki said, still on the subject of *shaking the lettuce*. "We just wipe our dicks on our jeans."

Jamie had clapped him on the back of the head and called him a disgusting pig. Yuki just grinned and sauntered away whistling.

Since then, Tom had been thinking about April all the time. He'd been looking forward to this camping trip so much that, for at least a few days, he'd barely had a chance to think about his dad at all.

Tom left Yuki to get the fire going while he set up the tents. He liked to get it done before it got too dark. They pitched them opposite one another, either side of the fire. Once the tents were up and the lines were tight, he threw in the girls' sleeping bags and pillows.

Yuki had bought Jamie a Purple Ronnie cushion that said: 'Groovy chick', because he knew how much it would annoy her. She used it for camping, but refused to admit that it was comfortable. April had brought one of her pillows from home, which was currently covered by a Rainbow Brite pillow case. Every couple of months (or when Jamie got too drunk and spewed on it) she dragged all the bedding home and washed it. Her mum worked every Saturday, so she could sneak the stuff in and out of the washing machine before she got back in the evening.

Tom sniffed April's pillow before tossing it onto her sleeping bag. It smelled like vanilla and oranges: just like her.

By the time the girls arrived, the fire was roaring. The cushions from Yuki's old shed-sofa had been placed near it, and the 'kitchen table' (some old crates) was loaded with beers, cider, fags and Space Raider crisps (because they were the cheapest).

"What took you so long?" Yuki moaned as they finally arrived, lugging rucksacks laden down with god knows what in Jamie's backpack, and probably books in April's.

"Sorry," April said, smiling at them both. "Jamie's mum insisted on driving us to my house, then checking all the doors and windows were locked. Then she made us promise not to use the oven, or toaster". She breathed a sigh of relief as she took off her bag and dropped onto a sofa cushion. "What have we missed?"

"My nan cooking Yuki a bowl of rice with a load of cinnamon and nutmeg on the top," Tom said. "And he ate it. And she called him Yucky."

"Ha, Yucky!" Jamie cried gleefully as she ripped a can of cider from the pack on the table and pulled back the tab. "Suits you" she said, raising a mock toast to him before taking a massive swig.

"Nutmeg can get you high," April said, shuffling closer to the fire.

"Really?" Yuki asked, looking very interested.

"Yep, for about ten minutes before you start having spasms

and pass out." April said this while pulling food from her bag. When she'd unpacked her contribution to the table, she picked up a bag of marshmallows and perched on the floor next to the fire.

"I don't think I had enough," said Yuki sadly.

"It's not funny," she replied fishing around for a stick to dig in the marshmallow she was holding. "It can be super dangerous."

"All drugs are dangerous," Yuki intoned, in his best Jim Morrison voice "Drugs are a bet with your mind."

Tom and Yuki started discussing how much nutmeg they'd need to get high. April refused to tell them.

April had the odd toke on a joint when it got passed around, but never more than two. And if you looked closely, you could see she wouldn't take it back properly. When it came to April, Tom looked very closely. He'd become an expert in April; if she was a GCSE subject, he would get an A*.

Tom, Yuki and Jamie came here to take drugs and drink booze, but April seemed happy just to be outside. Open spaces seemed to be her high. She'd sometimes get up randomly, often in the middle of a conversation, to walk around the perimeter of the field, tugging at the long grass, or pulling loose leaves off the branches.

He watched her now while she searched for a stick that she deemed worthy to bear her marshmallow, before stabbing it through the centre. It was a tradition they'd started ages ago. April had wanted to make s'mores after they'd been mentioned in an American film that she'd watched. But none of them – including April – knew what the exact ingredients were.

This week she'd brought a packet of Penguin biscuits with her. When the marshmallow was hot enough to turn to goo, she quickly sandwiched it between two of the chocolate-coated biscuits and nibbled at it, laughing at the sticky mess she was making.

She looked great tonight. She was wearing a pair of baggy blue jeans, a white t-shirt and a checked shirt, unbuttoned over the top. She'd rolled the sleeves up before tackling her s'more. Her wrists were tiny and delicate, and her arms looked thin and pale poking out from the sleeves. She had a leather friendship bracelet wound around her left wrist that Jamie had bought (or stolen) for her.

Her hair was down and fell to the bottom of her back. She and Jamie had experimented with Sun-In hair lightener earlier in the summer. April's hair had grown-out since, so the roots were her natural dark colour, but the ends were almost white. She never wore make-up, except sometimes a lip-gloss or whatever it was that made girls' lips all shiny and sticky. Sitting there with her stick and her s'more, she was so beautiful it made his chest ache.

Jamie was the opposite and either had far too much make-up on, or none at all. Tom thought that she looked better with none, but he'd never tell her that. She'd only find some way to take it as a criticism.

April was reading out the joke on the back of the Penguin wrapper. It was rubbish as usual, but Jamie laughed anyway. Jamie was as fierce as a pitbull, but unwaveringly loyal. She laughed whenever April made a joke and would take on anyone who tried to take the piss out of her. Tom knew how much Jamie cared about April, and that meant a lot to him; she needed people to look out for her.

April was super bright, but she was also super green - innocent in so many ways. Jamie cared for her in all the ways Tom would like to but couldn't. He got the walks to and from school though, and the headphone-sharing.

As if sensing him watching her, April looked up and asked, "Wanna s'more?"

He was full of his Nan's dinner, and the two ciders he'd downed nervously before she'd arrived, but she was already delving into the marshmallow bag, her tongue poking out slightly as she concentrated on spearing a hand-picked marshmallow onto her stick. She looked up and waved it at him before holding it over the fire. He was full on the sight of her, but he ate his s'more anyway, and another one after that.

"You skip dinner?" he asked, after she'd eaten her third.

"I told Mum I was eating at Jamie's," she explained, wiping her thumb over her lips to swipe away any traces of chocolate.

"I thought I'd have time to make some sandwiches, but everything got a bit *Mission: Impossible*. Jamie's mum is scary. Like, *really* scary."

"I'd love to see Jamie saying: 'yes mummy, no mummy'." He said in a sing-song fashion – his version of a *posh* voice.

"She'd kill you. She even hates me seeing it. It's uncomfortable viewing."

A comfortable silence passed between them before Tom spoke again. "Hey, you still hungry? I brought food." He stood up and sauntered over to the food and drinks table. He had some bread, and possibly some Primula cheese, unless Yuki had eaten it. Yuki pretended that he hated it, but everyone knew he ate it straight from the tube. Well, everyone except Jamie who'd never eat it again if she ever found out.

"I'm full, but thanks." April dropped back and lay on the sofa cushions, motioning for him to do the same. Above them the stars were coming out.

Tom was just about to do as he was told, what he'd waited for all week, to lie down next to her, when Yuki switched on his little boombox and 'People are Strange' started playing.

"No. Not The-fucking-Doors," Jamie said, her voice already a little slurred. "No more fucking Doors. All the fucking time."

She ejected the tape and carelessly tossed it in Yuki's direction, which was pretty near the fire.

He gasped and dived to save it, cradling the cassette reverently once it was safely back in his grasp.

He began to admonish her, but she'd already put in her own tape and 'Debaser' by The Pixies blared out loudly. The volume was so high that the little speakers distorted the sound. The music sounded naff, but Jamie didn't seem to care, or was too drunk to notice. She jumped up and down singing in an off-key voice, which was actually a pretty good fit for a Frank Black imitation.

They all sat and watched her, Yuki (calmer now) clutching his precious cassette tape to his chest as he smoked a joint, which he passed to Tom every second toke. Every so often, Tom stole a glance at April. She was still lying on her back, watching Jamie with a half-smile on her face.

They all sang the chorus together, Frank Black impressions all around on the last line.

5

APRIL

*T*he tent smelled stale when April woke up, and her neck ached from using her arm as a pillow.

She had given her actual pillow to Jamie, to keep her head propped up in case she was sick again. April wrestled out of her sleeping bag and over a still comatose Jamie to the front of the tent, pulling the zip open slowly. Bright morning sunlight assaulted her and she winced, bringing a hand up to shield her face as she emerged.

The coldness of the grass took her breath away as she walked over to the fire. It was early, only 8am, but she knew Tom would be up already.

"Meh" she said grumpily, as she made her way towards him, and down onto a crate by the fire.

"Morning," he replied cheerfully, setting a kettle on a tripod that Jamie had nicked from the science lab.

She didn't need to ask him to make her a cup of tea: he was already rinsing out a tin mug. She watched him as he added a slosh of milk and dug around for a clean spoon to add her one sugar. Yuki and Jamie would happily just use the wet spoon, but Tom never did. He wrapped the sugar back up in its bag once he'd finished and used a wooden peg to keep it sealed. He was always neat, always prepared. Jamie called him Mary Poppins because of the kind of stuff he'd sometimes pull from his battered record bag.

In a way, Tom appeared to be so much older than all of them. He was the one who kept the camp running. The one who insisted they air out the tents and wash-up the kitchen stuff before packing it away.

"You're a disgrace to teenagers everywhere," Jamie would grumble, as he made her roll and then re-roll her sleeping bag each week.

April vaguely remembered him going to Cubs when he was younger, and maybe he'd gone on to Scouts too, but that had all stopped after his dad had died. It had been over a year now, and he still didn't talk about it, not to her anyway. Maybe he spoke to Yuki about it, but she wasn't even sure of that.

The kettle began whistling. Tom poured the hot water into the cup, added a teabag, stirred it and handed it to her with the spoon still in it. Then he did the same for himself.

"Thanks," she said and cradled her hands around the mug, the steam warming her face and sending curls into the morning sunshine. April stirred her teabag, watching the swirls of milk in her mug bleed from white to brown.

They sat in companionable silence for a few minutes, sipping tea and listening to the birds sing and fidget overhead. April loved this time of day, when everything was fresh and new. Outside, in a place like this, she could breathe. No doors trapping her in, no bells harassing her. If she wanted to get away and be by herself, she could wander off into the spinney in the corner of the field. The funny thing was, when she did have the option to go off on a whim and be alone, she rarely felt the need to do so. It was when she felt that she couldn't, that she needed to so badly. The rational part of her knew her panic was irrational, she just didn't know how to stop it happening.

She took the last sip of her tea and stood up to refill her mug with coffee for Jamie. Her cold feet made her clumsy and she tripped on the edge of the crate, stumbled back and landed on a pile of bottle caps.

"Ow, ow, ow!" she hollered, grabbing her foot and hopping around grimacing.

Tom rushed to her side. "Here," he said, leading her back to the crate and helping her sit, then kneeling to look at her foot. He held it gently between his palms and turned her ankle towards him.

"You're going to get dirt all over your cords," April mumbled. He ignored her, staring instead at the sole of her foot. A small trickle of blood was running down the back of it and dripped from her heel.

"This might hurt," Tom muttered, then firmly pulled at the bottle cap which was sunk into her heel. Blood flowed faster, as he pressed the sleeve of his shirt to the wound hard.

April's foot throbbed and her head was pounding. Or maybe her foot was pounding, and her head throbbed - she couldn't be sure. Tom was very close, and the blood was making her eyes feel blurry. After a few minutes, he lifted his shirt from the wound and looked at her foot again. The bleeding had slowed, but he continued to study the cut in her skin, looking worried.

His face looked so serious she felt panic starting to creep over her. Maybe she was going to get blood poisoning and die. Her heart raced and she willed it so slow down, telling herself maybe she'd just lose her foot to gangrene, or a nasty infection.

She was just about to ask him what was wrong when he bent his head and laid a brief kiss on the underside of her heel. It was so quick she almost didn't feel it. It was just the lightest touch of his lips before he sat back again and looked up at her.

She felt stunned. He'd just kissed her foot. Her bleeding, dirty foot. With his mouth.

"Your shirt," she said (stuttered, stammered, whatever) "… it'll be ruined."

"Doesn't matter," he replied, sitting back on his heels and rolling up his bloodied sleeve before standing and brushing dust and ash from his cords.

"Can I see it?" she asked suddenly. "The bottle-top?"

"If you want," he passed it to her. It was from one of the bottles of Merrydown Cider that Yuki and Tom had been drinking the night before, the jagged edges red from her blood. "My fault then," he said, leaning over her shoulder to peer at it.

The air felt charged between them. He was so close, so close that when he spoke the hairs on the back of her neck prickled, so close she could smell his Flex shampoo. For a crazy moment, she thought about turning around and leaning into the warmth of his chest. She could pretend she was scared of blood. He'd hold her and stroke her hair, she knew he would. Instead, she shook her head to rid herself of the image and took a step backwards.

Tom took her headshake to mean that he was off-the-hook for the bottle-cap and said. "I should have gathered them all up last night before I crashed out, but I was knackered. Yuki was chatting nonsense till like, 3am. You were lucky you escaped when you did."

"Oh yes, I was so lucky. Jamie, as usual, downed three cans of Helen Brau in half an hour and then spent the next hour vomiting while I held her hair back." She replied with a smile, so he knew she didn't really mind. She'd do anything for Jamie, and she knew Jamie would do the same for her.

Tom laughed that easy laugh of his and the atmosphere relaxed again. "Here, pass it over and I'll throw it away with the rest" he said, holding out his hands for the bottle cap.

"It's okay," April said. "I'll do it. I'll just go put my trainers on." Her foot hurt a little when she walked on it and she winced again.

"You okay?" Tom said, frowning slightly. "Need a backie?"

"I'm cool," she replied, smiling at him and treading lightly over to the table where the food and drinks were kept. Even the thought of wrapping her legs around Tom at that moment in time (even from behind, as the very name for a 'backie' suggests) was making her lightheaded. What if she lost her mind and shouted out 'I love you!'? Her mind told her lies, it was not to be trusted.

She found the coffee, dumped a huge spoonful into the mug, added three sugars and then poured in the water from the still steaming kettle that had been resting above the smoking campfire.

It almost seemed to April like years had just passed, between sitting down for tea with Tom and the moment he'd kissed her foot. That one small action had done more to accelerate the growing tension between them than months of walking to school together had. For her, life would forevermore be split into before Tom kissed her foot, and after.

She carried the mug over to her tent. When she crouched down to unzip it, she slipped the bottle cap into the front pocket of her jeans, where it would stay, like a bloody little lucky charm.

"Rise and shine, sleepyhead," she said softly, holding the mug under Jamie's nose so the smell of coffee wafted up to her. "Here's your coffee." April took a careful step back to a safer distance and added: "It's your turn to cook, so hurry up. I'm starving."

"The light," Jamie croaked, fluttering her eyelashes painfully. "Who told it to sun?"

April poked her gently in the side with the toes on her non-wounded foot. "Come on, drink this, you'll feel better. I have some paracetamol in my bag."

Jamie sat up to take the coffee from her, hissing and spitting at the light streaming in through the open flaps of the tent's entrance.

April rummaged around in her bag for the box of pills and popped two out of the foil packet for Jamie, who tossed them down her throat and washed them back with a swig of coffee, grimacing slightly as she did so.

Jamie looked down at the back of her foot, close to the heel where the cut was. It was the perfect outline of a bottle cap. The wet grass had cleaned it and it wasn't bleeding anymore. She carefully pulled on a pair of clean socks and then her trainers.

Her hair was wild and knotted. She'd plaited it down one shoulder before she'd gone to sleep, but it had come undone at some point in the night. She dug out a hairband and pulled it up and back off her face into as tidy a bun as she could manage without a mirror. She added a swipe of clear lip gloss and then sprayed herself, and Jamie, with a liberal dose of Vanilla Essence from The Body Shop (*cruelty-free*, April thought. *Jamie would definitely approve*).

"Gah! Stop it. I don't want to smell like a fucking cupcake!" Jamie protested loudly, flapping her hand about.

"Would you prefer to smell like vomit and beer?" April asked sweetly.

"Fair point, spray on," Jamie relented, reaching around for her zip-up top. She paused, "Did you undress me?" she asked, sounding slightly embarrassed.

"I did your top and jeans. Tom did your trainers," April replied, passing her the jeans which she'd rolled up for her the night before.

Jamie looked miserable as April handed them over. "It's no big deal, Jamie. I don't mind doing it. You'd do it for me".

Jamie scrubbed a hand over her face and groaned slightly. "I know. I just wish you were the vomiting-drunk friend and I got to be the tipsy-drunk friend, who puts you to bed for once."

April's reassuring reply was interrupted by Yuki hollering, "Women, come and cook my breakfast!"

As April had carefully reminded her before, it was Jamie's turn to bring breakfast, which meant they would be having bacon sandwiches. Jamie always conveniently forgot that Yuki didn't eat bacon.

Yuki had anticipated this and brought along vegetarian sausages, which Jamie then proceeded to try and cook in the same frying pan as the bacon. Yuki rushed in and rescued them just in time: "Poor Tofu," he muttered soothingly to his food. "What did she do to you?"

"Tried to make them taste slightly nicer than rank mould!" Jamie replied, as she dumped crispy bacon onto Tom and April's plates.

Tom always brought the bread and April brought the condiments. Brown sauce for Jamie, red for her and Tom. Yuki liked his sandwich plain: "You're all a bunch of fucking slaves!" he declared once everything was served and they had dolloped out their HP and Heinz. "Where's your will to be weird?"

"You stole it off me," Tom said, biting into his sandwich and grinning broadly. He'd changed into an old army green t-shirt and had wet his hair to tame it.

"Mmmmm," Jamie said, shoving half her sandwich in at once and reaching for the second half. "*The Famous Five* were right - food does taste *soooo* much better outside." She said this in the posh voice that she used at home.

Tom and Yuki beamed at her and Tom said, "Oh yaaah, I agree. Jolly-bloody-hockey-sticks."

"Food also tastes great after one has emptied one's guts all over the floor," Yuki replied, trying really hard to pull-off his own posh voice.

"Shut up, Yuki" Jamie said. "You're no better if you drink too much."

"Which is why I stick to herbs, man," he replied, waggling his tofu sandwich at her.

"Leave her alone," April said, wiping her bread around her paper plate to mop up the last of the ketchup. "She's not in the mood for your pearls of wisdom this morning. Tell them to the washing-up." She dumped her greasy plate on his lap with a grin and walked to her tent to grab a book. She loved reading on the sofa cushions by the still warm fire. She picked up her Rainbow Brite pillow too, after checking it smelled clean.

When she got back, Tom was sitting on one of the cushions smoking a cigarette.

April spent a couple of minutes fluffing up pillows and re-arranging cushions before she settled down.

They sat in silence for a minute - Tom smoking, April reading.

"Sorry about your shirt," she said suddenly. "I feel bad that I ruined it."

"You didn't ruin it, and I don't care if you had. How's your foot?" He exhaled a plume of smoke into the air then chased it away with a ring.

April was reminded of a conversation she'd overheard in French class earlier that week. Claire was patiently explaining to her minions that if a boy blew smoke in your face he was "into you". Jamie had snorted loudly of course, and had rolled her eyes dramatically.

Tom hadn't blown smoke into her face (and she was rather glad he hadn't actually - gross), but he had kissed her foot. The memory of it made her face flush and she dropped her head down to rest on her knees. "Fine now, thank you."

"Hey, is Jamie okay?" he asked, taking another drag of his cigarette.

"I think so, why?" April replied lifting her head and tugging at a blade of grass next to her before wrapping it around her finger.

"She hardly even spoke last night. She just got here, got wasted, spewed and slept." He said this while tapping ash onto the floor by his feet.

"Maybe that was what she felt like doing?" April shrugged. "Her mum and dad have been on at her all week about where she's going to apply to after exams. They've given her a list of options to choose from. All of them are courses that they've picked for her, of course."

"Bloody hell," Tom said. "No wonder she needs to blow-off some steam." He plucked the blade of grass from between April's fingers and started tying it into a knot.

"Yeah, no wonder," April said, then paused before asking:

"Hey Tom, have you thought about what you're going to do after exams?"

Something in Tom's face closed-down. April sensed immediately it was the wrong thing to say.

"Nope," he said shortly, inhaling his cigarette deeply. Then he flicked the half-smoked fag over April's shoulder.

Before she could ask anything more, Tom had stood up and gone back to the others, where he began kicking dust over the fire to put it out.

6

———————

TOM

om had collected Em and was spending the rest of Saturday afternoon trying, and failing, to do homework while she made up elaborate games involving not putting a single foot on the floor.

She was using cushions, books and assorted teddy bears to get around the living room instead.

Tom hoped the noise might wake up his mother, but upstairs remained silent. He was hungover and dehydrated, and he just wanted to go to bed to re-live last night. He'd been rude to April and was feeling like crap about it. She'd stayed away from him after their conversation that morning. Her face was pale and drawn and he knew it was his doing.

Normally April always dragged her feet about leaving the camp, as if she never wanted to go home, but after Tom had snapped at her she'd put her book away and had started taking down their tent.

"I can help you with that," he'd said, going over to give her a hand. She hadn't said anything back. He'd thought about apologising but he didn't know how, and he really didn't want to get back onto the conversation about his plans after exams. April cared about schoolwork and doing well at school. Tom didn't anymore; he couldn't. It was one of the many differences between them.

Those differences hadn't seemed so huge that morning, when it was just the two of them and the sounds of the world waking up. Tom thought it had hurt him more than it had her when he'd pulled the bottle cap out of her foot. The skin there was so delicate he could see the pale blue veins under her skin. He wanted to draw over them - to draw her, lying asleep in their field of dandelions and daises, her long eyelashes on her cheeks.

He pushed his English essay aside and sighed, putting his head in his hands on the table. How could he write a thousand words on a book he hadn't even read? He grabbed his art folder instead and spent an hour sketching Em while she leapt from cushion to cushion. Then he drew the campfire from the night before, its flames rising to meet the darkening clouds.

When it started to get dark and his mum still hadn't appeared, he went into the kitchen and made dinner. Yuki knocked on the back door just as he was serving up their scrambled eggs and baked beans.

"Right on time," Yuki said and sat at the table next to Em, making a disgusted face at the amount of ketchup she poured onto her eggs, which made her laugh.

Tom shoved some more bread in the toaster and put the kettle on.

Then he took a plate of eggs and a mug of tea up to his mother and made a mental note to remove the untouched cheese sandwich he'd brought up for her earlier.

She was awake, lying on her side, staring blankly at the coverlet on the bed. "Thanks, love," she said softly when Tom placed the plate of food down.

"Try and eat something, Ma," he said, helping her sit up and then passing her the tea. She cradled her pale hands around the mug and he was reminded of April that morning doing the same thing. His mum gazed into the mug as if it held answers to life's unexplained questions.

"Mum," Tom tried, "Yuki's downstairs, we're just finishing dinner, and then we're going to watch a film. Want to come down and join us?"

She stared at her tea for a bit longer, and then said "Not tonight love, I'm tired. I'll come down later. You go and enjoy your film."

Tom sighed and stood up. "Em ate all her eggs," he said, "she likes scrambled eggs now, so long as she's allowed to smother them in ketchup." His mum closed her eyes and a tear rolled down from her face onto the duvet cover.

Tom couldn't understand why she was crying. He'd told her about Em's eggs success to try and cheer her up, to give her something to think about other than herself and her grief.

He tried again. "I bet she'd love your quiche now too, Mum," he watched another tear fall to join the first one on the bed. When she still didn't say anything, just kept silently crying, as if Em's progress with yellow food was sad news, Tom got up and left the room.

Once he got back downstairs, Em had finished her dinner and Yuki was running hot water into the sink to wash-up. Just like Tom had been when he'd first seen Yuki and his family, Em was fascinated by Tom's best friend. She would sit in silence for ages, which for Em was very rare, just watching him.

Yuki finished washing the plates and Em perched on a stool by the sink. While Tom dried the dishes and put them away, Yuki made her origami flowers from some old paper napkins Tom had found in the kitchen dresser drawer.

Once the kitchen was clean, sides wiped, table clear and mugs put away, they made their way into the living room to watch a film.

Em wanted to watch *Grease* while Yuki wanted to watch *Pulp Fiction*. Eventually they settled on *Jurassic Park*, which Yuki loved but would never admit to. Tom sat on the arm of the sofa, sketching a cartoon of the pair as they sat watching the screen. He drew images of cats and cupcakes in Em's head, snakes and chopsticks in Yuki's. Outside the blue glow from the TV that he'd sketched them within, the shadows on the living room wall stretched out into huge dinosaurs with arms outstretched and mouths open wide.

Em fell asleep before the end of the film. Rather than wake her to carry her up to bed, Tom covered her with an old orange waffle blanket and he and Yuki slipped outside to share a joint before Yuki called it a night.

"Thanks, man," Tom said eventually "…for coming over."

"It's nothing, man. You make mean eggs."

Tom choked up for no reason at that moment and had to swallow down a lump in his throat. He knew Yuki could be at home eating his mum's awesome noodles and listening to Jim Morrison, or whatever the hell he did when he was alone, but he'd given up his time to help Tom out, and it meant a lot. Tom hated asking people for help. Yuki seemed to know that and to offer it in a way that didn't make Tom feel as if he'd failed.

Sensing that Tom was having a moment, Yuki blurted, "I'd do that Ellie from Jurassic Park man, I dig a chick who digs archaeology. She could feel my fossil." He wiggled his eyebrows mischievously.

Tom burst out laughing and gave him a high five. Yuki was pretty switched on for a bloke who was attempting to be the reincarnation of a man who claimed to be a shaman.

7

APRIL

*T*uesday afternoon was the afternoon that April
dreaded the least.

She had double English with Miss Khan, who usually let
her go and work in the reading resources room. It seemed
ironic to April – who was so good at writing that she was
set different work to the rest of her classmates - that she
couldn't find the words to explain what was in her head.

Like April, Miss Khan was a big Sylvia Plath fan and often
tasked April with translating her poetry, or comparing it to
other poets of her time, while the rest of the class studied
something else.

April was pretty sure Sylvia would understand what was
going on in her head, if only she were around to talk to.

She pulled out her dog-eared copy of *The Bell Jar* and
flicked to find a favourite line:

*"To the person in the bell jar, blank and stopped as a dead baby, the
world itself is a bad dream."*

That was April, inside the bell jar, fingers pressed up
against the glass. Even if she could find her voice to tell the

65

world she was trapped inside her mind and its obsessive thoughts, would anyone hear? Would they help her, or would she be pinned down and locked up physically as well as mentally? Just reading the description of the McLean Psychiatric Clinic that Sylvia had attended made April tense.

In history class that week, they'd been learning about the Salem Witch Trials and the idea that all women were either mad or bad. "Sounds about right" one of the boys at the back had said and Jamie had turned around in her chair to glare at him. "She'd be a mad one," he'd loudly whispered to the girl next to him. The girl had giggled in response.

The teacher went on to explain that those suspected of being a witch were stripped, bound and tossed in the river. "People believed witches had spurned the sacrament of baptism, so the water would reject them. An innocent would sink like a cat in a bag, a witch would bob on the water," she said, casting her eyes around the room.

Jamie had been furious of course, and had hurled a tirade about the historical repression of women. Within minutes she was likening the treatment of witches to the treatment of the Suffragettes when they'd been imprisoned for their crimes.

"Demanding equality," Jamie said, her voice rising as she finished. "What a crime, huh?"

April was pretty sure that learning about the 'witches' in Salem wasn't on the curriculum for history class (like a lot of the other subjects their history teacher sometimes talked about), but at least it made things slightly more interesting. Their teacher obviously loved Jamie's passion for the subject and dug out stories to deliberately rile her up. It always got the class involved in the end, even if only to argue against her - Jamie's passion was impossible to ignore.

Maybe I'm a witch, April thought, and almost smiled at the idea. She wondered if she were tied and tossed in the river would she would sink like a stone or keep her head above water?

The smile faded when she remembered that either way it made no difference. If women accused of being a witch drowned when they were 'ducked', they weren't a witch (but they were dead). If they didn't drown, they were burned at the stake (same result – dead). April sighed and rubbed her left temple, willing her thoughts to stop their constant noise.

What if you feel sick and need to get to the toilet, April? The voice in her head would ask her. *What if you get lightheaded and pass out? What if you are allergic to something in the science lab and it suffocates you? What's the quickest route out of this room April, and will it be quick enough?*

Quick enough for what?? she wanted to scream. What was she so scared of? Maybe if she could work that out she could stop being such a coward, stop living a half-life.

April was in the top set of every subject, and that was with half her mind set against her. She sometimes imagined what she'd be capable of if she could just get it to calm down. The most frustrating part was that she knew her thoughts were just that, thoughts, but she couldn't stop believing them.

A tiny part of her brain (which was still rational) told her to stay put when she wanted to rush out of lessons, or to try and eat a plate of chips in the lunchroom one day. Maybe she wouldn't pass out, maybe she wouldn't choke. She wasn't ready for that though. Not yet, perhaps not ever. Her mind was a problematic equation that she couldn't work out.

God, she was so tired of herself.

April's head hurt. She lay it down on the cool desk top and

turned to stare out the window. The resource room looked out onto the back playground and playing fields where the Year 9 girls were out on the pitch playing hockey. She heard their shouts through the open window.

She longed to open the door, walk through it and not stop. She imagined her 'mad' thoughts dulling with each footstep away from school as she headed towards home.

Towards the camp. Towards peace.

Whenever she was at the camp she felt like a different person. The relief it brought her almost made her giddy. Not the giddiness that school halls and assemblies would bring; when she was at the camp with Jamie, Tom and Yuki she felt light. She could eat without worrying that she'd choke, she could lie on her back, spread her arms wide and touch… nothing. She was free.

A movement out of the corner of her eye made her sit up as Miss Khan walked into the room and smiled at her.

"Hello April, how are you doing?" April loved Miss Khan's voice. It was so light and gentle that when she read aloud April could close her eyes and almost feel as if she wasn't trapped.

"Fine thanks, just getting my stuff out." April said as she slid *The Bell Jar* under the table onto her lap and pulled the ring binder she used to keep her English work in towards her. Tom had decorated it with band logos and Adidas stripes adorned the front and back, painstakingly painted by April in Tipp-ex correction fluid.

She loved Tom's artwork. He'd always add hidden details that she'd spot weeks after he'd added a new drawing. The *inside* of the folder was covered in thoroughly crossed-out scribbles - comments Jamie had made about anyone and everyone in the classes they shared, which April always had to hastily erase.

"You've read *To Kill a Mockingbird* already, haven't you?"
Miss Khan asked her, carefully moving April's folder to the
side so she could perch her tiny frame on the desk.

Miss Khan wasn't like the other teachers. They all seemed
beige and washed-out in comparison to her. Somewhere
along the way, April thought, it was as if they'd all lost their
passion for teaching, but Miss Khan's brown eyes sparkled
whenever she talked about books.

She wore brightly coloured jumpers and a thick sweep of
black liner along the top of each eye. She never tied her hair
up and would kick off her shoes at the beginning of each
class. Miss Khan rarely sat properly at her own desk at the
front of the classroom, always preferring to perch on it, or
pull up a chair next to a student. She smelled of roses and
the bitter coffee that she always drank. April loved her. She
was sure Sylvia Plath would have loved her too.

"Yes, I read it over the summer. I loved it. I watched the
film too."

"Gregory Peck is wonderful in it, isn't he?" Miss Khan said,
"I must see if I can get a copy of it to show the class."

"You can borrow my copy. My mum got it for me when I
told her I was reading the book. She's a big fan; she loves a
good courtroom drama."

"Your mum sounds like a very interesting character herself.
I didn't get to spend much time with her at the last parents'
evening. Has she seen *12 Angry Men*? It's another classic
black and white courtroom drama."

"It's her favourite film," April said smiling. "It's what made
her want to work in law."

Miss Khan smiled and checked her watch. "I've got to go;
the class will be waiting outside for me. Can you do a quick
character assessment for Scout and Jem please? I want to
use them as examples for the rest of the class next week."

69

"Of course, I'll do it now," April said immediately and dug around in her bag for her copy of the book. As she did so, *The Bell Jar* slipped off her lap and onto the floor. Miss Khan bent down to retrieve it for her and smiled at the battered, but obviously well-loved, copy.

She flipped through the book and landed on one of the pages where April had folded down the corner to mark a place. She knew the quote that was ring-marked on the page before Miss Khan started reading in her calm steady voice:

"I wanted to tell her that if only something were wrong with my body it would be fine, I would rather have anything wrong with my body than something wrong with my head, but the idea seemed so involved and wearisome that I didn't say anything. I only burrowed down further in the bed."

Miss Khan looked up from the book, her brown eyes gazing steadily into April's. "Interesting that you circled that, April. It's not the sort of thread that you tend to pick out in class, what made you do so here?"

When they shared favourite Sylvia lines in class, April would always pick ones she thought would seem 'normal'. For example:

"How could I write about life when I'd never had a love affair or a baby or even seen anybody die? A girl I knew had just won a prize for a short story about her adventures among the pygmies in Africa. How could I compete with that sort of thing?"

April cleared her throat and looked down at the book as if an answer might appear from the pages. Eventually she said carefully, "I just like her description of being tired, that feeling you know, when it all just seems too much?" She glanced up briefly to see a slight smile creep over Miss Khan's face.

"Ah yes, the exhaustion of being a teenager, I remember it

well! A famous man once said, 'If you liked being a teenager, there's something wrong with you.' Can you guess who it was?"

April racked her brain, "Um, E.E. Cummings?" she guessed.

"Nope, Stephen King." Miss Khan hopped off April's desk and headed towards the door. "I'll be down the corridor if you need me. When you've finished the paper, pop it in my pigeon hole and we'll catch up on Friday."

April nodded and pulled her folder back towards her. She was grateful that Miss Khan hadn't been more alarmed about the quote that she had circled in *The Bell Jar*; but she was also strangely disappointed. A part of her had hoped that Miss Khan would somehow know the reason she'd highlighted it – the words could have been written by April herself, she identified with it so strongly. If she'd broken her leg, there would be no question, she would go to the hospital and a doctor would fix it.

But what could be done about a broken brain?

8

TOM

*T*om leaned against one of the pillars outside the chapel and checked his watch.

April was late, as usual, and almost everyone else had left. A sea of white shirts flooded out of the front gate and down the side of the sports field where a hole in the fence provided a shortcut for those who lived on the estate behind the school.

Whenever April was late, it would mean that Tom had even less time to get back and sort the house out before racing down to collect Emily, but he waited all the same. Luckily Em loved school. She had a different after-school activity each day, which was great on one hand, because it gave Tom time to get to her. On the other hand, it also gave him a headache trying to make sure he remembered (and washed) all the correct kits or equipment. She was into everything: Karate, dance, drama, Lego club, book club… the list went on and on.

If Tom was ever late to pick her up, she would go down to the reception block and play with their pet rabbit while she waited. She told Tom she wished that playing with the bunny rabbit could be an after-school class too.

Today she had Karate and her white suit was washed, ironed and packed into her bag. Em's energy was almost infinite. Some days she had two classes after school and still came out skipping and singing. After what had happened to their Dad, Tom knew Emily's teachers offered her extra attention and support and he was grateful for it. He just wished they wouldn't ask him so many probing questions all the time.

"How's your mum doing?" one of his old teachers would ask every time she saw him, tilting her head to one side in a familiar motion that he'd come to despise. He was sick of being given that look. Everyone had looked at him that way at the funeral, like they'd taken acting lessons in how to show sympathy, or contracted some hideous disease which had left their necks too weak to keep their heads on straight.

He'd slipped behind the bike sheds at lunch to share a joint with a kid from his maths class and it had left him feeling a bit spaced-out. He wished he hadn't bothered now.

He sighed and rubbed the toe of his trainer against a crumbling pillar. Their school had once been an old orphanage, and it had a chapel set in the front of the grounds. There was an abandoned crypt beneath it that had flooded years before in a storm. There wasn't much to see down there, except a couple of chairs floating about in stagnant water and some vintage orange and brown tiles on the wall.

Tom had only been down there once. The steps leading to it were set into the back of the chapel, hidden behind a faded red velvet curtain. Mostly people went behind there to snog, furiously.

He imagined being behind that curtain with April, running his hands through her long hair. He wondered what it would feel like if he touched it. It always looked so soft, like a river flowing down her back. She must wash it every night. He tried not to picture April in the shower, washing her beautiful long hair. Instead he focused on how, when she tied it back, hairs started escaping again within minutes. She'd sigh and lift her arms to sweep it back into another messy bun.

He pictured himself tying it back for her like he did for Emily each morning. He'd learned to do plaits after a frustrating week of practising on one of Em's Barbie dolls.

Tom leaned back on the pillar, shut his eyes for a second and saw his hands crossing over one another as they pulled April's long strands into a braid. She had the most beautiful neck. The changing room was full of boys talking about girl's tits and arses. April was slim and hid her figure under oversized clothes. He guessed that she had an incredible body, if the curve of her neck was anything to go by.

When she wasn't looking, he'd study her collarbone and the skin behind her ear. If he had the chance to touch April anywhere, he would run his nose down the skin behind her jaw. He didn't tell the other guys in the changing-room though. He didn't tell them anything, just laughed and nodded along as they ranked all the girls out of ten, on what felt like a weekly basis.

One week they'd discussed April. At the mention of her name, Tom had felt like punching a hole in one of the lockers. "Hmm April, a tricky one," Alex had said. He was the football captain and had blond hair that fell in two ridiculously neat curtains either side of his face. Girls talked about his hair a lot. Tom thought it looked like he had an open book on his head, but whatever.

"Keeps herself a bit too covered up for my liking, but I saw her in trampolining class once. Her legs go on for *ðaaaaaays*…" Alex drew the last word out salaciously.

Tom had bitten his lip and thrust his head further into his locker to stop himself from headbutting Alex.

"How did you manage to get a glimpse of the girls' trampoline class, man?" Joe asked, "We have classes in the science lab then."

"I was on my way to the Head's office for calling Miss Mitchell 'Mamma Mitchell'" Alex explained, sounding very pleased with himself. Miss. Mitchell was their sumo-sized chemistry teacher and knew full well what some of the students called her. Some days she called the kids out on it and sometimes she let it go. This perceived inconsistent behaviour led the boys into talking about 'Mamma Mitchell's time of the month'.

Tom thought what Alex had been sent to the Head's office for was lame, but the crowd around him laughed and offered him high-fives.

Tom decided he had heard enough, so he shoved the rest of his kit into his bag and began to head out of the changing room. Just as he pushed the door open, Alex piped up again: " 'Course, Tom might know something about those legs, he's always sniffing around her. Tell us, Tom - does she have a tight arse to go with her tight attitude?"

Tom was back across the changing room and fisting Alex's shirt under his fingers before he even realised he'd moved. "One word, *one-fucking-word* about her and I swear to god you'll never be able to walk again - let alone play football." Tom's voice was low and steady, and he meant every single word.

Alex grinned at him, but Tom saw the slight panic in his

eyes. Tom never lost his temper anymore, and this was why. If he let his control slip, the angry black mass sitting on his chest reared up and he wouldn't be able to contain it.

A couple of seconds passed while they glared at one another. Tom had felt his heart roaring in his ears and he itched to wipe the smug look off Alex's pretty-boy face.

Just as he decided suspension would be worth it, he felt a strong arm on his shoulder and somebody said, "Chill out, man. He's only kidding, it's not worth it."

It was Joe. They'd been good friends once and Tom knew he was trying to help him. He shrugged Joe's arm away angrily but released his hold on Alex, who sat back and smirked even wider, but didn't say anything else.

Tom bent to pick up his bag and marched out of the room without another word, slamming the door behind him. Alex could report him, but as he had a bad reputation of his own, Tom didn't think anybody would take him seriously.

Just after his dad had died, Tom had been in a different fight every day. The school went easy on him at first, but as the months passed and he spent more and more time on the bench outside the Head's office with bloodied knuckles, they began to lose patience. They talked about suspension and Tom knew that he had to get a grip.

Since then he'd worked hard to keep his anger under control. He'd stopped playing football, as it presented too many opportunities to lose his cool, a cool he'd fought so hard to find. His coach had been disappointed, as were Alex and the rest of the team. Tom has been told more than once he possessed magic left foot and his leaving was a great loss.

He missed the feel of scoring a goal almost as much as he missed his old life, his life before it all went tits-up. He told the football coach that he didn't have time to go to Saturday practice or after-school games anymore, as he had to help with Emily. It was the truth.

His coach was understanding but had said: "Remember to still make time to be you, Tom. Your dad wouldn't have wanted you to take on so much responsibility, to grow up so fast." He had put his hand on Tom's shoulder and told him he'd always have a place on the team if he wanted one.

Tom hadn't said anything, worried that if he opened his mouth he'd just break down. That was when he realised he would have to work hard to keep his mouth shut, as well as working hard at not starting fights, or playing football or being late home. He was especially careful not to lose his temper with Em when she wouldn't get dressed. His life had become a list of things he couldn't do.

Tom sometimes wondered if he and April would have become friends if his dad hadn't died and she hadn't brought round dinner that time; if he hadn't had to stop playing football and grow up. He hated that he Aprils' appearance in his life bought him joy, but at the cost of losing his dad.

He'd noticed her before the day she'd knocked on his door. She'd often walk past his house on her way down to the village shop to get the paper, and he'd seen her at school occasionally. She always pressed herself against the wall and sort of slid along it, as if she wanted to be invisible. It only made her stand out more. He found himself looking out for her in assembly, he'd settle his gaze on her long hair. For some reason, it relaxed him knowing that she was in the same room.

She appeared so small, compared to everyone around her. She always kept her coat on, and a huge scarf wrapped around her neck. A lot of the girls wore short skirts, but April wore a long one that fell almost to the floor and a baggy V-neck jumper with the cuffs turned back.

He hadn't spoken to her back then, and he doubted he ever would have if it had been up to him to make the first move. She was posh and pretty and nothing like Tom. They didn't even share any classes. Tom wasn't stupid, but up until his dad had died he'd only cared about football and art, and after, he hadn't cared about school at all. His grades reflected it.

These days, he wondered if he'd have even bothered to turn up for school if it wasn't for April. Even though he didn't see her often, just knowing they were in the same place and that he'd get to walk her home, was enough.

She was Tom's compass; she kept him going in the right direction. She nagged him to do his homework and always wanted to see his art projects. She was actually the inspiration behind most of them. Even when he drew a still-life of a bowl of fruit, the curve of the banana would be her neck. She was under his skin and although he missed his dad (*really* missed his dad), a tiny bit of him was glad of the accident, because it had brought April into his life.

He hated himself for feeling the way he did. Like Jamie, he thought religion was a waste of time. Where was God when his dad had been dying alone on a railway? Churches and prayers were a waste of time as far as he was concerned. He hadn't stepped foot inside a church once since the funeral and he never planned to again. If there was a heaven, Jesus obviously didn't want him for a sunbeam.

Tom knew he didn't really deserve April. She was beautiful and smart and funny. She lived on the other side of the village to him, in a detached house with a paved driveway and a huge front door with stained glass windows. April was going to get straight A's in her exams and be accepted into a university miles and miles away from their tiny town. He'd be lucky to get a full-time job at the corner shop. He wasn't going anywhere.

So, he would cherish their walks home and the opportunity to teach the brightest girl he'd ever met about music.

Maybe through doing so, she'd still remember him long after her amazing brain took her far away from him.

9

APRIL

*T*om looked as if he was in a daze.

His eyes were a million miles away and she wondered what they were looking at. She cleared her throat, but he didn't seem to notice, so she poked him in the arm instead. He looked startled, then saw it was her and relaxed. Smiling, he pushed off the wall and began walking.

"Sorry I'm late," she said, falling into step beside him. "I was talking about this poem with Miss Khan after class and time just... went."

April loved talking to her teacher after class when everyone had gone. When the room was empty save for her and Miss Khan, she finally felt able to relax. This was mainly because she could leave whenever she wanted, not when a bell told her to. They'd talked about poetry, but Miss Khan had also talked to her about where she was going to apply for college and what universities she'd been thinking about.

April was surprised. She hadn't even considered it. She was so desperate to finish school, she couldn't imagine voluntarily applying to go to another *institution*. But she loved English and she loved books. They were alternative universes she could get lost in. She could wander around someone else's mind and take a break from her own. She'd never admit it to any of her friends or classmates, but she often asked for extra English homework Miss Khan must have thought it was to swot up for A-levels, hence the slightly awkward conversation they'd had that afternoon.

"Have you thought about what you'll do after GCSEs, April?" Miss Khan had asked while they were stacking books. "I imagine you could get in anywhere you like, if your final grades are as good as your predicted ones."

Miss Khan had predicted April an A* in English Literature and English Language. April knew she was good at writing, but she hadn't expected predictions as good as that.

She'd looked down at the books she'd been holding and mumbled a 'thank you'.

"Of course, I'd love to continue teaching you through your A-Level if you chose to stay on in the sixth form," Miss Khan had continued. "I've had a look at the upcoming prospectus and there are some wonderful books in the mix." April looked up, her interest piqued. "Oh yes, some really strong female authors," Miss Khan had gone on, her eyes sparkling. "Alice Walker, Jeanette Winterson…"

"Oranges are Not the Only Fruit?" April had interrupted.

"Oh, you've read it?" Miss Khan had said then, looking impressed.

"Yes, I read it a couple of months ago," April had replied. "Jamie has a copy, it's great."

April would often run out of books and resort to reading Jamie's. Some of them were a bit angry feminist rather than empowering feminist for April's liking, but she read them all anyway.

"Anyway, I'm here now," she said to Tom, shaking the conversation with Miss Khan away. "How was your day?"

"It was *blah*," he said, "same as usual, yours?"

"Yeah, mostly just *blah*," April replied. "What are we listening to?"

"*Aha*! I have a treat for you today," he said excitedly and pulled a tape out of his pocket, which he rattled slightly before inserting into the little portable cassette deck. "You are about to experience the wonder of The Smashing Pumpkins."

When Tom spoke about music his whole face lit up. His eyes shone, and all his features became animated. April could watch Tom's face as he talked about music for hours.

"Billy Corgan is, like, the best guitarist of all time. It's insane. He has this way of making music so that, within two seconds of a song playing, you know it's the Pumpkins. Here, I'll show you." He lifted April's hair up and gently fitted the speaker bud in her ear. As he pulled his hand away, he let it trail through her hair, before tucking the loose strands back behind her ear.

Through her single earphone, Billy Corgan cooed at her. She grinned at Tom to let him know she loved it, immediately loved it. Her grinned back at her, turned up the volume, and they walked home slow enough to listen to the whole album.

When they reached the bottom of her road, he slid the tape out and gave it to her. "Here," he said, "for you."

"I can't keep it!" April reeled at his generosity. "It's the original copy, it must have cost a fortune!"

"I made a copy," he said, slipping the tape into her hand. "Take it. I can tell how much you like it." He pulled the cassette cover out of his bag. "The lyrics are in there too…."

Tom knew April loved lyrics, he'd seen some of her favourite lines scribbled inside her folder, amongst all of Jamie's angry graffiti.

She relented and took it. "I'll just borrow it for a while," she said, hugging it to her chest.

1 0

TOM

*T*he rest of the week passed uneventfully.

Tom took Em to school and ballet class and walked April home. He took tea up to his mum in bed before he left for school and made Em eat her broccoli. He washed and ironed school clothes and hoovered the living room. He didn't get time to do any of his homework.

Each night, once Em was asleep, he slipped out to Yuki's shed to share a joint with his friend, then return home to do more washing up, and more cleaning. He went through the bills and worked out which needed to be paid first. The railway had paid out some money after the accident, and his mum still got family allowance for him, as well as Em, but he still worried about money; he didn't know how long it was going to last or how soon he'd be able to get a job that paid enough to support them.

Tom had become pretty good at budgeting. He hated charity of any sort, but he'd accepted the second-hand school uniform for Em that a mum down the road had offered. The ballet kit was a hand-me-down too. His paper

The rest of the week passed uneventfully.

Tom took Em to school and ballet class and walked April home. He took tea up to his mum in bed before he left for school and made Em eat her broccoli. He washed and ironed school clothes and hoovered the living room. He didn't get time to do any of his homework.

Each night, once Em was asleep, he slipped out to Yuki's shed to share a joint with his friend, then return home to do more washing up, and more cleaning. He went through the bills and worked out which needed to be paid first. The railway had paid out some money after the accident, and his mum still got family allowance for him, as well as Em, but he still worried about money; he didn't know how long it was going to last or how soon he'd be able to get a job that paid enough to support them.

Tom had become pretty good at budgeting. He hated charity of any sort, but he'd accepted the second-hand school uniform for Em that a mum down the road had offered. The ballet kit was a hand-me-down too. His paper

84

round didn't pay much, but the little cash he earned helped. Tom didn't really buy anything for himself anymore, always too busy thinking about his mum and Em. His priorities had gone from saving all his cash for new albums, to making sure the cupboards were full and the bills were paid.

He and Yuki had recently managed a rare shopping trip to Camden though. Yuki drove them up in his mum's car. Tom had picked up some second-hand cords and a couple of Ben Sherman shirts. He'd also found an awesome brown and gold zip-up Adidas top and some shell top trainers. The entire lot had cost him twenty quid, and the guy selling the stuff had thrown in a couple of old green t-shirts too.

Yuki had been more adventurous with his purchases. He'd bought a pair of union jack trousers and matching jacket, then a top hat and a long cigarette holder. They'd grabbed a load of 'Morning Rain' incense cones and then, despite Tom's perpetual lack of personal funds – they'd hit the record shops.

It was the best day he'd had in ages. London was so busy, so alive, so different from their boring middle-class town. He wished that April could have been with them too. She would have loved all the unusual colours made by the scores of stalls within the market. There was a zip-up red and white Adidas jacket that would have looked amazing on her, and although it was only five pounds, it was five pounds that he didn't have to spare. And what would he say when he gave it to her? "I bought this for you because I love you, please be my girlfriend?" followed by "I have nothing to offer you except second-hand clothes and a little sister who needs a mother." Yeah, not likely.

He did save her a couple of cones of incense however, and a pre-owned copy of Suede's *Dog Man Star*, which he knew she'd played so many times that her copy had broken. She'd spent most of the last Friday night at camp twisting the reels patiently with a biro, trying to mend it.

Tom waited until the next camping trip to give April her gifts. She had been delighted with the tape. She was so happy that she actually went to hug him, but then stopped just shy of it. Instead she'd said "Let me pay you, please?" Tom refused, but allowed her to make him a s'more with a Kit Kat base and a salt and vinegar crisp topping.

He'd deliberately waited until Jamie and Yuki had gone to find firewood before presenting it to her. He could hear them bickering as they headed into the spinney. He desperately wanted the hug that she'd taken back at the last minute.

Instead April tucked the tape carefully into her bag and lay face-down on the sofa cushions by the fire to continue reading her book, *The Bell Jar*.

"How many times can you read that book?" he'd asked her. She'd looked at him over her shoulder and made a *shushing* sound, before turning back to her reading. Tom was irrationally jealous of the book.

"What do you love about it so much?" he'd asked, flopping down on his back on the cushion next to April, sending her up in the air and causing the book to fly out her hands. She rushed to snatch it back into her arms, replying "Girl things. You wouldn't understand with your... um... boy bits." She made a sweeping gesture at him and he laughed.

"Boy bits, eh?" he'd waggled his eyebrows at her "We can still read you know, even with a *penis*."

April went so red so fast it made him blush too. He felt he might have shouted the word 'penis' really loudly and wanted to groan in embarrassment. It just wasn't a cool word.

They'd both sat there glowing like beacons for a moment,

before April finally said, "Are you really interested, or just bored?"

He was bored, bored of her obsession with the book. But instead of saying that, he'd answered, "I'm interested. Read me something." Tom had sat up as April rummaged around in her massive bag. Eventually she pulled out a slim paperback, which she'd handed to him with the sort of caution you might reserve for a new-born baby.

"Read for yourself," she'd said as he took it from her. "This is some of Sylvia's poetry. Maybe try that first before committing to her book." She'd patted his hand and went back to her reading again.

Tom had sighed and flipped open the first page to read the sleeve:

'The poems in this book were all written between the publication in 1960 of Sylvia Plath's first book, and her death in 1963.'

"Wait, she's dead?" he'd asked, surprised.

"Duh," April said and flipped over a page. Tom leaned over her shoulder and saw that she had written stuff in the margins and highlighted some paragraphs. He was about to read one aloud when she'd snapped the book shut and glared at him.

"Okay, okay," he said, giving her what he hoped was a winning smile. "I'll just crack on with this then." He'd opened the poetry book again and flipped through pages of poems that made no sense to him, before landing on one called 'Daddy'.

He almost dismissed it and was about to turn the page when the first line caught his attention:

"You do not do, you do not do, anymore black shoe, in which I have lived like a foot."

87

Tom stopped turning the page immediately and read the rest of the poem. And then he read it again, the last line over and over:

"Daddy, Daddy, you bastard. I'm through."

He was so lost in the words he hadn't noticed April was watching him. "You like it?" she'd asked, her voice sounding slightly nervous.

He didn't know what to say. He hardly understood most of it, but the bits he did understand felt like direct blows to his nervous system. It was like the woman who'd written those words had walked around in his head, collected all the thoughts about his dad and had laid them out neatly on paper.

She got it. How he was furious at his father for dying and effectively killing his childhood. How he still loved his dad as much as he hated him, and how he hated himself for feeling this way. Sometimes he felt so ashamed that he felt physically sick. This Plath chick seemed to get it. Love and hate were both just four letter words.

"I wasn't sure you'd want to read that one…" April has said, obviously worried he might be upset.

"It's good," he'd said finally, not sounding entirely like himself. "It's really good."

April had grinned and squeezed his arm. He only had a t-shirt on and when her hand closed around the skin above his elbow, he felt like he'd been mildly electrocuted. She never normally touched him - she mustn't have noticed she was doing it. A few seconds passed, and she carried on squeezing him tightly, looking at him like he'd just told her he'd hung the bloody moon.

Poetry reading, Tom thought. Who knew? He'd have to do it more often. He would have Sylvia Plath quotes tattooed all over him if it meant April kept looking at him like that.

For the second time that morning he didn't know what to say, so he placed the hand of the arm that was not having the life squeezed out of it over hers. He thought she'd pull away, but instead she let go of his arm, and as the blood rushed back into them, she slowly linked her fingers through his.

He was holding her hand.

April's hand became everything. It was an entire world that he wanted to explore. A small, warm one.

Without thinking, he'd stroked his thumb over the base of hers and felt her jump in response.

Tom had pulled away before she could and got up hurriedly, running his hands through his hair before shoving them into his back pockets. "Want a drink?" he'd asked, his voice croaking as if he'd smoked too much the night before.

"Please," she said, smiling up at him with her shy face. He loved that face.

"Beer or Hooch?" he asked her.

"Beer. No, Hooch! No, beer. Hang on - what beer is it?" Tom had wondered if she might be a little flustered herself.

"*Trampaigne*," he said doubtfully, which was their nickname for the cheap German beer they always bought. It was cheap, but it had one of the highest alcohol percentages.

April had screwed her nose up adorably. "Yuck, Hooch please." She'd turned back to her book, but Tom knew she was still smiling. He could tell from the set of her shoulders.

That night and the next morning passed easily, like they always did at the camp. They spent the evening talking

ERICKA WALLER

about what Tom and Yuki had seen at Camden Market and listening to The Bluetones album Tom had managed to get for himself. The next morning Tom and April had sat around drinking tea again. April reading and Tom drawing, while Yuki and Jamie slept on in their tents.

Jamie was never allowed to sleep in at home. Her mum always had her up and about at 7am doing her school work. It must be hard to have a parent who loaded on that kind of pressure, Tom thought whenever Jamie moaned about her. Tom knew it wasn't a competition, but having a mum who didn't even get herself out of bed, and didn't seem to care at all anymore... well, he was pretty sure that was worse.

April had lay on her front on the sofa cushions again, swinging her feet in the air behind her as she read. She'd looked completely relaxed. At school, she always seemed a bit stressed out. Tom guessed she didn't like being late for class or something. Whenever the bell rang, she would jump to attention and scuttle off.

But when she was here at the camp she was a completely different person. In comparison to her behaviour at school, she was so laid back it was as if she was stoned. That thought made Tom smile, and he was glad she had somewhere where she felt at peace.

Even at school, where she seemed at her most anxious, April was approachable and friendly to everyone. She helped coach some of his old football mates in English sometimes. Some of them had even come to rely on her; they knew she'd always help them if they asked her.

A few of the lads who she had helped had become very fond of her (platonically or not, Tom couldn't be sure in every case) and told Tom that he'd "done well there". He didn't bother explaining that he hadn't done anything. He didn't necessarily want people to think that he and April were a couple when they weren't, but their assumptions that he was dating her meant that none of them were likely to hit on her, so went along with it.

Tom's days of having a temper weren't far behind him, and his reputation was still such that he knew nobody would touch April if they thought she was going out with him. God, how he *wished* she were going out with him.

April didn't seem to have the faintest clue, but she was more than pretty enough to be in the 'popular' group at school with Claire and the rest of her minions. She didn't have it in her to snub or bully people though - just another way in which she was different from a lot of other girls their age.

Claire was in Tom's form room, so he often overheard the daily trials and tribulations of her overly-dramatic life. It was hardly eavesdropping - she always talked loud enough for everyone to hear. She was always nice to Tom and it unnerved him. He supposed it was a legacy left over from when he used to play football and be 'popular' too.

He'd gone to a couple of house parties that Claire had hosted in the past and he vaguely remembered snogging her once. They had been in her parents' massive kitchen, wedged against the island in the middle of the room. He had an awful feeling it might even have gone a bit further than snogging, but he'd blocked it out. He did a lot of blocking stuff out.

Tom's football and party days seemed so long ago, although they were probably only a year or so in his past. His life had changed so suddenly that he couldn't even imagine the sort of freedom that he'd used to have. He used to be able to leave on a Friday morning for school and not come home until late on Sunday night. Now he couldn't go anywhere without making sure Em was okay and that there was somebody to look after her. Then there was his mum – he worried about her too. Even if all he could really do to care for her was to make sure she was conscious.

They'd still had an hour or so at the camp after the poetry, before they needed to head home, so Tom went and smoked a joint with Yuki, who was practising guitar. Then he put the kettle on and made everyone a cup of tea.

The joint had made him feel buzzed and creative. On a whim, he decided to do some work on his art project. He'd grabbed his bag and pulled out his sketchpad. "Mind if I sit here?" he'd asked April.

"Nu-uh," she'd replied distractedly, not looking up from her book. She rolled over to give him some room, and lay on her back with her book held up high above her face.

The theme for his art GCSE was *Encounters, experiences and meetings*. How the hell Tom was supposed to translate that into a piece of art, using 'various types of media', he had no idea.

He drew a picture of *The Flintstones* instead. It was Em's favourite cartoon and she would make Tom watch it with her all the time.

Once he'd finished the sketch, he re-read the brief for his art project and tried to think of an idea. It counted as a massive part of his GCSE grade. Not that his art grade was going to make much difference, or any of his other grades either. He wouldn't be going to college or sixth form, he would be getting a job. He'd probably be better off studying the job pages of the local paper.

Tom had sighed at the thought and looked back at April. They were lying top to toe and he'd stared at her bare feet. They were slightly tanned on the top from the late September sun and she had chipped silver nail polish on her toes.

The mark from where she'd trodden on the bottle cap was still visible on the underside of her arch, healing to leave a perfect circle of ridges. It reminded him of Em's ballerina tutu.

Without really thinking, he'd grabbed his biro and began gently tracing over it, filling it out to make a dress, and then sketching Em inside it. He'd drawn her hair in a tight bun and one leg bent next to the other.

"That tickle?" he'd asked April.

"No, feels nice," she said sleepily wiggling her toes.

Next, he'd drawn Brian, Nan's ginger tom cat next to Em, his tail snaking up her leg. Then he'd drawn a ballet barre, which turned into a snake with a long tongue that forked out. He added Yuki running away from the snake, April lying in a field of daisies reading, and Jamie asleep on her side. He'd covered April's whole foot in his artwork while she read.

Only when there was no space left did he stop. He would have kept going if her feet hadn't been so dainty. April had sat up and looked down at his work.

"Hey, that's amazing," she'd said, tracing her finger lightly over the drawing of Em. "So beautiful." She'd sat gazing at it, twisting her foot this way and that to study all the details he'd added, like stars and mushrooms in the grass.

He had drawn a tree with branches that turned into a pair of Hamsa hands, open eyes inside them and intricate patterns over their palms. The tree's roots swirled like ribbons and flowed under her heel, ending in the shape of an ammonite.

"Where do you get your inspiration from?" she'd asked.

You, Tom thought, but he said "Weed" and April laughed.

"What are you going to do for your art coursework?" she'd said, still looking at her foot as she traced over the patterns with her finger.

"Dunno," he'd sighed dropping his pen and lying on his back.

She'd lifted her legs in the air and waved her feet at him. "My other foot looks naked, practise on that?"

Tom had grinned and picked up his pen.

APRIL

*S*he could have lain there all day, with Tom holding her foot as he drew intricate designs over it.

The sun seemed to vibrate in the sky, pinning her down with a sleepy lethargy. Birds chirped, and a light breeze made the dying leaves whisper.

She was aware of everything and nothing. Nothing except Tom's light fingers on her foot.

TOM

*H*e drew her name in the leaves on the trees, and the swirls of the roots, and then his name beside it.

He carved her initials into the base of a toadstool that went up the arch of her perfect little foot, in the ends of the tendrils of her hair as it spread out around her and turned into fire.

He spelled her name out in stars, so tiny that only he could see; only he would know.

APRIL

*L*eaving the camp on Saturday morning was always a subdued affair.

April wasn't the only one who packed up slowly; they all had crap at home that they didn't want to go back to.

Jamie would have to study all day and night to prove to her mum that her weekly sleepover wasn't affecting her grades. Her mum was forcing her to learn stuff that wasn't even on the GCSE curriculum, like Japanese and human biology.

Sometimes she'd badger Yuki into teaching her stuff. He kept telling her he was Chinese, not Japanese but Jamie would always respond the same way: "Whatever, just teach me some stuff that sounds like Japanese. That'll do."

Yuki would sigh, but then he'd teach her stuff anyway.

Yuki would clean the office his mum worked in on a Saturday. He could theoretically do it whenever he liked but he picked Saturday afternoon because everyone was always busy, and no one would be there.

April couldn't imagine Yuki *professionally* cleaning

anywhere, even though his garden shed was always tidy enough.

Tom had a paper round on Sunday mornings, so he went to bed early on Saturday nights. He delivered the posh Sunday broadsheets and supplements to the rich townies who lived at the top of the valley. He took Em with him, which April thought was extra sweet because she knew it slowed him down. April occasionally went with them too, if her mum was working away for the weekend.

As they made their way around the houses, Em would make up names for them and the people inside. She would have to be dragged away from the windows if she saw any animals inside.

The sight of them together always made April smile. Tom was a brilliant big brother, always patient and intuitive of his little sister's needs. He would pull out a peanut butter sandwich a second before Em would say she was hungry. Ten seconds later he'd produce an Um Bongo, before she could even complain her mouth was stuck together and she needed to drink from the 'tropical river'.

In contrast to her friends, April didn't have much to do when she got home. Her brother James might be home from university, which would be great. She didn't get to see him much and she missed his noise in the house.

Her mum's job as a divorce solicitor gave her the opportunity to work weekend surgeries and make extra cash, but she loved her job and probably would have worked anyway. Kate hadn't gone back to work until April was eleven and was on her way to secondary school. April knew how much of a sacrifice it must have been for her mother. After just a few years back at work, her mother had been promoted to partner – the firm's first ever female partner. That had been a couple of years ago now. It was the only time April had ever seen her mum cry.

Their dad had left when she was eight and her brother was twelve. April knew that he'd had an affair, although her mum had never told them that specifically. She knew because she'd knocked the hall phone off the hook as she was running up the stairs one day. When she'd picked it up to put it back in its cradle she'd heard her dad whispering to a woman who wasn't her mum.

Even now, if she thought about that overheard conversation, it made April feel sick. She hadn't known what to do, so she quietly put the phone down and spent the rest of the day in her room. Her mum hadn't seemed to mind, but her dad had demanded that she come down for dinner.

She'd spent so long lying on her bed crying that her throat was raw and swollen by the time she went downstairs. She'd toyed with her dinner, scraping her fork across the plate, till her dad lost his temper and ordered her to eat it.

She took a bite of her lamb chop and half-heartedly chewed it a few times, but when she tried to swallow, she started to choke. The lump of half-chewed meat was stuck in her throat and she couldn't breathe. Tears stung her eyes, and her heart pounded. The more she tried to breathe or swallow, the more she choked. Her vision started to blur, and her hands went numb.

"April!" Her mum raced around the table to bang her on the back. The piece of half-chewed meat dislodged, and April spat it onto her plate, sucking in huge breaths. She was badly shaken and could do nothing but sit for a few minutes. Her dad got her a glass of water, which she couldn't drink because she felt it was tainted.

After a little while, April she said she felt sick was excused from the table. She went back up to her room and her mum had brought her up a cup of tea and some fig rolls. "Are you okay April?" she'd asked. April had hidden under the covers and said she was fine.

When her dad had come in to say goodnight she'd pretended to be asleep.

She hadn't slept at all though. She just laid awake wondering what to do. Every time she made up her mind to tell her mum, she imagined how she'd phrase such a thing, and then found that she couldn't find the words. She couldn't repeat what she'd heard; those awful crude words – even without having to hear that terrible strange voice her dad had used – the words alone would hurt her mum beyond imagining. April had wished, and still wished that she could just erase the whole thing from her mind.

As time went on, April struggled with her terrible decision and the mere sight of her father began to make her feel physically sick. The things he'd said on the phone that night appeared to her to have stained his skin - she couldn't bear for him to touch her. She would even rewash a plate if he'd used it and moved her toothbrush and flannel to the downstairs bathroom. She couldn't bear anything of hers touching anything of his.

April had carried her dad's secret around with her like a stone on her chest, a fist in her gut. Before she knew it, she'd been doing so for six months and still hadn't found the courage to tell her mum. The guilt she experienced had felt like it was killing her.

It had all exploded with no warning. Early one Saturday morning she was woken by her mother who said that April and her brother were going to be staying with their Aunt for a few days. When April and James got home, their dad had gone. Her mum had sat them down and told them that he'd got a new job, and would be away for a while. She had seemed relieved when neither April nor James had asked any questions.

'Okay,' April had said, then asked if she could go to her room. Her emotions had been all jumbled up, the biggest being a huge sense of relief, and she needed time to process her feelings privately.

Her brother also seemed relieved. Maybe he'd known about the affair too. If he had, he'd never talked about it to April. Instead, he just asked if he could move into the big bedroom and their mum have the smaller one, which she agreed to. The next day their mum went out and bought him an Atari and a game called *Double Dragon*, which he and April played all night long. It was the first time they'd been allowed to stay up as long as they wanted.

Time passed, and their dad didn't come back. April's mum told them that he'd decided to live in another house, closer to work. He'd phone twice a week – at least to begin with - to speak to them. They were difficult conversations, punctuated with long awkward silences. He didn't seem to want to be on the phone any more than April or James did, and she could hear *her* – the other woman - in the background, clanging pans or asking questions loudly. He never invited either of them to visit, and they never asked.

When April thought about it after, she'd realised that her dad had never been around much, even before he'd left officially. He'd been a Health and Safety Manager for some huge company in London and was always at training events, or so he'd said. Whenever he'd been at home, he'd be overly strict and snappy with them. He'd always have a go at April's mum for the smallest of things, like washing on forty degrees instead of thirty, or leaving the kitchen window open.

The house had changed overnight after he'd left. Her mum hardly ever used to have people over and the house was always quiet. Within a couple of days, classical music filled the silence and her mum's friends began visiting. They came and went at all hours and would sit up late drinking red wine and smoking cigarettes. April would get up in the morning and wash up the red-stained glasses rimmed with lipstick smudges and empty the ashtrays into the dustbin.

Life had moved on so easily without their dad around that April occasionally wondered if he'd ever been a part of their life at all. Her mum had replaced the stuffy armchairs that he'd liked with two old swivel chairs in brown velvet. She'd tossed out the hideous dark wood dining table and chairs (that they'd inherited after April's grandmother had died) and had replaced them with a battered pine table and a school bench she'd found in a skip. These replacements weren't fancy, sure, but April had thought they were much nicer. They were comfortable.

Her dad, Nigel, had always hated bright colours and had been just as strict about this as he'd been about everything else when he'd been around. The walls all had to be magnolia and April and James weren't allowed any posters on their walls. He didn't even allow houseplants; he claimed they were a safety risk. He'd said that about anything he didn't want in the house.

April now realised that the whole time, the only health risk had been him.

She didn't think he'd recognise the place now - not that he'd be welcome. The carpets had been ripped up to expose the old floorboards, and the walls were painted white (rather than bland old *magnolia*) and covered with huge posters. Her mum was an avid reader, just like April, and piles of books were stacked haphazardly on every surface. They now also had two budgies (called Thelma and Louise), who dropped millet seed all over the kitchen floor and never shut up.

The kitchen window was cluttered with geraniums because her mum loved the smell. The electric fire had been taken out and replaced with an open one. Logs, old newspapers and kindling were stacked up next to it, and an old sheepskin rug lay in front of the brown hearth tiles her mum found at the reclaimer's yard (her dad would have had a Health and Safety episode about that, for certain).

April would often lie on that rug to read when no one else was around. The afternoon sun would stream through the patio window and make a pool of light on the dusty floorboards where April rested her book. The old TV was still there, but it was rarely used. A battered old RCA radio was kept on low all the time instead, and April's mum would march over to turn the news up when she was home, telling Thelma and Louise to be quiet so she could listen.

Kate hadn't met anybody else since Nigel had left. She didn't seem to want to, she seemed happy being alone. She'd always loved her job, and when she was home, she seemed perfectly content. She'd spend hours in the garden or curled up in a chair with the newspaper or a book. She drank wine out of huge goblets and dyed her hair with henna over the bathroom sink. She lazed round in a silk kimono on Sunday mornings watching documentaries or researching some new law about to come into force.

She was pretty laid-back about what April did and where she went. April was pretty sure her mum smoked weed at the weekend with her friends. April could smell it whenever she was in bed, but she never did it in front of April, and April never asked.

She never would either – she figured that everyone was entitled to a little privacy, as long as they weren't hurting anybody, and a little weed between friends never hurt anybody.

Her mum was a *strong independent woman*, a fact her friends reminded April of all the time, slurring the words and sloshing red wine, which they raised in toasts to 'Kate, the Great'. April was 'lucky to have such a wonderful woman as her mother' they'd tell her, before turning up the record player and blasting Blondie.

She knew her mum's friends thought April should be more in awe of her mum. Although her mum never said, nor would ever say, April knew she was slightly disappointed by her daughter. Kate had tied herself to trees in protests when she was a kid, and been editor of the school paper. April was quiet and shy and lived in the safe world of books.

The weekend their dad had left, Kate moved on. Just like that. By the time April and James had returned home from their aunt's place, all of Nigel's stuff had gone. The house was full of flowers and the radio was blaring out. It was as if he'd never been there. If his leaving had left a hole in her mum's life, it closed again pretty damn quickly.

April couldn't ever imagine her mum being nervous or anxious, like she was. Nothing fazed her at all. She even took care of all the jobs in the house, from changing fuses to DIY, even plumbing work.

About a year ago, she'd spotted an old claw-footed bath (in another skip, that woman found some crazy good stuff in skips) and told April to help her drag it home. April was immediately mortified and replied that the bath was 'disgusting' and 'good for nothing', but Kate didn't listen, and they struggled all the way home with it – with April complaining loudly most of the way.

Kate spent the next two Sundays repairing it and cleaning it, painting the clawed feet a deep gold. She even plumbed-in the taps herself. Once finished, April had to admit that it was a beautiful bath. It was so deep she could sink down into it, so nothing but her face and her hands (holding a book) poked up above the surface of the water.

It was obvious why all of her mum's friends told April how

wonderful her mother was and how lucky she was to have such a strong role model.

April would nod and agree, but she felt that her role models were Sylvia Plath and Emily Dickinson; she understood them better.

TOM

*W*hen Tom opened the door, his mum was in the kitchen.

She was standing at the kitchen sink with her back to him, staring out into the garden. He shut the door noisily to let her know he was home and clattered into the kitchen.

"Hi Mum," he said, attempting to keep his voice light and casual. She didn't seem to hear him though. He moved closer to her, so that they were standing side by side. He looked out of the window too, into their small garden. The grass badly needed cutting and loads of Em's toys were dotted around. Another bloody job to add to the list.

"Mum," he said again, brushing her arm with his. She stiffened slightly and turned to him, her eyes vacant and watery. They used to be the same striking bluey-green as his and Em's, but her once beautiful hazel irises seemed to have been bleached of colour. *Probably from all the crying,* Tom thought.

"Hello, love," she said in her quiet voice, trying to smile convincingly, and failing. "How was school?"

He leaned across her to switch the kettle on: "It was fine, good. Have you been up long?"

She stared at him for a moment before she replied: "I... I'm not sure... I came down here to make Emily's tea and then I just..." she looked down at her hands for a long time. When she finally looked up at him again, she had composed herself a little. "I was remembering when your dad built that swing set out there. Took him all day. It started raining and I told him to come in, but he wouldn't, not till it was done."

She pressed her hand to her mouth and - knowing what was coming - Tom slipped his arm around her too-thin waist to help her into a chair at the table, pushing piles of paper and the fruit bowl filled with overripe bananas to one side. Her shoulders shook as she cried pitifully into her hands.

"Sorry, love," she said when she was finally done, wiping her eyes with the edge of her dressing gown. "How was your day?"

Tom sighed and pulled down two mugs from the cupboard, then dropped tea bags into them. He poured boiling water over them and used the minute it took for them to brew to control his annoyance. When he spoke again he sounded calm: "It was good, Mum. You already asked me that. Have you eaten?" She looked at him and considered his question, like he'd asked her the meaning of life.

Tom wanted to grab her arms and shake her. It had been over a year of this crap. He wanted to scream at her to *WAKE UP! Snap out of it!* He wanted to shout that Dad wasn't coming back, that they'd buried him. He wanted to tell her to crawl out his bloody coffin.

Yes, her husband was gone, but her kids were still here, and they needed her. They needed her to be a mum again.

He said none of this though, nor did he touch her. He placed her cup in front of her and leaned against the draining board to take a sip of his own. She stared into the mug the way she'd stared into the garden, and for a moment Tom wondered if she was going to start telling him about all the times his dad had sat in her chair drinking tea...

His dad was still everywhere in the house. She'd refused to pack any of his stuff up, or give his clothes away. She'd kept the book he was reading on the bedside table and still slept on the left-hand side of the bed they'd shared. His slippers were by the door, and his coat was on its peg. His dressing gown was behind the bathroom door and his wallet and car keys sat in the basket by the front door, as if he might still need them.

Tom knew why his mum was up; she'd been waiting for him. In her mind, it was Monday the 5th March the year before. That was the day his dad had left for work at 5am and never come back.

"Mum," Tom said, as gently as he could, "Dad isn't coming home, okay?" She nodded briefly, but didn't stop looking at the door.

"I'm going to make you something to eat," he said eventually, when he could no longer face the silent staring. He jumped up and pulled a loaf out of the breadbin.

Tom took great care in making her sandwich, as if the right combination of cheese, cucumber and salad cream would fix her. As if she'd take one bite and say: *I'll just finish this and then I must go and get Emily from school!* Maybe his magic sandwich would make her start ordering him around again: *You peel some potatoes and I'll pick up some sausages on the way home.* Or perhaps, Tom fantasised, she'd want to treat them both for managing without her for such a long time: *Do you want to go to the cinema this week? They're showing the Star Wars*

Trilogy at the Odeon for the twentieth anniversary. We can go out for pizza after, if you like?

She didn't even take a bite of it, she just looked at it like she didn't quite know what it was for, then reached into her dressing gown for her pills.

Tom collected them every four weeks from the chemist. They were prescribed for her by the GP after the accident, for the shock. Tom wondered if she'd be better without them, but she refused to try. "They're nothing," she'd tell him when he tried to talk to her about it. "Just my little pills, they just help me get to sleep, love. You know, since..." She would usually then trail-off and start crying and Tom would give in and get them for her.

Still, he was sure that the pills were making her into the zombie she'd become. Tom sometimes wondered if the mother he'd known was even in there anymore. Was she trapped inside this shadow version of herself, screaming to get out? The pills made her practically comatose. Yes, she cried a bit less on them, but she didn't do anything else either. Even walking down the stairs seemed to exhaust her these days.

The doctor still phoned every two months to talk with her. Tom would answer the phone, and every time he'd tell himself that he was going to tell him that the pills were making her worse. More precisely, they were stopping her getting better. He never did though. His mum got so upset if he suggested that she think about stopping them and he wasn't strong enough to handle it. Her desperate pleas with him not to push her, not to rush her, were more than he could bear. He always gave in and passed her the phone.

"Yes, Doctor," she'd say carefully, enunciating each word, "I'm feeling okay. Just tired, you know?" Tom assumed the doctor must think she was tired from raising two children alone because her prescription was always put through, and was always waiting at the chemist when Tom went to collect it for her.

Tom had eavesdropped on enough of the phone conversations to have a good idea of what the doctor said to his mum: *I'll put the prescription in at the chemist for you and your Tom can pop along on his way home from school. Maybe you can stop in at the surgery next month?* His mum always agreed that she'd make an appointment soon, but she never would and the pills were re-prescribed regardless.

"Mum, I've got to go and get Em now," Tom said slowly "do you want to come? She'd love to see you." He waited patiently for his mother to process what he'd said.

Finally, she replied: "Not today, love. Could you get her? I'm a bit tired, is all. We'll go tomorrow, okay? We can feed the ducks by the canal." The mention of the word canal set her off again. Her eyes filled, and tears slid silently down her face.

The railway ran behind the canal. The railway his dad had worked on for twenty years.

It had been raining the morning of the accident. Tom's mum had got up at 4:30am to make his dad a fried egg sandwich, like she did every day. Then, like always, she wrapped it in kitchen roll and filled a flask with tea to go with it.

By the time Tom got downstairs at 7:15am, his dad had gone to work, and the kitchen was draughty from the window his mum opened to air out the smell of fried egg.

She'd been on her second cup of tea by then, having done two loads of washing and cleaned the kitchen. She'd put toast in for Tom and made porridge for Em, stirring in honey and brown sugar. The radio was on back then, filling the kitchen with morning news and chatter.

His mum's blue dressing gown used to sway while she moved to get the butter from the fridge. She'd always been so light on her feet, having been a dancer before getting married. She'd occasionally help out at Tom's school if the dance teacher was sick, or on holiday, but she'd not worked properly since having Tom, and then Em had come along a few years later.

"You're my job," she used to say, ruffling his hair. "You and your sister and your dad. The best job in the world."

Sometimes, when a song she loved came on the radio, she used to force Tom to dance with her in their tiny kitchen – his feet slipping about on the lino in his socks.

His mum never wore socks or slippers, but would glide over the floor like it was an ice rink. When Em was a baby she used to hold her in her arms and pirouette in endless circles to make her laugh. Tom remembered watching her, her foot pivoting on the spot, her body spinning in perfect waves, with Em clutched to her chest.

The morning of the accident there'd been no dancing, their mum being busy with making packed lunches and chopping veg for dinner. She met up with a group of other mums in the village on Mondays after the school drop-off and wanted to get a head start, making sure the house was clean and tidy for when their dad got back at 2.30pm. He would leave early and get home early and their life revolved round his timetable.

On the day of the accident, Tom had tickled Em in the ribs and kissed his mum hurriedly on the cheek before dashing out into the rain. Back then he left early to meet Alex back then, so they could play football before school.

He'd ran down the road, stamping in puddles with his hood pulled up against the wind.

He was thirteen years old and had absolutely no idea that his dad would be dead in an hour, and his mum would have turned into a ghost by the time he'd got home.

APRIL

"*T*ickets will be sold out," Tom said. "It's The Bluetones."

Yuki explained, again, that he'd already phoned the booking line and ordered them and he and Jamie were adamant they were *all* going. "How much did they cost?" Tom asked looking worried. April guessed he didn't make a lot of money from his paper round and she knew his mum didn't, or couldn't work.

"It's cool, man," Yuki said easily. "I sorted it. You can sort me out whenever."

Tom relaxed a bit but still looked uncomfortable. "I'll get it to you this week, okay?" he said, then turned to look at April. "You going to come?"

"Yes! She's coming, going, coming, whatever," Jamie chimed in before April had a chance to answer, "and it's going to be fucking awesome." Jamie grinned and turned to look at April, tossing an arm heavily around her shoulder. "What are you going to wear? Actually, forget that - what am *I* going to wear?" She looked around and asked nobody in particular, "Will we need ID?"

"Well, I won't," said Yuki smugly, then he quickly cast an eye over them all. "Jamie and Tom, I reckon you'll be fine. April… Dollface, I think you're going to need to um… tart-up."

April blushed and stared at the floor, feeling like the baby of the group. Yes she was less *sexually* experienced than Jamie and Tom, and younger than Yuki and, okay, she didn't have much of a chest and her body was boyish at best, but she *was* a girl dammit!

She felt tears fill her eyes, which Jamie must have spotted because she squeezed her tighter and said, "April, you are a babe, but you don't look like an eighteen-year old one. That's what Yuki-the idiot meant to say, didn't you?" She narrowed her eyes at Yuki who nodded looking scared, then turned back to April, "But you will once I've finished with you."

She grinned, Yuki grinned, Tom even grinned and April couldn't help but grin back. It was so good to see this version of Jamie: happy and positive. The last few months she'd been prickly and negative about everything all the time. April knew Jamie loved her, and she really wasn't scared of her best friend, but she never knew how to ask her if she wanted to talk about it.

"Okay, fine," April relented. "But I have two rules, no cutting my hair and no fishnet tights, *eurgh*."

Jamie grinned even more, held out her hand out and said "Deal." Then she turned back to Yuki and began questioning him furiously: "Are you going to drive? Will your mum let you use the car? What time do the doors open? We want to be there, like, two hours before so we can get right down to the front."

Tom groaned, "I'm not hanging around outside the front for hours before, like some kind of bloody groupie."

"*You* don't have to," Jamie said gesturing to both Tom and Yuki. "You can wait in the car, but *we…*" she turned and grabbed April's arm "…are waiting out the front. I'm not wasting a single second of the one exciting thing that has *ever* happened within fifty miles of this boring bloody backwater!"

Jamie was right. The Bluetones were amazing and when they'd announced they were going to play at Watford Colosseum, everyone they knew wanted to go.

Claire's tickets had arrived in the post already (of course) and she was showing them off to anyone and everyone. "I'm sure I'll manage to get backstage," she'd told her enraptured minions as they all got changed for PE. "Daddy knows someone who works at the Colosseum and he's going to sort me out a pass."

April wondered what Claire would say if she knew that she and Jamie were going too. She really didn't want to bump into her at the gig; Claire could be mean, and April knew she'd ask her what the hell she thought she was doing there.

During the week leading up to the concert, April listened to Jamie prattle on about clothes and make-up and what time they needed to leave. She'd stolen her dad's roadmap and had made Yuki memorise the route, even though it was only in Watford (where Yuki had taken his driving test), and he already knew his way around perfectly well.

Jamie was so excited that as the date drew closer, April couldn't help but start feeling the same way. Both girls had stayed in at lunchtimes to get all their homework done, and Jamie had been pulling out all the stops at home. She hadn't stayed at April's house for the two weeks leading up to the concert, instead she stayed in with her parents for 'family games night'.

She'd even joined in the Mother and Daughter pageant

which her mum had organised for the church. They'd worn matching floral dresses (which Mrs. Fenton-Jones had made herself) and matching straw hats. April had come along to watch and clap with the rest of the church audience, trying her very hardest not to laugh.

She didn't tell Jamie, who would only go on about how cool Kate was, that she'd asked her mum if she could go to the gig and been granted permission immediately.

"How exciting!" Kate had exclaimed clapping her hands. "About time you got out and about, April. There's more to life than books, and I say that as someone who loves them!" She then offered to give April and Jamie a lift to the concert. April wanted to go with Yuki and Tom, but her mum was so excited to be involved in some way that she accepted.

Kate had given her fifty pounds to cover the cost of the ticket and to get some new clothes to wear. She'd offered to go shopping with her too, but April had explained that even she had no say in that; Jamie was overseeing her outfit.

Kate had laughed at that, "Oh god, lord knows what she'll dress you in then…fishnet tights, too much eyeliner…"

April had laughed too and had assured her mother that she would NOT be wearing fishnet tights. Then she'd decided to tackle a slightly harder subject, one that had played havoc with her anxiety ever since Yuki had bought the tickets. "Mum, you do know I have to pretend to be eighteen to get in, right?"

Her mum had rolled her eyes at her good-naturedly. "Yes April, I do. Do you think you're the first person to go to a gig underage? I went to see The Stones when I was your age. Best gig of my life."

Kate had gone over to the cabinet by the stereo, dug out her favourite Stones album on vinyl and had placed it on the record player to spin. They'd listened to it as she taught April how to apply eyeliner to the top of her eyelids. "Forget what Jamie says," her mum had told her while she rummaged in her make-up bag "subtlety is key." She'd paused and changed the subject: "April, you're the most responsible fifteen-year-old I know, and I trust you. I'm so pleased that you told me about this gig and didn't try to lie. I don't ever want you to feel like you can't talk to me." She'd looked her daughter in the eye as she said it, and April had found herself getting a bit choked up.

April had thought her mum was finished and was about to reply when Kate continued: "I know Jamie's mum is…" she'd paused, as if looking for the right words "…full-on. Is that the right term? When April nodded, she carried on "She crowds Jamie, like your dad used to crowd me." She'd looked down at her hands then and said, "I'm sorry. I shouldn't have said that about your dad."

"I know he had an affair," April had suddenly blurted out, because she couldn't stand seeing her mother blame herself for anything, not for a second. "I heard him on the phone once, talking to her."

Her mum had sighed and said gently, "Oh April, I'm so very sorry you had to hear that. I imagine it must have been horrible for you." She took her time putting the lid back on the black liquid liner she was holding, then sighed again and said "I'm sorry I didn't tell you or your brother what was going on at the time, but I didn't want you to think I was turning you against your dad. You were both still so young when he left, and I didn't want you to have to carry any of that. I planned to tell you when you were older and could make up your own minds. He cheated on me, not you. He's still your dad."

"He's a liar and a cheat and I hate him." April said vehemently, feeling as though a great weight had been lifted off her, now that her mum knew the secret she'd been carrying around for years. At the same time, the anger she was still holding for her father roared into life again. "When he cheated on you, he cheated on us, and the life we lived," April had continued fiercely. "I don't want anything to do with him. He's a selfish idiot."

"Well, he is certainly an idiot," her mum had agreed. She'd looked down again before saying, "I was happy when I found out. Is that bad?" April hadn't known what to say to that and before she could think of anything, her mum had rushed on: "We got married when we were so young, and he got old so quickly, and I… didn't. He stifled me, and he bored me." Kate had taken a deep breath to finish. "When he told me that he'd met someone else and was leaving, I cried with relief and leapt up to pack his things for him." She'd finally looked up at April and asked her: "Am I awful? Should I have asked him to stay?"

"NO!" April had said loudly and firmly. "God no. *He* was awful, Mum - not you. We are all happier without him."

Her mum had kissed the top of her head, "I've enjoyed today so much, April. I never wanted to be like your dad - bossing you around and telling you to be quiet - so I gave you space. By doing that, sometimes I felt like I'd lost you a little. My job is so involved, and you're so capable - I just always assume that you're fine. Are you fine?"

"Yes, Mum. I'm fine," April had said, pushing down the sudden temptation to tell her mother that she was obsessed with Sylvia Plath putting her head in an oven, and panicked about everything all the time. Instead, she'd put her arms around her.

"Excellent," Kate had said, sounding relieved. "Now then, who else is going to this gig? What's the band called again? Any of their lyrics on your wall??"

April had smiled. "They're called The Bluestones. I have their tape - wanna listen?"

"Sure," her mum had said, and leaned over to kiss her on the top of the head again.

TOM

*J*amie's enthusiasm for the gig was affecting everyone.

Even Yuki was excited about going, at the risk of losing his cool - Jim Morrison never showed excitement about anything.

Tom had done a couple of extra paper rounds to make enough money to pay his friend back for the ticket. They'd stopped camping now that the weather had cooled enough to make it an uncomfortable idea, so he'd taken on a Saturday morning route as well. Dragging himself out of bed at 6am (when he was used to getting up just before 8am) was a killer.

Getting up at 8am on a Saturday hadn't been mandatory, and it wasn't as if he took his alarm clock camping or anything - but he knew April would wake up early and want a cup of tea, and he loved being the one to make it for her. Then he got to see her face when she took her first sip. Some girls his age seemed to want so much from people (especially boys), but April never seemed to demand, or even politely ask, for anything. The smallest things could make her happy. Which was just as well, small things were all he had to give.

April's mum was going to give the girls a lift, which suited Tom and Yuki. They were both excited, but not excited enough to leave at 4pm, or whenever Jamie had said they were going.

Tom knew it would have been far easier to jump on the train to Watford, but he hadn't been on a train since his dad's accident. In fact, he hadn't even been to the train station. He'd never said anything about this to Yuki, but his friend already seemed to know that getting the train wasn't an option. The idea hadn't even come up. Sometimes Tom felt like he owed Yuki more than he'd ever be able to give him.

April and Jamie had been locked in 'what are we going to wear?' discussions all week. When he wasn't hearing it from them, Claire was busy telling everyone in their class about her outfit choices, and her backstage pass, and the limo 'Daddy' was hiring to take her there.

Tom and April listened to The Bluetones non-stop on the way to and from school. April would even sing along sometimes, which was new. She normally held herself back, watching and taking it all in.

He loved being the one that she relaxed with, even if her singing was rubbish.

17

APRIL

"*J*amie, I'm not wearing this," April said from inside the changing room. "It's too short and too sparkly. I look like a Christmas bauble."

"Just shut up and come out and show me," Jamie had demanded, trying to open the curtain which April was holding tightly closed. "I'm sure it looks great, April. Just let me see!" She gave a hard tug and the curtain opened.

April was crouched behind it, trying to hide any exposed flesh with her small and wholly insufficiently-sized hands. They were in H&M in Hemel Hempstead and had been there for *hours*.

Jamie had sent April into the changing room with at least ten different dresses. The few dresses which April had liked made her look too young, according to Jamie. Any dresses which Jamie liked, were too daring for April.

The one she had on when Jamie burst in was black and short, shorter than anything she'd ever worn before. It had silver glittery thread woven into the fabric, which reflected the light when she moved. It was high necked, which April liked, but the back was so low-cut that she felt naked.

"Oh my god," Jamie had clapped her hands to her mouth in wide-faced awe. "You look amazing. That dress was made for you."

April had tugged it down again. "I feel *naked*. I can't go out like this." She'd pulled her hair down out of its usual messy bun and tried to use it as a shawl to cover her back.

"No, you're tying your hair back," Jamie had said, stepping behind her and pulling it back up. "That dress was made to be seen. *You* were made to be seen. Stop bloody hunching over. You look like you're in pain!"

"I am!" April replied, her voice wavering, "This is painful for me."

Jamie had looked at her in the face for a moment, and considered something. Then she ran her critical eye over the dress once again. "Fine, wait there. Do NOT take it off!"

She'd returned a couple of minutes later with a leather jacket. The collar was bright blue, the same colour as the two thick stripes running down either side of the waist. The rest of the jacket was red. "Try this on," she'd said and thrust the coat into April's arms.

April had slipped the jacket over her shoulders, liking how the cotton lining felt cool and silky on her bare back. Normally she struggled to find a coat that didn't dwarf her narrow shoulders, but this one was like a second skin.

"Louise Weiner wears one like that," Jamie had informed her. She *loved* Louise Weiner and so did April. "Now will you wear the dress?"

April had looked down at the price tag and hesitated. Jamie saw her face and said slyly, "Don't worry about that…"

"NO!" April interrupted her friend before she could attempt to shoplift the heavily security-protected leather jacket for her. "I'm paying for my outfit." Her tone was so fierce that Jamie didn't even attempt to argue. April felt a little guilty, so decided to add: "…and anything you buy."

Jamie had looked relieved, despite her bravado. "Well, in that case…" she went back out, returning a minute later with a necklace made up of bright red beads, a matching bracelet and some sheer black tights for herself.

April carefully took the leather jacket off and folded it over her arm along with the dress. Jamie had picked a leopard print dress which she was going to wear over thick black tights. She also planned to match the outfit with chunky black Buffalo trainers which she'd saved up six weeks' worth of dinner money to buy.

It meant that she'd had to do other people's homework in exchange for cigarettes, which she hated, but for the shoes she'd decided it was worth it. The teachers were surprised to see Jamie helping others for once and asked if she wanted to start a tutor group for some of the lower sets. She'd refused, obviously.

After they'd paid for their new clothes (and picked up some new lip balms and sparkly eyeshadow), they wandered to McDonalds. Jamie had a Big Mac which she ate in three seconds whilst muttering, 'Mmmmm junk food, I love you.'

April just had a milkshake. Dress shopping and the crowded shopping centre had made her feel tense. She worried her throat would close up, as it always did when she tried to eat when feeling like this.

When they'd finally got on the bus to go home, April was exhausted.

Jamie had wanted to go back to hers and practise make-up ideas, while April wanted to go back to bed, but she went along with what Jamie wanted. It was easier that way.

The days before the gig seemed to drag on. When Friday

afternoon finally came, Jamie *whooped* at the sound of the bell ringing and ran out the door, dragging April behind her. Tom was waiting for them by the chapel and laughed when he saw Jamie charging towards him, with April stumbling behind her.

"Tom, have you spoken to Yuki?" Jamie demanded, "What time are you leaving? Are Watford playing at home tonight? There might be traffic. Have you considered traffic? There's no way Yuki would consider traffic. He probably plans to ride his bloody snake there."

"Chill out, Jamie," Tom said, offering her a cigarette "…and let go of April, she's not going to run off."

April smiled at him in gratitude as Jamie released her to snatch a cigarette from Tom's packet. He lit it up for her, and she took a long drag before saying to April: "COME ON! We need to get to yours and get ready and get there and… and just hurry up!"

April sighed in mock anguish while Tom laughed and let Jamie hurry them both home along the canal. When the path got too narrow for them all to walk side by side, Jamie charged ahead.

Tom grabbed April's arm as she went to pass him and asked conspiratorially: "Do you want me to push her in?"

April laughed, "Tempting, but can you imagine what she'd do to you when she got out?"

Tom made a face that said he could. "You're right, it's not worth it."

"Hurry *up!*" Jamie hollered from around a bend in the path ahead of them. "We're going to be late!"

"She does know the doors don't open till 7pm, doesn't she?" Tom asked, and April nodded. "And she does know it's

now…" Tom pulled up his sleeve to look at his watch "…
3.30pm?" April nodded again.

"Jesus, what does she have planned for you?" Tom said.
April thought of the dress hanging on the back of her
bedroom door and felt tense, then she thought of the
beautiful red leather jacket and relaxed slightly.

"You okay?" Tom asked her. "You have your worried
face on."

"My worried face?" April said, now sounding worried to go
with it.

"Yes, you normally only wear that face to school."

April forced a smile over her previously 'worried face' and
explained. "It just feels like we *are* at school when Jamie is
like this. Come on."

She grabbed Tom's arm and broke into a run.

18

TOM

They left in Yuki's car at 6pm, which they'd both decided was more than enough time to make the twenty-four-minute journey (Jamie had worked out the time using a very complicated maths equation) to Watford for the gig.

Yuki was wearing his Union Jack jacket and his top hat. Tom wore his brown cords, blue Ben Sherman shirt and white Adidas shell tops. The blood from April's foot injury weeks before had left a small stain on the cuff of the shirt, which he rolled back so she wouldn't notice and feel guilty about. He liked the shirt even more for it.

The journey took exactly twenty-three minutes, but finding parking took another fifteen. In the end they parked at the hospital at the top end of the town. By the time they got to the Colosseum, there was already a huge queue outside.

"Sad-o's," Yuki declared, pulling up his leather trousers.

They finally found the girls. They were about twentieth back in the queue. Tom recognised Jamie immediately; her tight leopard-print dress and stacked black trainers made her even taller than normal and she towered over the people around her. He looked around for April, but couldn't spot her. He was just starting to think that she must be off getting a drink or something, when the girl standing next to Jamie turned around and Tom felt his mouth drop open in shock.

April looked amazing. She was wearing a dress that showed her long legs, and sparkled under the streetlamps. Over it, she was wearing the coolest red and blue leather jacket Tom had ever seen. The dress was tight, and for the first time he could see how tiny her waist was. Her red Adidas shell tops made her feet look tiny, which he found ridiculously attractive. Her hair was piled up in plaits and twists all over her head. She had eye-liner on and her lips looked darker than normal. Finally, he noticed she was waving, looking slightly nervous.

Oh god, he'd thought. How long had he been staring at her? Yuki had already made his way over and doffed his hat to them. "Ladies. Looking lovely tonight..." Jamie had scowled at him in response, Tom could see it from a distance. "...as usual?" Yuki tried, making her scowl even more.

"You're late," she said, "and what *are* you wearing? You look like Willy-fucking-Wonka."

"Oh Jamie, my dear, you have so much to learn." Yuki said as suavely as he could under Jamie's glare. "We aren't late," he continued "obviously. Look..." he cast his hand around to show the huge queue of people and the still-closed main door. "We're right on time, like Black Box once sung about." Yuki must have been in a good mood to admit to knowing 90's pop bands,

Jamie ignored the reference and asked, "Did you even follow my map and directions?"

"Jemima, you are a woman, what do you know about

directions?" he'd replied, wiping his hands down his leather jacket.

Jamie's eyes had widened in incredulity for a second, before she launched into a furious rant, pushing him so hard his hat fell off.

"I don't know why he likes winding her up so much," April said to Tom shaking her head.

"You look great!" Tom had blurted out in response. "Like, seriously great. I love your jacket."

April had blushed and said. "Thank you, you too," then stared down at her shoes.

Tom hadn't said anything else, worried what might blurt out of him, so they stood and listened to Jamie and Yuki arguing like an old married couple. Thanks to their loud squabbling both boys managed to join the queue, without any shouts of 'Queue-jumping scum' from the other people in line, just before the doors opened and the line began to move forward.

The security guard on the door had swept an eye over Jamie and April, nodded at them and said nothing. He'd nodded at Yuki and Tom in the same way as they followed them in. Tom had noticed how he blatantly checked out April's legs as she'd passed through the entrance and felt his fists clench. A few seconds later they were all through the door and he forced himself to relaxed.

April looked fantastic, but it made it hard for him to concentrate on anything else. Every time she moved, her dress caught the light and drew his eye to a different part of her body, which, for once, was on display. Forget her neck, her legs were insane. Yuki had to ask him for a lighter three times before he heard him.

Once they'd got their bearings inside the Colosseum, Jamie had headed for the front, pulling April along with her. Tom was sick of seeing April be dragged about, but April always let Jamie do it. If *anyone* got to drag April around tonight, he'd thought, it should be him, to a dark corner to kiss off her dark lipstick.

Tom had decided he needed a drink, many drinks in fact, enough drinks to make April and her dress blurry.

"They're not going to come on for ages," Yuki had said, lighting up a joint and interrupting Tom's reverie.

"Yuki! You can't smoke that in here!" April had exclaimed, panicked. She'd lowered her voice to a loud whisper: "We'll all get kicked out."

Yuki had smiled at her, looking completely relaxed. "Look around you, man. Or *smell* around you – everyone's doing it."

He was right, Tom had noticed. The hall had been filled with the pungent smells of weed, cigarette smoke and cheap perfume. Jamie had plucked the joint from Yuki's hand and took a couple of drags. When she 'd offered it back to Yuki the butt was covered in purple lipstick.

"Nice," Yuki had said distastefully as he looked at his artfully-rolled joint, now defiled, "real classy."

Jamie had grinned at him in a way that said *like I care, bro* then said; "I'm going to the bar, who's having what?"

April had asked for a beer and Yuki - who was happy to smoke and drive, but *never* to drink and drive - wanted a lemonade.

"I'll have a beer too, please," Tom had said, then out of politeness and no desire to leave April for a single second: "Want me to come to the bar with you?"

Jamie had shaken her head vehemently and said, "NO! I don't want you cramping my style," before fluffing up her hair and marching off.

While she was gone, the support band had come on and the crowd started moving forward. Someone pushed Tom into April from behind and he'd put his hand on her waist to steady her.

"Sorry," he'd muttered in her ear. He could smell vanilla and oranges and had tell his hands to let go of her several times before they obeyed.

Jamie came back with the drinks, grinning from ear to ear. "What are you so happy about?" Tom had asked, feeling slightly nervous.

"Nothing, nothing," Jamie said coyly, and held drinks out for everyone to toast the evening. "Here's to being young! And free from my fucking mother!" She'd downed her beer in one and let out an impressive *belch*.

"Classy," Yuki had said again.

She'd stuck her tongue out at him, held her plastic cup out to Tom and said: "Your round. Same again. Beer with a shot of Sambuca. If Yuki is paying, make it two shots."

Tom sighed and took the cup, knowing Jamie was going to be hard work, but also knowing he owed her a drink and preferred to get it before the band came on.

"Want anything?" he'd shouted in April's ear over the music. She'd turned to look at him and held up her glass to show it was still full. "I'll go and get her highness one before the band comes on."

She'd nodded at him, half-listening to something that Jamie was shouting to her at the same time.

Tom approached the bar and waited to be served. The place was filling up by the second and Jamie, April and Yuki got swallowed up by the crowd the second he moved away from them. He'd hoped they'd stay in the same place or he had no idea how he would find them. People jostled against him, their plastic cups of beer spilling over his shirt. He was about to be served when he heard a familiar voice beside him say: "Tom, *fancy* seeing you here."

He'd turned to see Claire, with a couple of her mates either side of her. She was wearing a low-cut white dress that left nothing to the imagination. Her long hair was pulled up in a high ponytail and she was wearing bright red lipstick.

"Claire," he'd acknowledged shortly, then turned back to the bar, putting up his hand to try and get the barman's attention.

"Who are you here with?" Claire had asked, unperturbed by his shortness, then leaned closer to him, her cleavage pressing against his arm. Tom had sighed and moved his arm away. He hadn't wanted to talk to Claire, he'd just wanted to get back to April. "Yuki and…" he began, then stopped. He didn't want to tell her that he was with Jamie and April. Knowing Claire, she would march over and cause a scene. April had looked nervous enough already for some reason, and he didn't want to make it worse. Maybe she'd been nervous that she wasn't going to pass for eighteen, but they'd all got in easily and she'd still seemed tense.

He scanned the crowd for his friends again, worried that he'd lost them.

Claire had moved closer again and whispered something unintelligible in his ear. "I can't hear you" he'd said as he turned to the bartender and gave his drinks order, handing over a tenner. Claire had moved even closer, her ample chest pushing against his shirt sleeve again.

She'd looked down at her cleavage, then looked him in the eye, smiled slowly and stood on her tiptoes so she was inches from his face. "I said I was hoping to find you here tonight, Tom." Her breath had tickled his ear, but not in a nice way. She smelled of too much perfume and far too much hairspray. Tom had tried to pull back but she had him wedged into the bar.

You never come to my parties anymore," she'd said and pulled a sad face. "We used to have so much fun." Her pout reminded him of Em when she had one of her sulks. He found it cute on Em, he didn't find it cute on Claire.

He'd shrugged in response and said "I've been busy" then turned around, so his back was to her. The barman came back with his drinks and he'd taken them gratefully, pocketing the change before turning around again. Claire hadn't gone anywhere though, and gave him another slow smile which she'd probably thought it was sexy.

"Is one of those for me?" she'd cooed. "I have two backstage passes. Maybe after we've finished these we can go and meet the band?" She tried to take one of the beers, but Tom had held on tightly and in an even tighter voice said "Sorry, I'm with…people," before moving away from the bar.

He hadn't got far before Claire snaked a hand around his belt buckle and said, "Come find me later, I'll be waiting."

Before he could stop her, she'd moved closer and pressed a kiss to his mouth. He hadn't been able to push her away because his hands were holding the drinks. She'd opened her mouth slightly and Tom had felt the tip of her tongue on his lip. He'd snapped his head back and glared at her, but she'd just smiled at him and said "later" then beckoned for her friends to follow her as she headed to the side of the stage.

Tom had battled his way back into the crowd. The Bluetones had come on already and were thrashing their way through 'Cut Some Rug'. He made his way back to where April, Yuki and Jamie had been standing but couldn't see them.

The beers in his hands were splashing everywhere and he'd felt a slight surge of panic. He moved back a couple of paces, then he checked to the left and right of the stage, saying "sorry...sorry..." as he barged his way through people.

Finally, he'd spotted the top of Jamie's head by the stage door and made his way over.

"Why the hell did you move? Where's April?" he'd demanded as he looked around for her. "And what have you done with Yuki?"

Jamie had looked at him with glazed eyes as she took the drink from his hand. "I don't know, I thought they came to find you? You took ages, dude." She'd giggled and gulped at the drink.

"The queue was massive," Tom explained as he looked round frantically. "Christ, it's packed in here. I need to find them." He'd turned back to Jamie who was still giggling away to herself. "Stay here, okay? I'll come back to you."

Jamie blew a raspberry at him and said "No need, I don't need a babysitter." She swayed whenever she moved, and her voice was slurred when she spoke.

"Shit Jamie, how much have you drunk already?" he'd asked, pinning her in one place with his hands on her shoulders as she muttered something he couldn't hear.

He'd sighed and marched back into the crowd, knocking back what was left of his drink as he did so.

The night was turning out to be a disaster.

19

APRIL

*a*s soon as Tom had left for the bar, Yuki had said he needed a piss and went off to find the loos.

The support band had finished their set and Jamie began talking to the people next to her. Tom seemed to be taking forever. More and more people were making their way down to the front ready for The Bluetones.

People pushed and shoved her. She couldn't see the green signs of the exit lights she'd made a point of locating when she'd first come in. She couldn't see much of anything. Around her, people cheered and sloshed beer on the floor. A cigarette burned her leg and she jumped back in alarm, pouring some warm beer onto it, not knowing what else to do.

The room felt hot and panic started creeping in. April looked up to talk to Jamie, hoping she might distract her, but Jamie had wandered off with the bloke she'd been stood next to. She called out her name, but Jamie didn't hear her, or wasn't listening. April had started following her, but the lights went out completely as the band came on, launching into 'Cut Some Rug'. They sounded nothing like their tape, April thought distractedly.

Feedback screeched in her ears. She'd dropped her cup on the floor and clapped her hands over them. The crowd surged forward for the chorus and April was pushed into the bar at the front of the stage. She'd pushed back off it with her arms, as waves of hot white panic washed over her. She'd considered crawling under the bar and running away, but before she could do anything, she was shoved hard from behind. Her hands broke their hold on the railings and she hit her head hard on the bar.

Her head swam as her body crumpled beneath her and she passed out.

TOM

*T*om looked up from his battle with the crowd when he saw a commotion at the front of the stage.

There was the limp figure of a girl being passed over the bar to the security guards and even from the distance, he could tell it was April. Her sparkly dress blinked at him as she vanished from view. He started running, forcing himself though the crowd, pushing and punching wildly to get to her.

"She's with me," he panted to the security guard when he'd finally made his way to her side. April was lying in his arms, eyes closed, with a huge lump coming out on her forehead.

"Is she okay?" Tom demanded. "Have you called an ambulance?"

"Tom?" April croaked, opening one eye. "Tom?"

Tom reached over and went to take her from the security guard. "Have you been drinking?" the guard asked him.

"One beer," he said clearly. "I'm fine. Give. Her. To. Me."

The guard looked at him for a long second, measuring him with his eyes. Finally, he said: "You need to take her to the medic. The office is at the side door next to the bogs. I'll show you."

Carefully, Tom took April from the guard and lifted her in his arms, amazed at how light she felt. She slid her hands around him and hid her face in his neck. He felt her tears on his skin. When he knew she was safe and well, he was going to kill Jamie and Yuki for leaving her.

The medic checked her for a concussion and gave her an ice-pack. "You seem fine, apart from the bump," he said, helping her to her feet. "I don't recommend going back out there though."

April shrunk back from the direction of the audience at the idea. "I don't want to go back out there," she turned to Tom. "I want to go home."

"I'll get you home," he promised, putting his arm around her waist. "Is there a back exit, mate?"

The medic pointed to a door at the back of the room. "Out there, turn right, right again and the door at the bottom will take you out to the car park." He looked at April and said to her: "If you have a headache, blurred vision, feel sick – anything - go straight to A&E. I'd take some ibuprofen when you get home too."

April thanked him quietly and Tom led her to the door.

APRIL

*J*f Tom hadn't been holding her, she wasn't sure she'd have been able to stay upright.

Her legs wobbled, her head throbbed and her stomach was in knots. As they made their way down the corridor to the car park - and the noise lessened considerably – April finally began to breathe easier.

"Where the hell were Jamie and Yuki?" Tom asked her angrily, pushing open the fire exit and leading her out into the frosty night air.

April drew in a deep breath before replying. "Yuki went to the loo. Jamie went off with the bloke who was standing next to us. I tried to follow her, but then the band came on and I got pushed to the front of the stage."

Tom led her over to a bus stop and helped her sit.

"I'm so sorry that you got hurt," he said to her. He didn't seem angry anymore – just concerned. He brushed the hair that had fallen out of its intricate plait back from her face, so he could see the lump on her head.

"Bloody hell," he said, "that was some knock you took."

April tried to smile but it came out as a sob and her face crumpled. Tom moved closer and put his arm round her. She felt overwhelmed and exhausted. Fighting the panic, being knocked out, and then hearing Tom's voice as she'd come to. It was all too much, too strange. She gave in to the comfort of Tom's arms around her, rested her head on his shoulder and cried.

Tom held her and let her cry. He didn't shush her, or tell her to stop. Instead, he carefully pulled out the pins and plaits in her hair, so it fell down her back. She sighed in relief and moved closer into him, her hair around her face, like a veil.

Hidden under her long hair and in Tom's arms, she almost felt safe again. Her legs stopped trembling and the pain in her stomach lessened. Tom smelt of Flex shampoo and incense. So close to him she could hear the slow heavy rhythm of his heartbeat, as he ran his hands through her hair and planted a soft kiss on top of her head.

"I need to find Yuki and Jamie," he'd said, when she'd finally stopped crying and sat up straight on her own again.

"I'm not going back in there," April declared, fear racing through her again at the thought.

"It's okay, you don't need to." He'd reached into his pocket and pulled out Yuki's car keys. "His leather trousers are too tight for him to fit stuff in the pockets," Tom explained "so he gave them to me to look after. I'll let you into the car and then I'll go back and find the others, okay?"

April nodded and stood, then they'd started walking away from the bus stop and down the road that led them to the hospital car park, where they'd left the car. Tom muttered curses about Jamie and Yuki under his breath but April hadn't feel like talking.

She just wanted to be at home, out of this stupid dress and away from this whole stupid night.

TOM

*A*pril was quiet the whole way to the car.

He wondered if she was embarrassed about being knocked out and carried out of the crowd by security. Jamie would think it was hilarious and crow over it for days, if it had been her. But April would have hated being so exposed.

He looked at her as she walked. Her sagging shoulders, hair hung over her face and her feet dragging along the pavement. She looked broken, and he hated it.

When they reached Yuki's car, Tom unlocked it and April climbed into the passenger seat. He slipped into the driver's seat, then turned to her and asked: "You okay now?" April had nodded, leant her head back on the headrest, and closed her eyes. Tom noticed she was shivering slightly and he turned the engine over, so he could put the heating on. The stereo came on at the same time and 'Slight Return' by The Bluetones was playing.

April smiled sadly. "I was so looking forward to tonight." A tear rolled down her face and Tom wiped it away with his finger.

"I shouldn't have left you," he insisted, "it was your first gig."

"It was your first gig too," she'd said, "and I ruined it." She looked so small, hunched in the seat, with her arms wrapped around herself, like she was trying to disappear. She put her head on her knees and sighed glumly: "I just, couldn't handle it."

Tom turned the heating up another notch, wound down his window and lit a cigarette, exhaling smoke into the cool night air. "It was pretty intense in there," he said. "I didn't like it much myself."

April lifted her head up and looked at him. "Really?" she'd asked, perking up a little. "You didn't like it either?"

"It was crazy. Loud and dark and full of idiots." He took another drag on his cigarette.

April had shrank back into her seat again and covered her face with her hands. "You're right. I *am* an idiot."

Tom turned to look at her, surprised at her reaction. "April, you are NOT an idiot." He smiled at her as he added: "You idiot."

He'd hoped she'd know he was joking and it would make her smile. Instead she put her head back on her knees and said: "I wish we were at our camp." Her voice was a whisper.

"I wish we were at our camp too," he'd said softly. He'd been thinking exactly the same thing as they'd been walking to the car. He could have made a huge fire to keep her warm, and a mug of tea that she could have cradled in her hands. They could have sat up talking all night with The Bluetones on the stereo, not in a dark busy room with feedback screeching in their ears.

He'd finished his cigarette and made a move to get out the

car, but April had touched his arm before he could. "Please don't leave me," she said quietly.

He sat back again and sighed. "I don't want to, but I need to get Jamie and Yuki. She was so pissed. Lord knows where she is, or what she's doing."

April didn't let go of his arm "You can drive, right?" she asked. She knew Yuki had been giving him lessons; Yuki had been moaning to them all about Tom's poor clutch-control for the past few weeks.

"Well yeah, but I'm not legal."

April shook her head. "I don't care. Drive us back to the gig." Tom looked at her for a second, not sure if she was serious. At that moment, there was nothing Tom would have liked to do more than lean over and kiss her, running his hands through her beautiful hair.

His fantasy was ruined when he remembered Claire's kiss earlier. He recoiled inwardly at the memory. April looked more beautiful to him now, sat with a huge lump on her head, kinks in her hair and mascara running down her cheeks, than Claire ever could - even when she pulled out all the stops. He would never have kissed her voluntarily – not anymore.

Tom sighed for what felt like the hundredth time that night, and turned the engine over again. He dropped the clutch and slipped the car into first gear, then pulled very carefully (painfully aware that he was breaking the law) out of the car park.

23

APRIL

The gig had finished by the time Tom had pulled up to the Colosseum.

There was even space to park on the kerb outside. Groups of people still hung around by the main door, where some guy was selling t-shirts and posters.

Tom killed the ignition and turned to April. "Wait here and I'll go find them."

April felt like a wimp for not going with him, but even looking at the building made her shiver. "Sorry," she said as Tom opened his door.

"Stop bloody apologising! You have nothing to be sorry about. Stay here, stay warm, and I'll be back as soon as I can." He got out of the car and jogged towards the building.

April sat and watched out of the car window as people made their way home. Everyone looked hot and dishevelled. She touched the lump on her forehead and winced at the pain, then pulled down the sun visor and looked in the mirror, grimacing at her reflection. Her mascara had run down her face and her skin was red and blotchy. She used the hem of her dress, the dress she'd never wear again, to wipe her face clean. When she was finally satisfied she look marginally less shit, she shut the sun visor again and looked back out the window.

Jamie was being helped out of the main door by Tom and Yuki. She was all over the place; her hair a matted mess and her tights ripped. All worries about herself disappeared at the sight of her friend, and she opened her door to run over to them. "Jamie? What happened? Are you okay?" She looked to Tom and Yuki for an answer.

Tom spoke first: "I found her and Yuki by the toilets," he said, lifting Jamie slightly so she didn't trip on the kerb. "She was lying on the floor talking a load of bollocks. Yuki was trying to persuade her to get up." Yuki stayed quiet, struggling under the weight of a very drunk Jamie.

Once they reached the car, April opened the back door and Tom and Yuki slipped Jamie into the seat. She giggled to herself and sighed in satisfaction, rubbing her hands on the leather seats and making small, chirpy noises.

"She's had more than just alcohol, man." Yuki said quietly. He was looking at Jamie through the back window as he continued, "I'm sure of it. When I found her she was twirling around, trying to get her dress off."

"What do you think she's taken?" Tom asked. They both looked at Jamie, who was lying in the back of the car singing to herself and tracing patterns in the air with her finger.

"I dunno…acid, a pill? Hard to tell." Yuki said, looking as concerned as April felt.

"Well, have you asked *her* what she's taken?" April demanded, leaning into the car to speak to her friend. "Jamie! What have you taken? Did someone give you something?"

Jamie smiled up at her and slurred: "April, my beautiful friend! Where've you been? I told you that dress would look killer on you. Doesn't she look killer, Tom?" Jamie reached her arm out and fondled April's dress.

April sighed in exasperation. "Jamie, tell me, please - what did you take?"

Jamie looked at her for a long minute with unfocused eyes. Then she suddenly asked her, "Can you see that?" She started stabbing the air with her finger, pointing at something that wasn't there.

April backed out of the car, suddenly furious.

She turned to Yuki. "Did you encourage her to do this?" she shouted at him. "Did you buy the drugs for her?"

"No!" Yuki said. "I didn't, I'd never do that, man! I don't touch chemicals; that shit is a *big* bet with your mind." He sighed and looked away from Jamie finally as he admitted, "I knew she was looking to try something new tonight. She asked me what she should take."

He signed again as he took off his jacket laid it over Jamie. She took it and began 'ah-ing' and 'ooh-ing' as she stroked the fabric. "I told her not to take anything tonight. I told her if she wanted to try something new, I'd get some 'shrooms and we could do them at the camp. But she was adamant she wanted to get *really* high tonight. I planned to stay with her and keep an eye on her."

"Well, why didn't you then?" Tom said, looking furious.

"Man, I went for a piss!" Yuki shot back. "I was gone, like, five minutes. And I didn't leave her alone, she was with April!"

Before April could say anything, Tom jumped in to defend her. "Jamie marched off the second you left, man. April went to follow her, and got swept into the crowd. She ended up being slammed onto the bar at the front and knocked unconscious! I found her being lifted out of the mosh pit by security."

Yuki turned to look at April looking horrified. "Shit man, I'm so sorry. I should never have left you guys," he said.

"No, you fucking shouldn't have!" Tom shot back. "She could have been killed!"

Tom shoved Yuki in the chest, and Yuki went to shove him back. But before either could throw a punch, April stepped between them. "Stop it, please! I'm fine. Tom, it's not Yuki's fault." She sensed both boys backing off from each other as she continued. "I'm fine, but Jamie isn't. We need to find out what she's taken and get her home. Now."

April climbed into the back seat, shoved Jamie along and tried to get her seatbelt done up for her. Jamie batted her hand away and said stroppily, "I can do it, April. I can do anything. No help needed for Jemima. Jemima… has it all worked out."

Tom and Yuki got into the car and Yuki started the engine. "I don't want to go!" Jamie said loudly from the back seat. "Back to fucking Berko, with its fuck-all to do. Let's drive to London and go to Camden Market?"

Tom turned around to look at her. "It'll be closed now Jamie. Fancy telling us what you took instead?"

Jamie grinned at him, "Just a little something to pick me up. Nice man next to me offered it to me." She frowned slightly. "Well, not *that* nice. He wanted me to do something in return," she looked down at her ripped tights. Before anyone could say anything, she carried on, "But I told him that wasn't going to happen." She waggled her finger about at them all. "No way, not with him, not with anyone. There's no one for me. I have all this love and all this… feeling. All these things I want to do. But no. Bad Jamie, not allowed to feel this way... must be a good girl and do what her mummy wants her to do."

April let out the breath she didn't know she'd been holding. "So, you're not hurt?"

"Hurt?" Jamie asked her, incredulous. "I live each day in fucking *agony*. Each day I pretend I'm someone I'm not. I have to say the right things and walk the right way and not look." She looked right at April, "I must *never* look. Must never been seen looking"

"What the fuck is she on about, man?" Yuki said to Tom, pulling onto the bypass. Tom shrugged and looked at Jamie.

They drove along for a couple of minutes, listening to Jamie babble before Yuki declared he needed a McDonalds. April held Jamie's hand and watched the cars and lights blur past them, feeling blurry too. When Tom asked her if she minded stopping, she shook her head, but all she wanted to do was go home.

They pulled into the drive-through with Yuki trying to cheer them up by talking about food. "Fish, I quite like you, but not as much as when Ronald McDonald fries you in batter. Then, you are delicious!" He turned to the others, "What do you want, gang?" April could tell he felt guilty for the state of Jamie, even though it was not his fault. Jamie did what she wanted to, and always would.

"Big Mac, chips, chocolate milkshake," Tom recited his usual and tried to give Yuki some money, which he refused to take.

April wanted a hot chocolate. She too tried to give Yuki some money, which he again refused to take.

"Want anything, my little drug monkey?" he asked Jamie.

"Claire," Jamie said, quite clearly. "I want Claire."

147

Yuki laughed and placed their order through the window, then turned to Tom and said, "Oh yeah, we bumped into Claire by the loos. Her dress…" Yuki's eyes got very big and a bit misty as he remembered "…well, Jesus Christ. She asked where you were, man."

Tom rolled his eyes. "Yeah, I saw her by the bar."

"Did she offer you her *backstage pass*?" Jamie asked in a very suggestive voice from the back.

"You saw Claire?" April asked, sitting forward. "You never told me. *Did* she offer you her pass?" She realised she'd said the last bit out loud and blushed.

"Looks like she offered him more than that," Yuki said, pointing to Tom's shirt. April saw him look down at the lipstick mark on his neck.

"Nice lipstick," Yuki grinned. "Got it anywhere else?"

April felt sick. She wanted to get out of the car and run away. She couldn't believe that Tom had been with Claire.

Claire had probably offered him a backstage pass and no doubt backstage sex to go with it, and all April had done was sob and demand to go home. Furious with herself, she bit her lip to stop more pathetic tears falling.

"Do you think she's a good kisser?" Jamie sat up and asked Tom. "Knows what to do with her tongue?" she waggled her own at him and gave a spiteful giggle.

"I didn't bloody kiss her!" Tom roared, turning around in his seat. "She was at the bar when I went to get the drinks. She invited me backstage and I said *no*. As I walked off, she sort of…" he stopped and looked at April, as if he didn't know how to finish.

"She what?" Jamie asked him. "Thrust her chest into your hands, whispered in your ear?"

Tom sighed yet again, "It wasn't like that. I had drinks in my hand, I had *your* bloody drink in my hand!" he said, glancing from April to Jamie.

"Oh, so it's my fault you snogged Claire?" she demanded, sitting forward. "It's my fault you've got her lipstick and perfume all over you?"

April sniffed the air for a trace of perfume, but all she could smell was stale beer and the Fillet o' Fish that Yuki was holding.

"I didn't kiss her!" Tom insisted, "*She* kissed me."

April's stomach lurched and for a moment she wondered if she might be sick all over Yuki's car. She opened the back door and ran onto the verge area next to the drive-through.

"April!" Tom shouted, jumping out of the car and running over to her.

"Just… fuck off, Tom," April said flatly, turning away from him and trying to get air into her lungs. She'd never told him to fuck off before, but she needed him to leave her alone and it was the only thing she could think of to say. She saw the hurt flash across his face, but he didn't stop heading towards her.

She felt closed like a fist. Her stomach twisted, her head pounded, and the sound of the cars crossing the bypass made her dizzy. Her legs wobbled and she sank to her knees.

"April… shit, are you ok?" Tom bent down next to her. "Does your head hurt? Do you need to go to hospital? I'm taking you to hospital. Yuki!" he yelled at the car, "She needs to go to hospital!"

April put her head between her knees and said, "I am not going to hospital, Tom. I want to go home, take some painkillers, get this fucking dress off and go to bed."

She had never spoken to Tom so rudely, to anyone so rudely. But he'd kissed Claire. Tom, and Claire. *Her* Tom. As if reading her mind, he said, "I didn't kiss her, April. She kissed me, and I moved my head away. I have no interest in Claire. I…." He went to carry on, but April stopped him.

"It's nothing to do with me," she said, taking in deep breaths and trying to steady them.

"It's everything to do with you, April!" Tom insisted. "I don't like Claire. She's everything I don't want in a girl."

April forced herself to stand up. Her legs trembled and she wanted to lie down, but not as much as she wanted to be at home. "Tom, I don't want to hear about it. Please can we just go home?"

Tom's shoulders sagged as he stood up and made his way back to the car. Yuki and Jamie must have had words as well. Yuki was staring out the window silently, and Jamie, had stopped wittering and was now lying on the back seat grinding her teeth.

They made their way home in silence.

When they got to April's house, Tom went to help get Jamie out of the car, but April refused. Jamie pushed past Tom and stumbled, before running to April's front lawn and throwing up everywhere.

"You going to be okay with her?" Yuki asked. "I can take her back to mine?"

April sighed and rubbed her eyes. She was furious with Jamie for leaving her and taking drugs and saying that stuff to Tom about Claire, but she was her best friend and she'd never leave her like this.

"I'll be fine," she assured him wearily, going over to help Jamie up.

"Sorry April," Jamie said. "I'm so fucking sorry. I love you so much."

April put her arm round Jamie's waist and led her around to the back gate.

"Don't worry about it," she said "Let's just get indoors. I'll make you a coffee."

April didn't look back at Tom as the car pulled away.

24

TOM

*E*ven after two joints Tom couldn't calm down.

If anything, he felt more tense. Yuki was quiet. He put The Doors on and lay on his futon with his arm over his face. Everything felt wrong.

"I'm sorry I left them, man," Yuki said from under his arm. "I had no idea how serious Jamie was."

Tom sighed, "It's not your fault, I left them too."

Neither of them spoke for a while, then Yuki said suddenly, with realisation in his voice, "If she took an E, she might be thirsty, but she can't drink too much water."

He sat up and looked at Tom, "I didn't tell April that." He stood up hurriedly, "That girl in the paper, Leah Betts, she died from drinking too much water."

Yuki grabbed his car keys from the table by the door. "We need to tell April not to let Jamie drink too much."

Tom and Yuki ran to the car and sped up the hill to April's house. They parked a couple of houses down and Tom leapt out.

"Stay here," Tom whispered to Yuki before closing the door quietly; it was really late and he felt nervous as he padded over to April's house.

He knew her bedroom window overlooked the front of the house. It had Rainbow Brite curtains. He picked up a handful of gravel from the driveway and threw a small stone at the middle pane of the window. When she didn't appear right away, he threw another. It took three more before she opened the window and poked her head out.

"April! Come down, I need to talk to you," he hissed up at her. She didn't say anything, just closed the window and the curtains fell back into place where she'd been. He wondered for a long moment if she was going to come back, when then heard the chain being pulled across the front door as she opened it. She frowned at him, then made a *shush* gesture by putting her finger to her lips and gesturing with her head towards the other upstairs window – her mum's room.

She was wearing a massive long t-shirt and fluffy red socks. She'd had a shower and her wet hair was piled on her head. Tom thought she looked adorable.

"What's up?" she asked, not as angry as earlier, but not exactly friendly either.

Tom explained, "Yuki said if Jamie took a pill you can't let her drink too much water."

She nodded, and without missing a beat said: "Leah Betts?"

Tom remembered the photo of Leah he'd seen in the paper – it had made national news. She had tubes coming out from all over her face, her skin blotchy and blue. He felt sick at the thought of it.

"She's not drunk much water," April sighed. "I made her a coffee, she had some, threw up again and now she's tracing patterns on the floorboards and singing to herself."

153

Tom sagged against the door in relief. "Thank fuck," he said, "Yuki was so worried."

"It wasn't his fault about tonight," April said, tugging at the hem of her huge t-shirt. "It wasn't anyone's fault," she looked up at him then back down at her t-shirt. "I'm sorry I was so rude to you."

Tom smiled at her, relieved again. "I'm sorry I left you. And I'm sorry about…" he went to say Claire and then thought better of it.

"Sorry I ruined your night," April said finally.

Tom hated everything about the conversations. He'd gone out tonight thinking maybe he'd get to dance with April somehow, hold her in his arms as she laughed and twirled like his mum used to. Instead, he'd had her in his arms because she got knocked out. When she found out about Claire she looked like she'd been punched in her already bruised face, and it was all his fault. Tom was reminded again, how much he simply didn't deserve her.

She looked so young with her wet hair and her fluffy socks. Her thin legs poked out from under the t-shirt. He could see bruises forming on her knees from when she'd been pushed over in the mosh pit.

"You didn't ruin my night April. You were the best bit." It was his turn to look down at his shirt as he felt his cheeks flush. He wanted to tell her she was always the best bit of everything, but instead said "How's your head?"

She touched a hand to it, "Fine. I took some painkillers and washed all the spilled beer and lord knows what else off me."

"Yeah, I'm looking forward to washing this night off me too," Tom said, hoping she understood that he meant Claire.

"I'd better go," April said after an awkward moment. "I don't want to leave Jamie for too long."

Tom pushed himself off the doorframe and stood straight. "Me too, Yuki is waiting in the car. Are we..." He brushed a hand though his hair, trying to find the right words, "...are we cool, April?" He wanted to reach out and touch her face, but he chickened out and touched her arm instead.

"Yes Tom, we're cool," she said. She gave him an exhausted, but warm smile.

He was so relieved that they'd made up, he felt like crying. He hadn't cried since his dad died. He wasn't going to cry now. He gave April a dorky salute and turned to go, then turned back before he could think better of it and said, "Hey, April."

He looked her right in the eye as she peeked at him from the half-closed door before adding, "I loved the dress."

25

APRIL

*H*er mum got in at about 12:30am and tiptoed into her room.

"Did you have a good night?" she whispered when she saw that April was awake. For a moment, April wanted to tell her mum everything: about Jamie taking drugs and Claire kissing Tom and how she'd been knocked out and had freaked out in front of her friends in a McDonald's car park. She wanted to crawl into her mother's arms and be a kid again.

But she couldn't tell her mum anything. Her mum was cool, but she'd go nuts if she knew April had been knocked out.

After taking her straight to A&E, she'd hunt down whoever had been responsible for knocking her daughter out, and sue the crap out of them. If she knew Jamie had taken ecstasy, she might phone her mum and April couldn't let that happen. It would be the end of Jamie's life; her mum would never let her out of her sight again.

And the rest? Well, what to say? *The boy I like got kissed by another girl.* So what? Tom didn't belong to her, he could do what he liked. She thought about how he'd carried her out of the Colosseum, and had sat in the bus stop with her unpinning her hair.

April couldn't help feel that Claire suited Tom better than she would. Claire was confident and up for anything while April feared her own shadow. She'd hated the gig long before she'd been knocked out. The second the doors closed, and the room had begun to fill up, she'd wanted to leave. Everyone else had seemed to be buzzing while she'd just wanted to run.

She told her mum what a great night they'd all had and promised to tell her all about it in the morning.

April had struggled to get to sleep, even though she'd been exhausted. She'd kept kept leaning over to check on Jamie and when she hadn't been doing that, she'd replay parts of the night, the feeling of panic still at the forefront of her mind. She kept imagining Tom kissing Claire. Claire kissing Tom's neck and him liking it.

She thought of the moment before she passed out and the horrible sense of relief it bought her. For hours, her mind tormented her. She put her head in her pillow and begged it to stop. When she finally slept, it was filled with nightmares.

She got up 7:30am and went downstairs to make a cup of tea, while Jamie and her mum were still snoring. April had been too excited to eat dinner before the gig. Now her stomach churned and she decided food would help.

Deciding to make breakfast for everyone, she pulled out bacon, eggs and tomatoes from the fridge. She put the bacon under the grill to cook, whisked up eggs and salt ready to cook when the pan was hot enough and chopped the tomatoes. Her head throbbed and she thought about taking more painkillers once she'd eaten.

The bacon sizzled as she chopped. She wasn't concentrating

and the knife missed the tomato and caught the top of her thumb. It was a tiny scratch, hardly drawing blood. It reminded April of a snippet from a Sylvia Plath poem: *"What a thrill, my thumb instead of an onion."* Sylvia wrote about cutting herself, as if it was an accident. But really, she knew exactly what she was doing.

April looked down at the knife in her hand and thought of Jamie's enthusiasm for the gig last night, the fearless way she viewed life. Then she saw herself being lifted, unconscious above the crowd, how the knock on the head had been a relief, an escape from the prison of noise and people.

"… Homunculus, I am ill'" she whispered to herself, pushing the knife back into her flesh and watching the blood seep out either side of the blade. *"'Saboteur, Kamikaze man…'"* the knife dug deep enough to hurt. The blood flowed freely down her thumb, crimson red making the tomato juice look pink in comparison. Her head spun with the power of it all. She felt like she was bleeding out pain, bleeding out the wrong, the broken inside of her.

Her blood stained the chopping board, seeped into the pips and the pulp, the thickness of her blood mixing in with the watery fruit juice. It created a grotesque marbled effect. April stared at it, fascinated.

She felt like she was seeing herself from another room as she dug the knife in even more. *Is this what Sylvia felt, this release?* she wondered. Then the pain made her head throb harder as the room started to blur and sway. The sink looked like it was dancing.

The bacon sizzled angrily under the grill, bringing her back. She dropped the knife and grabbed a tea towel, wrapping it tightly over her thumb, then dumped the bloodied tomatoes in the bin, just as the smoke alarm started buzzing.

Upstairs she heard her mum clumping around. She pulled

off the tea towel and held her thumb under the tap, watching as the water flowed pinkly into the sink.

"'Dirty girl, thumb stump,'" she said, finishing the poem as the water finally ran clear.

She stuffed the tea towel into the washing machine and went to get a plaster. By the time her mum arrived, she was dishing up breakfast, a plastered on smile on her face and her hand covered by her long-sleeved hooded jumper.

"What's all this?" her mum asked, looking at the breakfast April had served up, then sat down and poured herself some orange juice.

"Nothing," April said, putting the kettle on to make tea, "… just felt like it". What April really felt like doing was climbing into bed and sleeping for years. She didn't want to eat, and she didn't really want to see Jamie either. But April always did what was expected of her, what other people wanted, and today would be no different.

She hoped that her mum would drop Jamie home, but it seemed she was heading off out somewhere. When April turned back to the table with tea, Kate was hastily making a bacon sandwich, which she ate as she rushed around gathering her glasses and paperwork.

"I'd love to stay and hear about last night, but I've been called into the office early," she took a swig of the tea April held out to her. "Shall we catch up tonight? I won't be late, we can make some dinner and watch a film maybe?" She didn't wait to hear April's answer, and two seconds later April heard the front door slam shut, followed by the sound of Jamie shuffling into the kitchen.

She looked awful. Her usually poker-straight hair was sticking out every which way and her make-up was all over her face. Underneath it, her skin looked pale and her eyes were red and swollen.

"Meh," Jamie said, sitting down and clutching her head. April didn't know what to say so she made her a cup of tea.

April hated confrontation. Just the idea of telling someone that she was upset with them, of speaking up for herself, made her feel itchy and uncomfortable. She didn't hold grudges and liked to get on with people. But she was still mad at Jamie about last night and she couldn't seem to get over it.

"Thanks," Jamie said as April passed her the tea. "I feel bloody awful." April took a sip of her own tea, the hot mug making her thumb throb through the plaster. Jamie gulped down the tea, and then poured herself an orange juice. "I'm so thirsty," she moaned as she drained the glass and went to pour herself another.

"Well, ecstasy will do that to you," April said, sounding stronger than she felt.

Jamie waved her hand at her, "I'm not in the mood for a lecture, April."

April's blood boiled at that. He head pounded, her thumb throbbed, her heart hurt and she lost it. She snatched the glass from Jamie's hand and bit out "Well, I wasn't in the mood to sit up checking on you all night in case you had some crazy reaction to the pill, or drunk too much water and killed yourself like Leah Betts, or…"

Jamie cut her off with another wave of her hand. "Calm down, April. And talk quieter, my head is killing me. It was just an E, no big deal."

April threw the glass into the sink so hard that it smashed. Then - unable to stop tears springing to her eyes - turned back to Jamie, who sat at the table looking shocked. "No big deal? You left me in the middle of a massive group of strangers to go buy drugs! I tried to follow you and ended up being knocked out in the mosh pit and pulled out by the security guard. You think *your* head hurts?"

April pulled her hair back off her forehead to show Jamie the ugly bruise that had formed there. "*This hurts*, Jamie. But no sleep for me, no sympathy. I had to sit up all night checking on you."

Jamie had the grace to look slightly ashamed. "I didn't know that had happened, I'm sorry. I just wanted to have some fun."

"So did *I!*" April exclaimed, tears falling down her face. "But you didn't care about that. All you cared about was yourself and doing what *you* wanted to do. You didn't think about me at all. You could have told me that you planned to take pills. You could have asked me if I minded babysitting you, again, but you never do. You just expect me to look after you all the time."

Jamie stood up so fast that her chair clattered to the floor. She glared at April, "I never asked for a babysitter! I go out to get *away* from people who think they know what's best for me! You have no idea, April. How would you? With your mum who is amazing and *drops you off to gigs*, and Tom who hangs on every word you say, and the choice of any college or Uni you like. You have no clue what it's like *not* to be in control of your life."

April turned back to the sink and started pulling the broken glass out, wrapping it carefully in kitchen roll. Her head was spinning. This argument was going too fast. She hated it. Jamie was wrong, so wrong, but how could April make her understand?

"I never wanted to be your babysitter, but you seem to have no respect for your life! You push everything to the limit. You didn't even know those people last night. What you did was *dangerous*. You keep stealing, smoking, drinking. Now class A drugs too. What next? Is there nothing you won't try?" She ran the cold tap to wash away the tiny shards of glass.

Over the sound of the water running Jamie replied, "Is there anything you *will* try, April? You never get drunk or stoned. You're never late or forget to do your homework. You live within such tight lines. Maybe you should loosen up a bit – you're a frightened rabbit, for fuck's sake."

Her words cut April deeper than the knife she'd used just minutes before had. So, Jamie had noticed that April struggled, but rather than offer her help or support, she'd thrown it back in her face. Her own best friend thought she was pathetic.

April had no idea what to say, so she walked outside into the garden. She followed the pebble-dashed wall down the side of the house and sat down on the bench backing onto it.

She hadn't been there long before Jamie came out and sat down next to her.

"I'm sorry, April," Jamie said softly, reaching over and gently touching her on the shoulder. "I'm sorry for being a bitch and for not telling you I was going to take the pills. And I'm sorry for expecting you to look after me again."

April tipped her head back as all the anger she had toward her friend ebbed away. She knew it was another sign of her weakness, that nothing was cool, but she was so tired of everything feeling wrong. Jamie and Tom were her pillars. She needed them, and she'd take them however they came.

"I don't mind looking after you, Jamie, but you really scared me last night." She said slowly, "and later in the car - the stuff you said about Tom and Claire - it was so *mean*." She turned and forced herself to look Jamie in the eye as she asked, "Why did you do that?"

"Tom and Claire?" Jamie said sitting up, her hand falling from April's shoulder. "What about them? What did I say?"

"You don't even remember?" April said, still looking at her

"I'm sorry," Jamie said again. "I drank a few beers and a few shots too. I don't remember much at all. What happened? Did I see Claire?"

April sighed and replayed the events of the night before – starting with when they'd lost each other in the crowd. Then she told Jamie how she'd asked Tom about Claire in the car, going on and on about them kissing.

Jamie groaned and rubbed her face. "Oh fuck, April." She was quiet for a long time before she continued. "I remember now, sort of." She sat up and fixed her eyes on April's. "I *never* meant to upset you by asking Tom all that stuff about Claire. It was stupid of me, really bloody stupid, and nothing to do with you." She rubbed her face again and then added "April, I see the way he looks at you. *You're* the one he wants. We all see it."

April waved her hand in the air, "It wasn't the question that upset me. Well, it did a bit. What really upset me was how you wouldn't drop it. You just kept asking him about Claire."

Jamie groaned again. "You know how much I hate Claire, April. I was just pissed off that she went near Tom."

"So was I," April said darkly, swinging her bare feet under the bench, then letting them scuff the patio tiles.

"So, why not do something about it then?" Jamie asked her. "You never talk to me about Tom, but I'm not stupid. I know how much you like him. And don't give me the 'we're just friends' crap. You know you could be more than that, if you wanted to be. What's stopping you?"

April suddenly felt a thousand years old. How could she tell her that she couldn't handle a simple day at school, let alone a relationship? How could she explain how hard she found getting up each morning, knowing all the challenges the day would bring? Jamie wouldn't understand. She couldn't.

April was under the bell jar, watching the world through the glass and she couldn't break out. Not even to reach through to her friends.

"I don't know," she said lamely, the best answer she could give. "I'm just… scared"

Jamie pulled out a cigarette and her lighter. April heard the lighter flick and felt Jamie inhale deeply beside her. She blew the smoke out as she spoke, "We're all scared April. I'm scared of everything, deep down. I've just learned to live with the fear."

"How?" April asked, turning to look at her. "*How* do you do that?"

Jamie inhaled again and blew smoke out the side of her mouth, away from April. "What's the alternative?" she asked.

April said nothing, but she knew the alternative; she was living it.

The argument seemed to clear the air between them. Jamie helped April clear the kitchen then they went up to her room. There was a mattress on the bedroom floor for Jamie, but when April lay down on her own bed, Jamie lay next to her. She wriggled about a bit, trying to find a space for her head in between the embarrassing number of stuffed toys still on April's pillows. Once she discovered that this was impossible without throwing them all on the floor, she leaned over to rest her head in April's lap.

"I'm really sorry I fucked up so badly last night," Jamie said, sounding exhausted.

"Was the pill good?" April asked her quietly.

"Not really, I don't remember much of it. Bits of it were pretty cool, I think, but feeling like this now is horrible. This is so much worse than a hangover - comedowns make pills SO not worth it."

Jamie sighed and changed the subject, "I've got to get myself together; I promised Mum I'd help her do some paperwork for Dad this afternoon. Then he's having clients over and I'm playing the bloody violin to welcome them into the sitting room, before drinks and nibbles."

"Yuck," April said sympathetically, "I'd hate to do that today, even without a hangover."

They lay in comfortable silence for a while until Jamie fell asleep and started snoring softly on April's tummy. Not wanting to wake her, April picked up the book on her bedside table and escaped into another world for a little while.

At 1pm Jamie's mum called to say she was on her way to pick her up. The call woke Jamie and she stumbled into the shower to make herself presentable. "Can I leave my clothes and stuff here?" she asked April when she got out. She sniffed her clothes again to emphasise her point, "They stink, I'm sorry to ask…"

"It's fine," April interrupted, "I'll wash them for you".

Jamie's eyes filled with tears and her bottom lip trembled, "Poxy MDMA, making me all emotional," she wiped at her face. A car beeped outside and she pulled April into an unexpected hug (Jamie never hugged her - April had been surprised enough when she'd rested her head on her earlier).

April hugged her back. "See you at school. I'll bring your trainers too."

26

TOM

*T*om had stayed up all Saturday night writing a letter to April to tell her how sorry he was that he'd left her, how good she'd looked in the dress, how much he'd hated Claire's kiss and how much he longed to kiss her instead.

He wrote about how his mum never got out of bed anymore and so he had to do everything on his own. He told April that the only time he felt happy was when he was with her, whether it was at their camp, a concert, or in a car park. It wasn't the place, it was her.

He told her how he was failing all his classes and he knew he wasn't going to pass his mock exams. He told her how instead of going to college or university, he'd have to get a crappy job in their crappy town. He told her how he would love to go to art college, but knew that he'd never make any money drawing. He poured his heart out to her. He wrote until the sun came up and his fingers ached from holding the pen.

Around the words that he wrote, he drew pictures of April in the dress she'd worn that night. Then he drew Yuki eating a fish fillet which had a sad face poking out of the bun. He drew April and himself in Yuki's car, her with her eyes shut, him staring at her. He drew her in her t-shirt and red socks, the pair of them listening to music. He drew her in his arms.

When he'd finished, he folded the note carefully, pulled out his lighter, and watched it burn.

27

APRIL

*T*om flicked his cigarette away as soon as he saw April approaching.

"How's your head?" he asked as she made her way through the hedge the Monday after the gig. His voice was slightly higher than normal. April wondered if he was nervous too. Even though they'd made up, things still felt a tiny bit strained between them. The 'I loved the dress' comment had come back to her more than once over the weekend.

She fought a blush at the memory and said, "Better than Jamie's. She was a mess on Saturday morning. She cried, and... she *hugged* me?!" She emphasised the last part like a question, as if Tom may have the answer.

He didn't, of course. He laughed instead, "How was *that*?"

"Kind of nice, actually," April admitted, realising how much she'd enjoyed seeing a softer side of her friend.

"How was the rest of your weekend?" she asked Tom, zipping up her jacket and putting her hands into her pockets.

"Quiet," he answered her as they started walking. He seemed to want to say something more, but stopped himself.

"No music this morning?" April asked when a couple of minutes had passed and he still hadn't brought out his Walkman.

"I thought your head might be too sore?" Tom turned his head to look at her.

"No, it's fine," she assured him, and grinned when he pulled out *Pablo Honey* by Radiohead.

Jamie was back on form by the time April met her by the dining room - full of angst about the row she'd had with her violin teacher at the weekend. Her hair was poker straight again and her make-up was perfectly in place. April followed as she marched off to the bike sheds, where she smoked two cigarettes in a row and filled her in on the wretched violin recital. The argument with her teacher had been swiftly followed by a row with her mother, who told Jamie that she hadn't put in enough effort.

As punishment, she'd been made to write five hundred lines saying: *'I will not disgrace my family with my insolent behaviour, especially in front of Daddy's clients.'*

On their way back from the bike sheds, they bumped into Claire, who was surrounded by her usual herd of sheep, tittering around like little birds. They were rolling up their skirts before heading off to watch the boys play football. *Impulse* body spray was being passed round. A sickly smell filled the air around them.

"Oh, hi April," Claire said flatly, then looked at Jamie, smirking as she greeted her with, *"Jemima"*.

Jamie stiffened but said nothing. April thought she looked nervous. She watched the two of them exchange looks before Claire turned her attention back to April, "I heard you got pulled out of the mosh pit at the gig…" she feigned

sympathy by putting a manicured hand to her chest," …
That must have been *sooooo* embarrassing for you," she
smiled sweetly and one of the girls next to her giggled. "I
was watching from the side of the stage, in the *reserved
seating*," she added smugly. "Poor Tom had to go and
rescue you."

April blushed but said nothing.

"Did Tom tell you we met at the bar?" Claire continued,
lowering her eyelashes and smiling coyly.. "Things were just
getting interesting between us when he had to rescue you.
He was very disappointed he had to leave me so soon. We
both were."

Suddenly her face hardened. Her eyes were daggers and
her voice was sharp when she said, "I don't know what you
were even *doing* at the gig, April. I'm surprised you even got
in." Her eyes flitted to Jamie as she aimed her next shots at
her, "And I hear you were off your head on pills. Tut-tut,
Jemima. Does Mummy know?"

Jamie held Claire's gaze, but April was surprised to see that
her friend's face was flushed. Claire had really rattled her.
She hated Claire's dig about Tom but she'd known it was
coming. Jamie looked caught off-guard.

Claire knew it, and she pushed even further. "I know she'd
be very interested to hear about it. She didn't know you
were even there, did she? I'm sure my mother will fill her in
though. They still play bridge together…" It was a threat.
April knew it, but she didn't know why. Jamie dropped her
head as Claire turned back to her friends and said "Just like
her daughter, she has no idea that nobody wants her
around."

April wanted to say something to defend Jamie, but what?
She knew that if she begged Claire not to tell Jamie's mum
about the gig, it would only make her more likely to do so.
She looked at Jamie, who still had her head down; she'd

rather die than beg anything of Claire, but to rise to the bait and fight back would be suicide – she was trapped.

A moment passed in silence, until April couldn't take it anymore. Finally, she broke in, "Claire, come on…" she didn't know what to say next so stopped mid-sentence, hands trembling at her sides.

"Come on what, April?" Claire snapped at her. "I don't owe *you* anything, and she…" she looked pointedly at Jamie "… deserves what she gets. She's pathetic, and so are you."

She turned her full attention back to April again jabbing her finger into her chest as she spoke. "Tom is *desperate* to be rid of you. He told me at the gig how you hang around him all the time, he can't shake you off."

April knew this wasn't true. Tom wouldn't bitch about anyone; he wasn't like that. Besides, he waited for her to walk to school with him each morning and afternoon. If he didn't want to spend time with her, he could easily walk another way. He wouldn't have invited her to camp. He wouldn't have ruined his shirt when she cut her foot, or carried her out of the gig.

She knew all of this – she knew Claire was wrong - but still, inwardly she wavered. Was Tom spending time with her out of pity?

She automatically looked to Jamie – usually her strong, fierce protector - for reassurance, but Jamie was still staring at the floor.

April wondered why Jamie was standing there taking it. Claire had called her 'pathetic' *and* had insulted her mum. Jamie hated her mum, but April knew she how loyal she was - there was no way she'd let anybody say bad things about her family – especially Claire. Normally Jamie would be screeching every swear word she knew at Claire, and her airhead friends too, but she was just frozen on the spot.

April had a horrible feeling she might even by trying not to cry.

The thought propelled her forward and she took a step closer to Claire, hands clenched into fists. Her friend was not going to stand up for them, she'd do it. What was the worst that could happen?

"You're wrong, Claire," she said, trying to sound confident. "Tom told us that he saw you, and you threw yourself at him."

Claire's eyes shot up in surprise, but April carried on. If Jamie wasn't going to defend herself, then April would have to. She took a deep breath and continued, "It's *you* he's not interested in, and it's no wonder why. You're a bitch." April shook slightly, worried that Claire might punch her, but when no retorts (or punches) came her way, she carried on, "If you tell Jamie's mum that she was even at that gig, I'll make sure everyone knows that Tom had to run away from you."

When Claire's red face confirmed Tom's story, April's confidence grew even more. Her heart beat twice as fast, but she felt twice as tall as she took another small deliberate step toward Claire, positioning herself protectively in front of Jamie.

What the hell? she thought, *may as well make it worth it.* "Everyone will know you offered yourself to him on a plate and got turned down," she said to the most popular girl in the year, not quite believing she could do it until she had.

"They'll never believe you," Claire said angrily. "Who wouldn't want me? Who would pick you over me? You are nothing - a no one! A frigid baby who creeps up her English teacher's arse and follows Jamie around like a puppy. I see you, shrinking along in the corridors, scared of your own shadow. You're a freak. Everyone knows you can't sit still for ten minutes without needing to run to the loo. They all laugh at you, don't you know? You and Jamie are nothing but entertainment for the rest of us."

April felt tears prick her eyes, but she held them back. Jamie was still mute - as if she'd been stunned into silence.

Before she could find her own voice, Claire flipped her hair over her shoulder, as if nothing had happened, and addressed her minions, "Come on, girls. We don't want to hang round here too long, in case we *catch* something from the freak." She took one more shot at Jamie as she walked past them, "Enjoy the punishment you've got coming, won't you?"

Once Claire and her cronies were out of earshot, April whirled on Jamie, her heart still pounding: "Why didn't you say anything?! You just stood there and took it!"

Jamie said nothing, just kept her head down looking at the floor. April saw her shoulders shaking.

"What the hell is going on, Jamie? I thought you hated her? I thought you wanted to rip her hair out? This was your big chance! She certainly gave you enough ammunition... Jamie, are you crying?"

April pulled Jamie's hair back from her face and sighed at her friends crumpled frown, "Come on, don't cry, please," her own voice wobbled as she said it. "We'll work something out. I'll ask my mum to call your mum if Claire says anything. We can tell her you were at mine the whole time. It'll be Claire's word over ours. Your mum'll believe you, right?"

Jamie shrugged and sniffed and still said nothing. April had never seen her like this before.

"Come on, have a cigarette," she suggested desperately. "We have time before class." April dug in Jamie's bag and passed her the packet of Silk Cut and her lighter. Jamie let April put the cigarette in her mouth and light it for her.

She took a shaky drag and finally spoke, a mumbled "Thanks."

"Why does she hate you *so* much, Jamie?" April asked. "What the hell happened between you?"

Jamie just shrugged again and drew on her cigarette. She looked exhausted. April had never known Jamie defeated like this. It felt wrong.

April wanted to shout at her to wake up and fight back, but she didn't want to make her cry again. Instead she said, "Everything will be okay, I promise."

Jamie finally looked up at her and said, "It really won't, April. Nothing is going to be okay at all."

She dropped the cigarette on the floor and walked away across the playground.

TOM

om saw Claire in registration and she beamed at him, "Hi Tom, did you have good night on Friday? Weren't the band great?"

He didn't even look at her, he just went and sat in his chair, putting his bag on the desk in front of him and resting his head on it. He wasn't in the mood for Claire. He was never in the mood for Claire.

She wouldn't be deterred though. She walked over to him, pushed his bag to one side and sat on his desk. "Did you get one of the t-shirts?"

"No," Tom said shortly. He wanted to say that he spent most of the night in the car park with April, but he didn't think it would be a clever idea.

"Are you going to see Suede next month?" she asked. "I can get us tickets…?"

Tom was saved from having to answer by the teacher walking in and calling for everyone to sit in their seats. Claire dutifully went back to her desk, smiling at him over her shoulder before sitting down.

ERICKA WALLER

After the teacher had finished the register, and told them to hand in their homework diaries on their way out, he dismissed the class. When Tom went to add his (empty) diary to the pile, Mr. Lloyd stopped him and said, "Please come back at the end of the day, Tom. We need to have a chat."

Tom said nothing in reply, he just dumped his book on the pile and walked off.

He knew what was coming.

APRIL

*T*om was in his form room when April walked past.

She'd been on her way to meet him outside the chapel after school, and as usual, she was late. He didn't look happy, he was sprawled in a chair with his record bag in his lap, fiddling with the strap. Whatever the teacher was saying to him couldn't have been good.

April stayed close to the side of the wall and peered in the window. The teacher was going through a load of papers, holding them up and pointing to Tom, who wasn't saying anything. April wondered if all her friends had turned into mutes.

She watched the teacher sigh, and scratch the side of his head. Tom's form teacher was Mr. Lloyd. April had him for science and he was nice. He rarely got stressed and he let them have lessons outside in the summer. She'd never seem him look so serious.

As April watched, Mr. Lloyd made his way over to Tom with the papers in his hand. He passed them over, shaking his head. April couldn't make out what they were saying, but she saw Tom shove the papers in his bag and scramble up out of his seat.

Mr. Lloyd called out something as Tom walked to the door. April didn't hear what it was but she heard Tom's reply: "Yep. I understand."

The door swung open before she had time to move away.

"April, what are you doing here?" Tom asked, sounding annoyed.

"Sorry!" she said immediately, "I was on my way to meet you. I was running late because I stayed to help Miss Khan laminate the new books..." she trailed off and touched his arm gently. "Tom, are you okay? Did you get in trouble?"

He sighed and ran his hands through his hair, so it stuck up in messy peaks all over his head. April didn't say anything else, just stood and waited. Finally Tom said; "I'm not in trouble. I'm just behind, like massively behind."

The papers his teacher had given him were poking out of his bag. April reached for them tentatively, "Can I see?"

Tom slumped against the wall, deflated, "Why not?"

The papers were reports from his teachers. They showed that Tom hadn't been turning in his homework for months, and his predicted grades were low - really low. April tried not to look as shocked as she felt.

She took a quick look up at Tom who was kicking his record bag with one foot.

April thought quickly for a minute, trying to work out what was going on. Tom was always so organised. He was always at her lock before her, and when they were at the camp, he made it run like clockwork. He was no slacker and he was certainly bright, but the grades that had been predicted meant he wouldn't even make it into the school's sixth form. April flicked through the papers again and stopped. Even his art teacher predicted a 'D' and that was his best subject.

"Right, it looks like we have some work to do."

Tom's head shot up. "What? No, you are *not* helping me with this, April. You have a load of your own stuff to do."

He went to grab the papers back from her, but she refused to let go. It seemed today was her day to be brave. She reminded herself of the time she cut her thumb, and how scary that numbness felt. Standing up to Claire, and arguing with Tom was scary too, but it was an alive, in the moment kind of fear, infinitely better than quiet detached dread. She wasn't a freak, she wasn't a mouse and she wasn't going to keep doing whatever was easiest for her to disappear anymore.

She looked down at the silver scar briefly before she carried on; "I'm on top of all my subjects, I have no little sister to look after and I *want* to do this. Don't say no, Tom. Please. You gave me Dinosaur Jr. You gave me Pavement and the Pixies…" she realised her voice was getting louder and slightly hysterical with emotion. "You gave me Yuki and the camp and the Beastie Boys. You gave me the Smashing bloody *Pumpkins*! Please…" she paused and drew in a breath, "…please, let me help with your schoolwork. It's all I have to offer in return."

She was breathing heavily and her eyes were filling with tears of frustration - frustration at the injustice that Tom was struggling when he didn't deserve to be. Frustration that this was all she could ever give to repay him. Frustration that she was a coward and a wimp who'd hid from everything and everyone, while Tom was so busy looking after them all that he never thought about himself.

He stared at her for a long minute, and just as April was sure he was going to refuse her help, he said "Ok, thanks" in a quiet voice and let go of the papers.

Relief seared her chest, but she kept her voice even as she said: "We start tonight. What time can you come over?" Tom had never been to her house, except for that one time to return the casserole dish. April had never been to his either, except for the time that she'd delivered said casserole dish. She thought of the stuffed toys on her bed and panicked.

Tom looked worried for a moment as he said, "I can't come tonight." He paused, sighed again and admitted "I can't come *any* night, April. I have to look after Em. Mum isn't well right now."

Alarm bells rang in April's ears but she ignored them, for now and said "Fine, no problem. Em can come too. We have a TV and a big garden and budgies."

Tom looked at her. April could tell he was weighing up the situation in his mind and waited patiently. "She loves animals," he finally said slowly, almost cautiously.

"Well, Thelma and Louise are friendly enough. Mum lets them out of the cage all the time, Em can help me catch them. I'll make dinner too," she added, "so we can crack on straight away. There's quite a lot do, but it's only catching up and I've done a load of this stuff already."

She could see that he was uncomfortable again. "This is no big deal, Tom," she said in a reassuring voice, putting the papers away in her own bag and making her way to the door so he had no choice but to follow. "We just need to make a plan and stick to it."

Tom caught up with her and they walked out into the weak November sunshine. It was getting cooler now, too cold to camp. A tiny bit of her was pleased that Tom needed her help with his schoolwork. She hated herself for thinking it, but it meant she had an excuse to see him.

"Shall we pick Em up from school and head to mine?" she asked, as they made their way past the chapel to the wrought iron gates at the main entrance.

"She has karate today," he said. "In the school hall."

"Okay, cool. We can start while we're waiting, if we have time," April said in a no-nonsense voice while hoisting her backpack onto her shoulder.

She was more than a bit worried about having Tom round her house. She pictured him in her small bedroom and her heart ramped up a gear. She imagined Tom lying on her bed as she read Sylvia Plath to him, and he cried and told her that Sylvia's poetry was almost as beautiful as she was... It was such a ridiculous image she almost grinned.

Em would be there too and they'd work in the kitchen, she told herself. She was sure her mum had some leftovers in the fridge that she could reheat for tea. April fumbled in her bag for her wallet and checked to see if she had some change. She had enough to buy Em some sweets and a couple of cans of coke for her and Tom.

She heard Tom light up a cigarette next to her and looked up to see him inhale deeply. He was looking at her out of the corner of his eye.

"What?" she asked, looking at him shyly.

"Nothing... just thanks, April. I really appreciate this."

Before thinking too much about it, she linked her arm through his. He widened his eyes in surprise and she grinned. "Don't thank me yet. I'm a very strict teacher."

"*Ooh-err*," he said playfully and did his suggestive eyebrow waggle.

She blushed and went to pull her arm back, but Tom held onto it, sliding his hand down until his palm met hers. He held their hands out in front of them, then carefully linked his fingers through hers.

So, this is what it feels like to be set on fire, she thought, staring at their joined hands.

TOM

*E*m was the smallest in the karate class, but always gave the loudest '*ki-ai*' when she finished a move.

She was so engrossed in her lesson that she didn't notice Tom and April watching her from the window outside.

"She's great!" April exclaimed. "She's like Hermia."

"Who?" Tom asked, watching Em as she kicked and punched her way across the old parquet floor.

"Hermia," April explained, "from *A Midsummer Night's Dream*."

It rang a bell, but he still didn't know what she was on about. "Nope, you've lost me," he said.

"Shakespeare...?" April supplied patiently.

"He rings a bell," Tom said.

"Well, he should. He wrote it. Shakespeare said: 'And though she be but little, she is fierce.' He was talking about a character called Hermia."

"I like that," Tom said, looking back at Em proudly.

"Just as well," April replied. "It's the play you're studying for English."

"Ah, I thought so." Tom lied, then grinned as Em saw him and came racing out.

"Tommy, *Tommy*, did you see my big kick?" Em was full of beans and talking a mile a minute. "Sensei says I'm ready for my green belt! I have to go to the grading on Saturday next week, you won't forget will you, I…" she broke off abruptly when she saw April.

"April!" she exclaimed, pointing at her.

"Em, don't point – it's rude," Tom said.

April just smiled down at her as she spoke, "How did you recognise me?"

Em smiled at her confidently. "Easy peasy! Tommy has drawings of you all over his room and your name is *allllllll* over his art folder."

April blushed prettily.

Tom blushed so hard he thought he might pass out. "No, I don't," he said, laughing like Em had made a great joke, and cuffing her gently over the ear. "She doesn't know what she's on about." He crammed Em's school uniform in her bag, so they could get going.

"Yes, I do and I'm hungry. Did you bring me some food?"

Tom pulled a banana out of his bookbag, peeled it and tried to shove it in Em's mouth before she could embarrass him further.

Em pushed it away, scowling at him. "A banana!? I don't like yellow food anymore and I *don't* want a banana. The Karate Kid didn't eat bananas after class."

"Yes, he did," Tom lied.

"Didn't!" she shot back.

Tom's blush had faded enough for him to risk a glance at April, who was smiling at Em the way Em smiled at puppies.

"Would you like to stop at Londis and pick a treat on the way home, Emily?" she asked her. "I'm going to help Tom with some homework. I thought maybe you could help me make dinner and feed our birds? They fly around the house all day, but at night we have to get them back into their cage. It's quite tricky."

"I will be able to do that. I can catch flies with chopsticks like The Karate Kid. Can't I, Tommy?"

"No," Tom said, laughing, "but you're getting better."

He turned to April, "We watched *The Karate Kid* last weekend, can you tell? Em now calls Yuki 'Dan-yal-san' and tells him to 'wax on, wax off' all the time. Drives him mad."

April laughed, and her eyes sparkled in the afternoon sun. "Doesn't quite fit with his Morrison image, does it?"

"No, but he does do a mean impression of Mr. Miyagi," Tom said. Then, in a very poor attempt at pretending to be Yuki impersonating Mr. Miyagi: *"Man who catch fly with chopstick accomplish anything"*

"Focus, Grasshopper," Em said solemnly.

April looked confused, "Sorry. I have no idea what you two are on about."

"You've never seen *Karate Kid*?" Em asked her, sounding shocked. "It's brilliant. We can watch it later, can't we Tommy?"

"Maybe, if you do all your homework," he said.

"And if you do all yours, Grasshopper," she replied sassily

and then linked her arm through April's as if they'd been friends forever.

"Can I have any chocolate bar I like? Ooh, can I have a Kinder Egg? *'It's a surprise, chocolate, and a toy,'*" she said in a perfect impression of the mum from the TV advert.

"If you like," April said to Em and then mouthed, *I love her* to Tom.

I love you Tom thought, but he said "You say that now, but try getting her to sleep. She has no 'off' button."

"Tommy sings to me at night time," Emily said proudly. "Anything I like, even Spice Girls."

Tom felt himself blushing again but April didn't seem to have noticed; she was too busy discussing chocolate bars with Em.

Tom sighed and walked behind them, wondering what the hell he'd got himself into.

APRIL

*E*mily held her hand all the way to the shop and never stopped talking.

Tom refused to let April pay for the sweets. While they were queuing up to pay, Em spotted some Love Hearts and said, "Hey Tommy, aren't you going to buy them for April?" She said it quite innocently, but there was a wicked glint in her eye.

April had never seen Tom blush before. It made her feel better, as she blushed around him all the time. She wondered if he really did have drawings of her at home, and her name all over his art folder. The thought of it made her stomach flip so hard she felt a bit queasy.

April lived halfway up Darrs Lane, a steep hill that led up to the top end of the valley. Tom lived along the road from the shop, right down the end, in one of the small terraced houses. She couldn't see Tom's house from her bedroom window, but she could see the corner of the field they camped in - only a glimpse, but enough so that she could picture herself there. She knew how that cool grass felt on her bare legs, and the sounds the birds made in the trees.

She knew what Tom looked like sitting next to the fire, and the sound of Yuki's guitar. She loved that view.

Her mum was never home before 6pm. April opened the back door, dropped her keys on the kitchen table, hung her bag on the bottom of the bannister and then stood awkwardly for a moment, not sure what to do now they were inside.

The whole house seemed to shrink now that Tom was in it, and everything she did suddenly seemed more intimate. Even the thought of taking off her jumper made her nervous. She was always hot after walking up the hill and normally ripped her top off as soon as she got home. But now she was worried that her shirt would ride up if she did that, and Tom might think she was doing some kind of sex show for him.

Em broke the awkward silence by demanding to see the birds 'at once!' April, relieved, pushed open the glass panelled door into the kitchen and pointed to the cage in the corner. Thelma and Louise were sat on top of it, pecking at millet seed.

"Ohh, hello birdies," Em cooed in her David Attenborough voice, tip-toing towards them with her hand outstretched. They flew off and landed on top of the giant Monet poster hung over the dining table.

Em clambered onto the table to get to them. Tom went to tell her off, but April touched his arm lightly and reassured him, 'It's fine, come on.' She pushed open the door into the living room and went to sit in the circle of light that the afternoon sun beamed onto the floor.

"Do you want to work here?" she asked him.

"I don't mind, it's up to you," Tom said, looking around. "Hey, I like your house, it's cool."

April watched him take in the piles of books and the art

prints on the walls. Her mum had hung mustard yellow curtains covered in giant red poppies up in the bay window at one end. The other end of the room looked out onto the garden, filled with the last of the summer blooms. Bunches of wilting flowers sagged on the mantelpiece, alongside photos of April and James. Fat church candles sat in dried pools of wax and a big, fat bronze Buddha smiled at them from next to the dusty fire, which hadn't been cleaned out since it had been last used in the spring. A stack of April's text books were piled onto the coffee table next to an overstuffed turquoise sofa, with a patchwork quilt thrown over one corner.

"It's so bright," Tom said, walking over to the record player and stooping to read what was on the turntable. "Cat Stevens," he said approvingly, "… cool. Can I put it on?"

April nodded, and the record crackled into life.

Tom did two more laps of the room before April managed to get him to sit down and get his books out. While he was getting set up, she went to check on Em who was sitting on the dining table whispering to the birds.

"I think they like me," she hissed to April. "They're listening to everything I say. I'm telling them about my Nan's cat Brian, but I've told them not to be scared because he's old and doesn't even go outside anymore, not even to do his business. That's what my Nan calls poos and wees," Em informed her, looking back at the birds.

April laughed, then covered her mouth when Em told her to *shush*, "Sorry," she whispered. Keeping her voice low, she asked, "Are you hungry, Em? Shall I make you some dinner?"

"No, thank you," Em whispered back. "The chocolate filled me up for now."

April made three glasses of orange squash and passed one

to Em, along with two custard creams. "We'll be just next door if you get bored with the birds, okay?"

Em had dragged her school bag onto the table and was searching for pen and paper. "Can I draw you please, Thelma or Louise?" she asked the birds. "I'm not as good at drawing as my brother Tommy, he's amazing." She stopped and looked at April over her shoulder. "The drawings he does of you look just like you."

April didn't know what to say to that, so she just stroked Em's hair for a second instead. "If you need us, just yell," she said as she left the little girl to get better acquainted with Thelma and Louise.

When she walked back into the living room, Tom was lying on his back on the floor with his eyes closed. Particles of golden dust danced in the air around him. He opened an eye as April drew nearer and grinned at her lazily. "Do you think if we spread the text books around us, the information might osmose into us while we sleep?"

April smiled back at him. "I think if you can understand the process of osmosis, you can easily understand Shakespeare."

She sat down and looked at the leaf of papers that she'd wrestled from Tom. "Okay, have you read any of *A Midsummer Night's Dream*?"

"That would be a no," Tom said.

April made a note on the page and moved on to the next one.

"Right, Physics. Do you know how to work out average speeds, acceleration and velocity? That seems to be the module you've missed the most of."

"Um, I sort of know how to?" Tom said it like a question, which was not encouraging.

"Okaaay," April said, making a note on that sheet too and then moving to the third report. "Geography," she said and then put on a voice like Bob Holness from Blockbusters: *"Tom, can you explain biomes, deciduous woodlands, coniferous woodlands and tundra?"*

"Yes, Bob," Tom said, grinning again. The smile faltered a little when he added, "If you let me look in my book first, just quickly." He was still smiling but his body language had changed since she'd entered the room. He'd seemed relaxed before, but now he looked stiff.

"You really don't like this stuff, do you?" she asked him quietly, as if she were whispering for the birds again.

"I hate it," he said honestly, finally losing the smile. "What's the point? How will knowing that coniferous forests occur in northern regions characterised by long cold winters and short summers help me, ever?"

He sounded just like Jamie, which made April smile despite herself. "Well, you might want to go travelling one day. Knowing the abiotic factors of ecosystems might help you then?"

She was trying to be light and funny, but Tom's shoulders sagged as he said, "Me, travelling? Not likely."

"Why not?" April asked, drawing her knees up under her chin and looking up at him. "Don't you want to?"

"It doesn't matter if I want to or not. I can't leave Em." He'd dragged an exercise book onto his knee and was drawing circles in the margin.

"What about your mum though? I mean, she can't expect you to have Em all the time?"

Tom stood up abruptly. "You don't get it April, okay?" His voice was hard. "It's okay for you, here in your big colourful house, and your mum who's out working all day and your text books stacked in alphabetical order, homework already done. You just don't get it." He broke off and glared at her.

She instinctively backed away as he started shoving his books back in his bag, then stood up too, not knowing what to do. One minute he'd been fine and the next he'd just exploded at her.

She was hurt, she'd only been trying to help. What was with Jamie and Tom these days she wondered. They were her pillars. She could not be theirs. She was the weak one. A tiny voice in her head told her she was a self-obsessed idiot and she straightened her spine. Learning she was not the only one who had problems was a comforting and horrible thought.

To Tom it might seem as if her life was easy, wonderful even, but he had no idea what it was really like to be her. If he ever asked, and she answered honestly, she'd have told him there was no way she was off travelling either. She could barely handle going to school up the road, and just the thought of getting on an aeroplane made her head swim. The idea of landing in a country she didn't know, struggling with a language she couldn't speak, all the exits she wouldn't be able to find… It made her want to lock herself in the safety of her room and never leave it again.

The reason she was so up-to-date with her homework, she longed to tell Tom, was because she was too scared to leave the house most of the time. Until she'd met him, and he'd introduced her to his music, all she'd had were books. She'd been so lonely that she would often think of fictional characters as her friends.

Tom had packed his bag and was standing in the middle of the room, looking awkward.

"Sorry," they both said at once, even though April was still feeling cross.

"You have nothing to be sorry about," Tom said, rubbing at his face. "All you've done is give up your time to try and help me, and I appreciate it - I do." He looked up at her and April saw the intent on his face, "I just find it hard to accept it, you know? I'm always the one doing the helping at home, it's hard to step out of that role and be... helped."

April nodded, but didn't say anything.

"My mum..." Tom said, then paused and rubbed his hand over his face again and tugged at his hair "How can I explain? She's still not doing so well, since my dad died."

April watched him carefully but still said nothing. She could see how hideously uncomfortable he felt talking about his dad. He'd been dead over a year. She knew it couldn't be easy getting over the death of your husband, but April didn't realise things were so bad. Again, she realised that everyone was battling something, not just her. She thought about how her mum moved on within seconds of her dad going, and was reminded again how different their home situations were. No wonder it made Tom mad to come to her house. She felt tears prick her eyes at the thought of Tom walked into when he got home each day,

"She takes these pills," he looked up at her again, "...and they just keep her in this... trance. She's like some kind of fucking zombie. It's like she's in a dream world and I can't get her out of it. I've begged her to stop taking them, to get up, get dressed, get on with life again. But she just lies in bed, or stands by the kitchen sink waiting for Dad to come home. And he's not coming home, April. You know? He's dead. He's fucking dead and now I have to be a dad to Em, *and* I have to look after my mum. I have to clean the house and do the cooking and work out the bills."

He was talking faster and faster now, like some dam had burst and all the stuff trapped inside him was spilling out.

"And I don't mind, you know? I don't mind looking after

Em and I don't mind looking after my mum. Before Dad died, she was a proper good mum - always there, always cooking, dancing around..." His eyes filled with tears and he swiped them away angrily. "But I can't do it all. I can't keep on top of my school work and Em's. I can't keep the house running and keep up with my subjects. It doesn't even matter what I get in my exams anyway, because I won't be going to sixth form, or college. I won't be going to uni. Family allowance will stop for me when I turn sixteen and then we'll only have Em's to live on...and the pay-out from the accident, which isn't enough. I'll have to get a job, any job.

"So, no, I haven't read *A Midsummer Night's Dream*, but I do read *Care Bears* to Em every night and I make up songs to help her learn her times table, or remember her spelling. I don't know the physics equations I need to know to pass my GCSEs, but I know how to cook a roast dinner, and plait hair. I know how to rewire a plug, and how to clean out the drains. I, I ..."

He broke off panting. It was the most April had ever heard him speak, and it seemed to have left him exhausted. He dropped his bag on the floor and sank onto the sofa.

April tried to take it all in. She'd guessed that his mum was still struggling from the amount of time he'd spend with Em. She'd assumed he was behind on his work because he was a typical boy, more interested in getting stoned with Yuki each night than revising. She'd had no idea things were so bad.

What a weight he must be carrying, she thought. She wondered if Yuki knew what Tom's life was really like. She felt momentarily jealous of Yuki if he did.

Then she thought back to what he'd said about his mum living in a dream world, and shuddered to herself. April thought that she lived in a 'bell jar', but hearing Tom talk about his mum being a zombie made her realise, with some relief, that she wasn't in her own little world all the time. Her horrible dreamlike feelings weren't constant. Sometimes they'd threaten to overwhelm her, but at other times, especially when she was at the meadow with her friends or walking along talking about music with Tom, she felt fine.

She was at her most relaxed when she was reading a book she loved, or listening to a tape that Tom had made her, in bed. *My mind is not* always *out of control*, she realised. I am normal, some of the time anyway. April was starting to wonder what normal even looked like.

She wasn't the only one struggling. They all had their problems; they were all struggling too.

Carefully, she sat on the sofa next to him and placed her hand on his arm. "I'm sorry, Tom. I had no idea."

He looked up at her, as if to say something, but she cut him off before he could. "I know you don't want my pity, and even if you did, you wouldn't get it. You don't need it. You're doing an amazing job. If your dad was here, he'd be so proud of you."

Tom frowned but April continued before she lost the nerve it took fifteen years to find, "And he would tell you not to burn any bridges, or waste any chances. Yes, maybe you'll have to go and get a job as soon as we finish school..." she crossed her fingers behind her back and prayed that wouldn't happen "...but even if that *is* the case, you'll still need good exam results. The better qualified you are, the better paid job you're going to get. You might even be able to get an apprenticeship somewhere..." Tom looked up again at this, a gleam of hope in his eyes. "*If* your grades are good enough," she finished. "And I don't mind helping. You..." she trailed off, wanting to stop, but feeling like she owed Tom this honesty after all he'd given her. "You've given me so much, more than you will ever know." He met her gaze and she forced herself not to look away.

His eyes were boring into hers. His expression was so intense, she almost wanted to duck her head down, to cover her face with her hair – that favourite retreat of hers. She could feel how hard her heart was pounding and the room seemed to have shrunk to the tiny space between them. Tom's face was only inches from hers. Had he moved closer? She felt his breath on her face, and saw the flecks of green in his blue eyes.

Nope, she couldn't do it. It was simply far too much. She lowered her gaze, bit her lip and wrung her hands together in her lap instead, all the while calling herself a coward.

"April…" Tom had said her name a million times before, but it had never sounded like this, "…look at me." It sounded a bit like an order.

She looked up and met his gaze again. All the anger had gone from his face, but the intensity remained. He slowly brought one hand up and cupped it gently under her jaw, his thumb brushing along her cheek. She forgot how to breathe. Tom's hand was warm, and she turned her head slightly to rest the side of her face in his palm.

"Tom?" she said into the heart line of his palm, her voice breaking slightly. She didn't know why she'd said his name. She had no idea what she was doing. Her treacherous heart pounded loudly, too loudly. She was sure Tom could hear it.

She felt the gentlest touch of his lips against hers… before the living room door burst open and Em skipped in. They sprang apart guiltily.

"I caught them!" she sang. "I told you I would. It was easy, I just covered myself in that long thing they were eating and pretended to be a statue like this…" She paused and stood on one leg, acting as frozen as April felt. "…and they landed on me and then I moved, inchy-inchy, to their cage."

Tom had already dropped his hands and moved away from her, but she could feel his eyes were still on her face.

April jumped up from the sofa on legs like jelly and ran over to Emily, her hands shaking slightly.

"Well done!" she said to Em, probably a little over-enthusiastically. "That's amazing!"

Em grinned at her. "I'm a bit hungry now. Can I have a chip sandwich with tomato ketchup and salad cream, please?"

"Of course," April said, moving towards the door. She stole a glance back at Tom who had a slightly pained expression on his face.

TOM

*H*e was about to kiss her. He had her in his hands.

Cat Stevens was singing "How can I tell you I love you?" on the record player in the background. Her face was small and fragile in his palm. Her skin was like velvet, her hair like silk. The his bloody, bloody, sister had walked in.

He'd *needed* to kiss her, especially after everything he'd just said. After she'd said, 'you have done so much for me', and the way she'd said his name like… like he was everything - like she was asking him to kiss her. He was sure she was asking him to kiss her.

She finally knew the ugly truth about his shit grades and she didn't care. She knew he wasn't going to college, or some fancy university, and she'd still wanted him to kiss her.

Tom had kissed a lot of girls. He'd done a lot more than kissing with a fair few, but those few seconds with April had been more intimate than any experience he'd ever had before.

He loved his sister, but her timing was rubbish.

33

APRIL

*T*om had been about to kiss her.

He *had* kissed her, for a second. Her lips were tingling from it and all she could think about was kissing him again. She didn't think she'd ever wanted anything more in her life.

Instead she'd followed Em out of the room and started digging around in the freezer for oven chips. Her hands were shaking slightly as she buttered bread. She flipped the kettle on to make tea for herself and Tom, pleased to have something to do, a moment to get her head together.

Claire *had* been wrong about Tom's feelings towards her, and the next time he went to kiss her, (if he ever went to kiss her again - please lord let him try and kiss her again) she was going to kiss him back. Even if he was just kissing her because she was helping him with his homework, she didn't care. She just wanted to feel the way she'd felt the second before Tom kissed her.

Em was still prattling on about the birds, and karate, and Yuki, and how lemons made her tongue fizzy. April listened to her chatter as she turned the chips over in the oven. Tom still hadn't appeared. She was becoming nervous about when he finally did - would it be awkward? Was he waiting for her to go back in to the lounge?

As if in answer, the living room door opened and he made his way into the kitchen. "Want a hand?" he asked lightly, not quite meeting her eye.

"Sure," she said. "You can do the ketchup, I'll make the tea." As she moved past him, he reached out his hand and caught her sleeve. She turned to look at him and he smiled at her. A slow, lazy smile. A smile that made her hands shake again.

Before she could do or say anything, he let go and made his way to the fridge.

34

TOM

*T*om's Nan automatically made food for Yuki every Friday night now, even though she still never got his name right.

She started adding pineapple chunks and tins of sweetcorn to the cinnamon and nutmeg rice. Yuki declared it 'delicious' and wolfed down every bowl. He even brought along chopsticks to eat it with. Tom's Nan was always transfixed by the speed with which he used them.

One evening, Em asked Yuki if she could have a go with his 'long tweezers' and he patiently taught her how to hold them. She scooped up a dollop of mashed potato with them and was very pleased with herself.

"Shak-shak," she said, which Yuki had taught her meant thank you.

"You *are* actually teaching her 'thank you', aren't you?" Tom asked. "She's not swearing or calling Nan a dog, is she?"

"Man, I wouldn't do that to her," he said, pretending to be offended. "I'm not Mouth from *The Goonies*, telling Rosalita to pack drugs."

Tom laughed, "Man, if you were one of *The Goonies*, you'd be Data."

"I find that offensive," Yuki said, not really offended at all. "Just because I'm Chinese, I have to be the Chinese one."

"Well, yeah," Tom said. "You do."

"Well, Data is the coolest one anyway, so I'm not that bothered. I suppose you'd be Mikey?"

"Yeah, man. But without the asthma."

"You can't not have asthma; that's like me saying I'll be Data, but not if he's Chinese."

After dinner, Tom's Nan brought out bowls of spotted dick for them all. Even Yuki had some when she refused to take no for an answer.

"Got some down you after all, man," Tom joked gleefully before they said their goodbyes and left to meet the girls.

It was too cold to camp now, so April and Jamie met them at Yuki's shed instead. Jamie was staying at April's and April had told her mum they were going to hang around in the village with some of the other kids. Her mum had been fine with it, she told Tom happily and he realised, with some irony, that she struggled to keep secrets from her mum, while he just struggled to keep his mum a secret.

"All she said was to be home before midnight and not to get in any cars with strangers. I guess that means no McDonalds trips with Yuki," she joked, and Tom laughed. "She also said to keep an eye on Jamie. She's going to call Jamie's mum and tell her we were in bed by 9pm."

April went on to tell him about the exchange she and Jamie had had with Claire at school. Well, some of it.

Tom sighed. "Bloody Claire. Why has she got it in for Jamie so badly?"

"I don't know, and Jamie won't say," April shrugged. "It's like she's scared of her - and Jamie isn't scared of anyone - but Claire really gets to her. She just shut down and... took it and she hasn't been the same since. Claire *can't* have told her mum about Jamie being at the gig, because if she had, Jamie would definitely know about it by now. She wouldn't be allowed to stay at mine tonight, that's for sure."

"So, what's she worried about then?" Tom wondered. "Claire's all talk."

"Maybe. But Jamie is sure it's only a matter of time. She thinks Claire is toying with her."

Tom could see that Jamie was unhappy. She'd said less than usual, but was smoking and drinking more. She and Yuki were sitting on the futon smoking a joint, while he and April sat on some cushions on the floor. After a while they all settled down - April got her book out, Yuki grabbed his guitar, Tom got out his sketchpad, but Jamie just brooded.

Eventually, Yuki couldn't stand her silence any longer and told her she could choose the music, which cheered her up. She put on a Violent Femmes CD, loudly, and ate four packets of crisps in a row. She followed the Femmes with a selection of what Tom thought of as 'angry girl music', after an hour of which, *he* couldn't take any more. He said he wanted to get some tapes from his room and asked April if she wanted to come along. He tried to ask her casually, as if the thought had just popped into his head, but he'd actually been trying to think of a way to get her alone for most of the evening.

He'd been practising what to say just before the girls had arrived and had been overheard by Yuki, who ribbed him so hard that Tom had had no choice but to give him a dead arm.

"Harsh, man - way harsh!" Yuki had cried, rubbing his arm

and sticking out his bottom lip, which made him look almost comically sad.

"Sorry, man. I should have done a Chinese burn, you must be immune to them." Yuki had tutted, disappointed in the cheapness of his joke. Tom had to admit, it hadn't been one of his best. "I'm just... nervous, you know?"

"I know, dude," Yuki had replied, voice full of empathy, as if he was wise in the ways of women. "You know what Jim would say? He'd say...."

"Do NOT tell me to ride the snake, or I'll punch you," Tom had warned him.

"You insult me *and* Jim. He would have said: 'Expose yourself to your deepest fear; after that, fear has no power.'"

"He was a right sage - that Jim."

"He *is*!" Yuki corrected him. He never liked to think of his idol in the past tense, and would rather live in denial. As if to prove his point, he'd sprung to his feet and switched on the little stereo. A few seconds later The Doors were playing, and Jim Morrison was singing, *'Come on baby, light my fire...'* "Just to set the scene for when they arrive" he'd said to Tom, with a wink.

The girls had walked in at that point and Tom had blushed furiously, grateful for the dim light in the shed. Yuki, delighted by Tom's discomfort, had laughed and turned the music up, trying to wink suggestively at April, who luckily didn't notice. She was too busy setting up cushions and candles to make the shed cosy.

Tom had thought that he'd recovered his cool quite well, but it had still taken him over an hour of pretending to sketch something to pluck up the courage to think of a way to get her alone. The idea to ask her to help him choose some music shouldn't have taken him so long to work out, but he was a bag of nerves and wasn't thinking entirely clearly.

"Um, okay" April said shyly, when he finally asked her. She stood up and put her book down.

"Won't be long," Tom said to Yuki, who winked at him lazily – he was good and stoned now.

"Ride on. Take your time, man. *Ride the snake…*" Yuki giggled at his own terrible and predictable joke and made a shooing gesture at them both.

Tom felt his ears burn as he blushed again. He didn't dare look at April as he opened the shed door for her. Jamie offered him a knowing smile, said "get yours sister" then went back to her beer and her brooding.

Tom pushed the broken fence panel aside and motioned for April to go through. They walked in silence up the garden. When Tom pulled out the key to his front door he said, "My mum probably won't be up." April nodded. "But if she is…" he paused, not knowing what to say next.

"It's okay, Tom," April said, as if she already knew he was trying to apologise for his screwed-up family. "Let's get inside. I'm cold."

Tom smiled and pushed open the back door. He saw the kitchen as April would, for the first time. It was tatty, small, and dark – nothing like April's house had been when he'd visited. He had cleaned up earlier, half knowing he was going to invite April back here tonight, so at least it was tidy. He'd been building up to inviting her over for a couple of weeks, ever since that afternoon at her house.

He'd been over to hers a few times since then, but Em had been with him each time. She'd disappeared a few times – mostly to chase Thelma and Louise around the house – but never for more than a few minutes at a time.

When Tom finally kissed April properly, he didn't want there to be any interruptions.

They made their way through the hall and he noticed April taking in his dad's slippers and the coat hanging on the bannister. The stairs creaked loudly as he began to climb. Tom stiffened, but when no noise came from his mum's room, he carried on up, motioning for April to follow.

Tom's room was next to the tiny bathroom. The door was covered in Beano stickers that had peeled and yellowed with age. He pushed it open, gesturing for April to go first. She crept past him silently, brushing him gently with her shoulder as she did so.

His room was tiny - and so was April - but she seemed to fill the space. Tom followed her in and took a deep, steadying breath as she looked round. He had an old wooden desk in one corner, a hanging rail for his clothes and a stereo on the floor. Stacked up neatly next to it was his tape collection.

He watched April as she looked around the room, her attention falling on the drawings all over the walls. Tom had started doodling on them when he was a little kid, and when his parents hadn't stopped him, he'd carried on. There was hardly any space left now.

There was nowhere to sit apart from Tom's single bed. He threw himself down on it with gusto, worried that if he did it any other way it might look too suggestive.

Tom loved Dinosaur Jr's album artwork and had included some of their trademark monsters in a few places. "Wow," April said, tracing her finger over one of them. Mixed among them were characters from *Dr. Seuss* that he'd copied years ago. Over time, he'd added extra little touches to them and now the Sneetches and the Grinch sat with their arms around each another. He'd also drawn Adidas trainers on their feet and they wore huge dark sunglasses.

"This is amazing," April said, now studying the Subbuteo table football game he'd covered another wall with. "You're so talented," she said, turning to look at him seriously. "You have to go to art college, Tom. You just have to."

He shrugged and said nothing. April studied the walls for a bit longer and then went over to his tape collection. She looked through them for a while, then pressed play on the stereo. The Jesus and Mary Chain filled the room and April smiled.

She pulled out a few tapes to take back to Yuki's, then perched on the end of the bed. Tom leaned against the headboard and watched her.

She looked great in his room, her scent filling the air and her quiet, intense energy seeping out like incense. He imagined particles of her, falling like glitter around his room. He liked the idea of finding bits of her on his pillow, or hidden inside his curtains.

"Is your mum asleep?" April said, worrying at a loose thread on his bedcover.

"Probably," Tom said. "She sleeps a lot."

She didn't say anything for a long moment and Tom could tell she had something on her mind that she was struggling to find the words to say.

"What?" he asked her softly.

She looked at him anxiously. "I was just wondering why your Nan doesn't help, or your mum's parents?" She looked down again, busying herself with straightening the stack of tapes in her lap.

Tom ran his hands through his hair and let out the breath he didn't know he'd been holding. "My Nan and my mum never really got on. Nan was only sixteen when she had my dad. My grandad died from a heart attack when he was fifty, so my dad was like, my Nan's whole life." He sat up a bit straighter on the bed, finding his own loose thread on the bedcover to pull at as he spoke. "She thought mum had stolen him away from her. Mum never said anything bad about Nan to us, but I know that Nan used to upset her all the time."

He laughed bitterly as he remembered a perfect example. "At the funeral, she told my mum that *she* was the one hurting the most. It was awful. She wailed when the coffin was carried in and…" Tom trailed off, not wanting to relive the moment any more than was necessary.

April waited patiently for him to continue, her eyes never leaving his face.

He stopped fiddling with the bedcover and looked back at her "She told Mum that she would have us every weekend. Mum just sort of nodded and that was that. We go there, she never comes here."

Tom readjusted the pillow behind him and sank back onto it. He hadn't brought April here for this and wanted to change the subject.

But she didn't let him and Tom worried it was the exact reason she'd come, to interrogate him. "Do you think your Nan knows your mum is um… struggling?" she asked.

"Maybe," Tom replied. "But I hope I'm doing a good enough job with Em that it doesn't show."

April grinned at that. "You're doing a wonderful job with Em! She's amazing and she adores you. You're a brilliant big brother. Actually, you're more than a big brother to her - you're her world."

"Yeah, and she's mine," Tom said, then "Well, apart from the bit that's, you know… yours." He hadn't meant to say that out loud and blushed for the millionth time that night. He can't believe that he been the line he'd come up with.

His life was full of the best lyrics ever written, why couldn't he have used one of them? Even 'Hey April, are we ever going to get it on? I'm dying over here' would have been better. He blamed it on the Dr Suess drawings.

When he finally dared look at April again, he saw she was blushing even more than him. Seeing him looking at her, she dropped her gaze down at her stack of tapes again and asked. "What about your mum's parents then?"

"Opposite story. My other Nan was fifty when she had my mum. They were just going into a retirement home when she and Dad met. They didn't live around here. Dad met Mum when he went away on a training course. She was working in the hotel he stayed at."

Tom smiled as he remembered. "He said he suddenly wanted to go on a lot more training courses, so long as they were in Blackpool." He checked to see he wasn't boring April, he certainly wasn't wooing her that was for sure. When she smiled encouragingly he continued. "They were pleased that Mum had met someone. They didn't want her to give up her life to nurse them. Dad asked her to move down here and they practically demanded that she did. They couldn't even come to the wedding; it was too much for them. Mum wanted to have it up there, so that they could make the smaller journey... but Dad's mum was adamant they should be married at her local church."

His smile faded at that. "They met me once, when I was just a year old. Then died within a month of one another, so, no help there either." He ran his hand through his hair again and thought 'Good job Tom, use a sad story about your dead grandparents and maybe she will snog you out of sympathy.

He knew the story of how his mum and dad had met off by heart. His Dad used to tell it to him all the time. His dad had used to say that the very second he'd seen her - behind the bar, laughing at something a customer had said – he'd known that she was the one for him. "I fell in love with that smile," he'd say, turning to look at his mum in a way that used to make Tom feel awkward, but now he kind of understood.

He knew he looked at April with that kind of wonder. His mum would blush when his dad had told them how he'd 'wooed her with his charm,' and then he'd kiss her, in front of anyone who happened to be around – mostly Tom and Em, who would cringe with embarrassment at their parents' regular public displays of affection.

Tom felt tears prick his eyes as he realised how much he truly missed his dad. Tom missed his calm voice, and his big hands that could fix anything. Tom remembered all the hours they'd spent playing football together, then Subbuteo when it was too wet or too dark to go out. They used to make their own sports report radio show, where his dad would comment on the highlights of the game. They had even made up their own daft jingles. When his mum bought them up chip sandwiches and cans of coke, she'd sometimes even join in.

He suddenly missed him mum too, the happy version of her that he remembered to go with his happy dad. Not the ghost next door, eaten up by pain, sadness and pills.

"Tom?" April said quietly.

He realised he hadn't said anything for a while and looked up, and that was when April kissed him. Briefly, sweetly and shyly. Just, like, that.

Eager to take back control he slid one hand up to hold her chin, and brought his other hand to fist in her hair, then he kissed her back. Hard.

He wondered if she'd pull away, but she responded immediately. He caught her bottom lip between his teeth and tugged on it gently. When she sighed in response he felt like he'd scored a hat trick.

Finally, he pulled away to look at her. "April, you have no idea..." he said, not knowing how to finish the sentence. Instead he pressed his mouth to the side of her neck.

He could feel her rapid heartbeat as he ran his nose down her skin and left a trail of kisses across her collarbone, before finding her lips again.

35

APRIL

*A*pril opened her eyes as he kissed her.

"*I shut my eyes and the world drops dead, I lift my lids and all is born again*" she thought, then closed them again and kissed him back.

36

TOM

Kissing April.

Fuck. How was he ever going to stop?

APRIL

𝒫lease. Never. Stop. Kissing. Me. Ever

3 8

TOM

I'm going to have to stop kissing her soon, before I go too far.

APRIL

*T*hey kissed for hours, or for what felt like hours.

The tape on the stereo ran through to the end, and neither of them had made a move to put on another one. They kissed until April's lips felt numb and her skin was burning.

When Tom finally pulled away, he leant back onto the headboard and pulled April with him, so she was lying on his chest.

"We'd better go soon," she said quietly, breathing in the scent of him.

"In a minute," he replied softly and dropped a sleepy kiss on the top of her head.

April smiled into his t-shirt and shut her eyes.

Tom woke her saying, "Princess, I'm going to fall asleep too if we don't move. You and Jamie have to be home soon."

She sat up immediately, panicked she was going to be late home. Away from the warmth of Tom she shivered slightly.

He must have noticed because he passed her his zip-up Adidas top from the end of the bed. She slipped it on and rolled the sleeves up.

"Suits you," he said with a grin.

She wanted to kiss him again.

TOM

*A*pril looked great in his jacket.

He wanted her to wear it to school, to let everyone know she was his. He didn't tell her that though, he told her he was going to check on his mum and he'd see her downstairs. She tiptoed past him on the landing as he pushed open his mum's door.

His mum was asleep, facing the photo of Dad that she kept next to her on the bedside table. She murmured something he didn't catch as he pulled the covers up and tucked her in, sweeping a stray hair from her face and leaning in to kiss her on the cheek.

"Mum," he whispered to her "I'm in love."

April was standing in the kitchen when he came downstairs, looking at the photos of him and Em on the dresser. "You were a cute baby," she whispered to him as he approached. He stood behind her and rested his head on her shoulder, then wrapped his arms around her waist. He felt her relax into him and he held her tighter. He was petrified that tonight was a one-off and the second they left his house the spell would be broken.

Now he knew what it was like to touch April, he didn't think he could bear to stop. They made their way back to Yuki's shed hand in hand. When they got to the door, Tom stopped and kissed April's knuckles. He wanted to say something profound to her, he wanted to ask her out, but it would sound so lame. Where would he take her?

Jamie was asleep on the futon and Yuki was sitting next to her playing the guitar quietly. He looked up as they came in, one eyebrow raised at Tom in a question.

Tom smiled at him over April's head and Yuki mouthed to him, "All the way to the river?" Tom shook his head fiercely, desperate for his friend just to be cool.

Yuki seemed to understand and changed the subject. He pointed at Jamie and whispered, "She's been out for a while. I tried to wake her, but she was having none of it."

April bent and stroked Jamie's hair softly. "Jamie, wake up, we've got to go."

She moaned and said groggily, "Piss off, I'm asleep."

April poked her gently and tried again. "I've got Findus Crispy Pancakes at home... cheese ones."

Jamie opened one eye. "Keep talking."

April smiled, she knew she was getting somewhere. Jamie wasn't immune to good old-fashioned bribery, especially when she had the munchies. "And Walnut Whips and Wagon Wheels..."

Jamie's other eye opened as she said, "Have you got tinned custard?"

"Yup," April held out her hand to pull her friend up "... loads of it."

Jamie let herself be pulled to her feet, then turned to high-five Yuki and went to leave through the door.

"Want a lift?" Yuki offered. "I've only had one beer. Not that much fun drinking alone." He nodded his head at Jamie. "She passed out five minutes after you guys left. And you were gone for ages..." His mouth turned up at the corners in a cheeky smile aimed directly at Tom, who couldn't stop grinning.

"What tapes did you bring us to listen to anyway?" he asked.

"Oh, I forgot to grab the tapes," April said as she looked at Tom with mild panic in her big eyes.

"Oh, you forgot them, did you?" Yuki asked, full of innuendo. "After all that time picking them, as well."

Tom glared at him, but Yuki just smiled and got up to gather his car keys.

Jamie sat in the front of the car and fiddled with the stereo. Tom sat in the back with April and held her hand in the darkness. He wanted to kiss her again, but he had a feeling she wouldn't be up for it in front of everyone. Besides, he didn't think he could bear Yuki's ribbing.

When they pulled up outside April's house, she leant over and kissed him quickly on the cheek then jumped out before he could offer to walk her to the door.

Once both girls were safely inside, Yuki pulled away in the car, turned down the stereo and asked Tom what he'd been dying to ask. "Well? Did you get some or what, dude?"

Tom climbed over into the front seat and pulled out a cigarette. "I'm not telling you anything," he said resolutely.

"Okay then," Yuki said defiantly "I'll just ask April."

"Don't you dare!" Tom warned, knowing exactly how embarrassed she'd be.

Yuki sulked. "Fine, I'll ask Jamie; April will have told her everything, like girls do."

Tom punched him on the arm, but offered: "McDonalds, my treat?"

"Good call, man," Yuki said, perking up at the idea of food and swung onto the bypass.

41

APRIL

*a*s promised, April made Jamie a midnight feast.

Her mum had waited up and was watching a film when they'd come in. She said hello, kissed them both on the forehead and went upstairs to bed, telling April to lock up once she was done.

Jamie devoured her food in silence for a long while, before she finally asked: "Well, did he kiss you or what?"

April felt dishevelled and disorientated from the whole evening. It felt delicious. She just smiled at her friend and sighed.

Jamie's red-rimmed eyes lit up instantly. "I'll take that as a *yes* then," she said excitedly, cramming in half a Wagon Wheel. "Did he use tongue?" April blushed and nodded cautiously. "Was it good?" Jamie asked, spitting chocolate on the table. April blushed even more and nodded again. "Cool," Jamie said, satisfied. Then she demanded, "Make me some tea, harlot!"

Once upstairs, Jamie fell asleep as soon as her head hit the pillow. April lay in the dark, running her finger over her lips, remembering Tom's kisses. She put her face into her pillow and grinned uncontrollably.

April spent most of her days feeling weak - a victim of her anxiety. But tonight, she'd felt in control. Well, until Tom had started tracing kisses down her neck and trailing his fingers down her arm. Oh arm, she thought, looking at it in the darkness, who knew you could feel so good ?

Jamie's mum was due to pick her up early the next morning, she had a violin concert she needed to rehearse for. April's mum got up at 8am and made them pancakes with bacon and maple syrup, which Jamie said might be her new favourite food in all the world.

It tasted even more amazing than usual to April. The birds sounded wonderful too.

When Jamie's mum arrived, Kate went out to talk to her. She told her what a lovely evening the girls had, watching films (*Heathers*) and eating popcorn (homemade!), and how Jamie had even done some homework.

Jamie's mum sniffed and made polite conversation, all the while looking Kate up and down judgmentally. April's mum was barefoot, wearing a silk kimono and an old tartan shirt over some old leggings. Her hair was held up haphazardly by a pencil, as usual.

"She's welcome here anytime," Kate called over to them as Jamie's mum turned on the engine. "Such a wonderful girl!"

She stood in the drive, waving the car off enthusiastically until it was out of sight around the corner. Then she turned back to April who'd wandered out to say goodbye too. "Thank Christ that's over! Poor Jamie, imagine having that woman for your mother. You're a very good friend to go to sleepovers at her house. She must put you to bed at 7:30pm!" Kate put her arm around April and they walked back towards the open front door. "Where did you go last night anyway? It's too cold to just hang around outside."

They made their way back inside and April told her mum about Yuki's shed, and a little bit about Tom. Then, as they were washing up the dishes from breakfast, she told her they all *sometimes* camped out along the road.

April's mum put down the tea towel she was holding. "I'm guessing you thought I wouldn't let you go camping if you'd asked?" April nodded and played with the water in the sink, making more bubbles. "And you're telling me now because it's too cold to go anyway, so who cares if I stop you, right?" April nodded again. "That upsets me, April. You should have told me."

Her mum looked disappointed and it made April feel a bit less wonderful. "I guess the boys go with you to this camp?" April thought for a moment before answering and then decided it was time to be honest . She told her about all the work Tom did to make it comfortable: the sofa cushions, the campfire and the s'mores. She knew that she blushed whenever she said Tom's name; she couldn't help it.

Kate listened quietly till April finally paused for breath, then sighed and said "It sounds pretty great, much better than sleeping over at Jamie's with that terrible woman around. I wondered why you rarely slept over here. I thought maybe Jamie's mother didn't approve of me..." April went to object, but Kate interrupted, "It's okay, I sort of hope she *doesn't* approve of me, April. You could have *told* me though. You don't need to keep secrets from me. I trust you, well I did anyway"

"I'm sorry I kept it from you, Mum" April said, feeling sick at the thought of her mum no longer trusting her. She swirled the dishcloth over a plate and watched the iridescent bubbles stretch and pop while she thought of what to say to make it better.

Her mum broke into her silence and said "Thank you for your apology... and for telling me the truth." She paused as if unsure of whether to continue then added. "Tom's mother never called me after the accident, you know? I don't see her around the village at all. Is she okay?"

April nodded quickly. It wasn't her place to say anything about Tom's mum. If he wanted people to know, he would have told someone. She understood the reasons for his secrecy, even if she didn't like them. She hoped her mum wouldn't ask if she ever saw Tom's mum to speak to. She *really* didn't like lying to her, especially after finally coming clean about their camping weekends.

Luckily, her mum didn't pursue it. "He was always such a nice boy. And I assume Yuki is the Chinese lad I see walking around in leather trousers all the time?"

April couldn't help but grin. "He thinks he's Jim Morrison," she said fondly.

Kate laughed as she declared, *"I am the lizard king!"*

"He says that all the time!" April told her mother, who was delighted. "He says it instead of goodbye sometimes."

"I'd like to meet them, April. You don't have to keep your friends hidden from me. I know when your dad was here the house was a bit... oppressive, but he's been gone a long while now. This house is your home to relax in. Your friends are welcome here on Friday nights now it's too cold to camp. It's much bigger than a shed."

April looked up at her, surprised into stunned silence. But her mum hadn't finished: "No boy sleepovers," she said firmly "and no drugs in my house. I assume if Yuki thinks he's Jim Morrison he enjoys a, um, smoke?" April blushed crimson and nodded carefully. "Well, he can do *that* in the garden, in the heating shed. Do you smoke, April?"

"I have a puff sometimes, but no, not really." April was relieved to have told her mum; she hadn't realised how much the guilt had been weighing on her until it was gone.

"Your dad hated me smoking," her mum confided in her. "So, I used to hide in the heating shed and do it. That's how I know it's a good spot."

April looked at her mum and felt a sudden wave of love. She threw her soapy arms around her in a hug and said, "Thank you, Mum. You're the best!"

Kate laughed and hugged her back. "I don't know about that. I suppose I'm pretty cool though."

They spent the rest of the morning in front of the fire reading in companionable silence, before April's mum went to do some paperwork upstairs.

On Sunday, her brother came home from university and they cooked roast chicken and apple crumble for him. He brought a load of washing with him, which April helped him do.

Over dinner, he filled them in on his course and how hideous living in halls on campus was. April shuddered at the thought of a massive block of flats, no privacy, no silence.

She had no idea what she was going to do after her GCSE's. James had passed his with ease, spent six months inter-railing with his mates and then had gone to Portsmouth to study economics.

"How's school, Sis?" he asked her once they'd finished eating.

"Fine, same as when you were there probably."

"Mamma Mitchell still there?" he asked, and April nodded. "And are you ready for your mocks?"

"Of course," April said tartly, as if he'd asked a silly question.

James called her a swot, she punched him on the arm and he wrestled her onto the carpet.

Her mum came back into the room and, ignoring their childish antics, put classical music on the stereo full blast and poured them all a glass of wine. Afterwards, James fell asleep by the fire and Kate fell asleep in the chair.

Before she went to bed, April went out into the garden to look at the stars and think about Tom. She wondered if he was thinking of her.

42

TOM

Saturday appeared to go on forever, and Sunday even longer.

When Tom and Em returned from their Nan's, his mum was sitting in the living room staring at the rug, with some half-folded washing on her knee.

"Hi Mum," Tom said gently, moving the rest of the washing to sit next to her on the sofa. Em hovered in the background and he waved for her to come in. She hesitated for a few seconds, then sat on his lap.

"Have you been up long?" Tom asked his mum, concerned. "Have you eaten?" She gave him a watery smile, and reached out to stroke Em, who shrunk back and buried herself further into Tom's lap.

Tom sighed. Em was always like this around their mum these days, almost frightened of her. It was a shame; he was sure that if Em could be her normal bubbly self around her, it might help.

"I made some tea," his mum said vacantly. "I made a pot if

229

ERICKA WALLER

you want some. I called you both, but maybe you didn't hear me."

"We go to Nan's on Sundays, remember?" Tom said gently, trying to move Em so she was sitting between them rather than on him. "Hey Em, why don't you show Mum your dance for the nativity play?"

Em had run out of school on Friday afternoon bursting to tell him that she was one of the angels in the school play. She'd gone on about it all the way home.

Em shook her head; "Why don't you show Mum some karate moves then?" he tried again. "She's a green-belt now," he said proudly.

His mum just smiled weakly, not really listening "That's nice, love." she finally said.

"Tommy," Em began in a whiny voice, tugging on his sleeve "I want you to come and sit with me while I have a bath."

She tried to tug his arm again to get him to stand up, but Tom refused. "Not yet, Em. Sit there and I'll put *Grease* on." He turned to his mum again, "You like *Grease*, Mum. You used to watch it with me and make me do the dances. Remember?" He realised he sounded desperate.

"Mum is a brilliant dancer," he gushed to Em, who gave him a suspicious look. It was the same look she'd give him when he told her there were no hidden vegetables in her dinner, even though there were green bits in it.

He stood up and found the video. Once it started playing, he sat back down - Em on one side and his mum on the other. He threw the waffle blanket over them, then found both their hands under the cover.

Em squeezed his back tightly, but his mum's hand was limp. Tom felt better when he thought about how April's warm hand fitted perfectly in his own.

As the film got going, Em cheered up, singing along to her favourite songs. His mum stared at the screen, but he had no idea if she was taking it in. Tom found himself thinking of April again.

When he fell into bed that night, he could still smell April on his pillow, but the bed felt lonely without her.

Monday morning was cold and rainy. By the time he'd walked Em to breakfast club, then doubled back to meet April at the canal, he was soaked and freezing.

He wanted a cigarette, but he didn't want to taste of cigarettes when he kissed her.

And he was *going* to kiss her.

APRIL

*A*pril was nervous as she made her way down to the canal.

Would it be weird between them after the weekend? Half of her wanted to run away, to walk the road way, avoid the awkwardness. The other half of her wanted to run to get to him quicker.

In the end she made herself walk normally. She'd plaited her hair the night before so now it hung in loose waves over her shoulders. She had Tom's Adidas top in her bag. She wanted to wear it (the thin blue cord jacket she had on was not keeping her warm), but she didn't know if he'd mind.

She knew he was going to be in his usual place when she slipped through the gap in the hedge, but her heart still beat faster when she saw him. He was leaning against the lock. His wet hair was plastered to his head and he was missing his morning cigarette.

She approached him shyly and held up her hand in a half-wave when he spotted her. "Hi," she said quietly when she got closer. He pushed himself off the lock, strode towards her to bridge the gap between them, then took her face in his cold hands and kissed her.

April dropped her bag, slid her arms round his back, under his jacket, and kissed him back.

TOM

They walked to school hand in hand.

Once or twice, he pulled her into a gap in the hedge, or down the side of a shop, and kissed her again. She tasted of toothpaste and vanilla. Her lips were soft, and she trembled in his arms when he held her. They were late to school.

APRIL

*J*amie had signed-up for the Christmas show at school, so April put her name down too.

But for painting stage props only, no way was she going to ask for an acting part.

Jamie loved the stage. Whenever they went to see plays with their English class, she'd sit stiller than April - from beginning to end - then argue with the teacher all the way home over who was the strongest actor. She'd wanted to take drama as one of her GCSE options, but her mother wouldn't hear of it.

The school were putting on a production of *A Christmas Carol* and Jamie auditioned for the part of Fezziwig. April went to watch her audition and saw Jamie light up on the stage. She'd never seen Jamie perform before and April's eyes filled with tears of pride when everyone watching stood up and clapped when she finished.

Jamie scowled, but April saw that underneath she was smiling.

When she discovered the part was hers, she and April high-fived. Jamie was so happy, she skipped her lunchtime cigarettes and spent her lunch money on two slices of millionaire's shortbread, which she and April ate in the back of the auditorium while poring over the script.

"You should ask Tom to help you with the set painting," Jamie said. "You can snog backstage." She snorted with laughter at her own joke. April blushed but said nothing. Jamie chuckled a bit more to herself and started practising her lines.

April told Tom about the play and asked him if he wanted to help. When she said she'd put her name down on props, he'd asked: "If I sign up too, can we snog behind the curtain?"

April giggled, blushed again, and nodded.

They'd continued going back to hers after school, at least once a week, to help him with his homework. One time, after he'd dropped Em at his Nan's, on the way she'd sulked and called him a meanie, but he'd produced a Kinder Egg and she'd forgiven him. As soon as they'd got inside – he'd pinned her against the front door and kissed her till her head swam.

Then he'd taken her upstairs, laid her down and kissed her on her bed, flinging her stuffed toys out of the way and saying, "whoops, sorry" to them when they bounced on the floor. She'd laughed, until he ran his hands down her arms, up her waist, and along the exposed line of flesh on her midriff above her skirt.

After that, she'd been determined to put homework before hormones, so the next week, she made them sit downstairs, where she read *A Midsummer Night's Dream* out loud while he sketched out the characters on her foot. When he ran out of space, he started on her ankle and drew up her leg.

April stopped reading when he reached the back of her knee. "Carry on," he reprimanded mock-strictly, tapping her with his pen.

By the end of the homework session, April had flowers all over her inner thighs.

TOM

*M*r. Lloyd had asked to see him after registration.

While he waited, he worked on his latest sketch from *A Midsummer Night's Dream*. He drew the moon with a serene face, and the stars distorted in the water.

He didn't realise his teacher was watching over his shoulder until he said: "That's amazing, Tom. Your art teacher told me how talented you are. I see you put your name down on props for the Christmas show too?"

Tom nodded, but carried on sketching.

"I've caught up with all your teachers," Mr. Lloyd continued. "And they all say the same thing…"

Tom said nothing, but he tightened his grip on his pencil.

"You're back on top of your work, Tom. Well done." His teacher was beaming at him. Tom relaxed his grip and grinned back.

"How did you do it?" Mr. Lloyd asked.

"I've had some… help," Tom said, smiling even more at the thought of April and how helpful she'd been.

"Well, whatever you're doing, keep doing it."

"Oh I will," Tom stated, putting his sketchpad in his bag and feeling happier and more relaxed than he'd been in years.

Then he headed off to science class, where he scored 85% in his test.

Later that evening, after he'd made Em her tea, he took a plate of food up to his mum. She was sitting up in bed and looked up when he came in to the room, looking tense.

"Hello, love," she said. "Did you pick up my tablets for me? I've run out."

Tom put her plate down on the bedside table, collecting the half-drunk mug of tea from that morning at the same time. "Sorry Mum, I forgot. I went to watch Em rehearse her play. She'd love you to go and see her in it. She's been practising like mad."

"I'll… I'll try, Tom," she said, sounding distracted. "Please can you bring the pills home tomorrow? I can't sleep without them, you see." She looked at him with her watery smile and for a second Tom felt like slapping her. He felt like telling her she'd been asleep for eighteen months and it was about time she woke up.

He nodded instead, not trusting himself to speak, and went downstairs to help Em make her costume.

She needed a big white t-shirt, so he'd dug out one of his dad's. He doubted his mum would notice. He cut the sleeves off, sewed gold tinsel around the neck and made some cardboard wings out of a cereal packet, which he coloured in with a gold pen that he'd nicked from the art room.

April had donated a white hairband that she normally used to keep her hair off her face at night, and Jamie had 'borrowed' some sparkly white tights and a gold belt for her.

APRIL

$\mathcal{T}$he weather gradually grew cooler and Christmas lights appeared in windows.

Em chattered non-stop about angels and Jesus and her costume. Tom's predicted grades went up, higher than ever before.

Tom had refused to let her return his zip-up top. She wore it everywhere and it felt like armour. She sometimes zipped up the collar to hide the smile that broke out whenever she saw him, but she could never hide it completely.

April felt like she'd been cracked open. Somehow Tom had pierced her bell jar. When she was with him, she was aware only of how she felt in that moment. She didn't worry about all the bad things that *might* happen next.

In class, she daydreamed about Tom's lips instead of looking for escape routes. Lunchtimes were now spent in the auditorium, behind the curtain, in Tom's arms.

"To think I used to spend my lunch breaks doing homework, when I could have been doing this," she said to him on one occasion. He'd just run his hand down her shirt and hooked his finger in the top of her skirt, when the lunch bell rang, leaving her reeling and Tom declaring he needed a cigarette.

People started to ask her if they were going out. April never knew what to say. They didn't really go anywhere. Tom never officially asked her out, but he stopped to kiss her if they passed one another in the corridor, and pressed her against the chapel wall at the end of school in front of everyone.

Her mum said that the boys were welcome round the house, but they all preferred the seclusion of Yuki's shed. The next Friday night, down there, Jamie made everyone practise her play with her.

Yuki had quite a flare for acting, which annoyed Jamie. April and Tom didn't really want to sit around practising for a play they weren't even in, when they could be practising kissing instead. But Jamie had thrown herself into something, at last, and she seemed happy. It was much better to have her bossing them all around than it was to see her silent and tearful.

By the end of the night, they'd all learnt Jamie's lines and she had them down perfectly. They'd practised everyone else's lines and all the songs too. It was beginning to feel a lot like Christmas.

The final weeks rolled by. Mock GCSEs took place the last week before they broke-up from school, which they all thought was decidedly un-Christmassy. April considered the fact that she wasn't going to do as well as she might have before she and Tom had introduced kissing into their relationship, but found that she just couldn't care. She'd spent so much of her life doing nothing but homework, she was confident her grades would be good enough.

April had watched *The Breakfast Club* with the boys in Yuki's shed one night and she'd loved it. She thought about her friends and how much they were like the characters in the film. Circumstance and location had thrust them together. They were all different, but the same. They were the four corners that completed a jigsaw.

For the first time, April felt like she knew how to be fifteen and happy. She and her mum were getting on, there were no secrets between them; Jamie was as happy as she'd ever seen her; Tom was… well, Tom was wonderful; Yuki was, reassuringly, the same as ever.

Not long before they were due to break up for Christmas, April skipped into rehearsals to report for prop duty. The drama teacher, Mrs. Hilton, asked her if she would consider joining the choir and April had decided to say yes. She already knew all the songs and she didn't have to worry about everyone looking at her, because the choir stood at the back of the stage, out of the spotlight.

She couldn't wait to tell Jamie, who'd been nagging them all to do it – even Yuki, who reminded her that he'd left school years ago.

The bounce in April's step faltered a little when she looked around the auditorium and saw Claire was on the stage. She looked for Jamie but couldn't see her.

"And… action!" Mrs. Hilton shouted.

Claire cleared her throat before saying: "Ebenezer?"

Joe (who was playing the part of Ebenezer Scrooge) replied: "Yes, Isabelle?"

Claire smiled at him (*even her smiles are evil*, April thought) and cooed: "My eyes are closed, my lips are puckered, and I'm standing under the mistletoe."

"You're also standing on my foot!" Joe declared, in the grumpy voice of Ebenezer.

"Perfect!" Mrs. Hilton said, clapping her hands, delighted

"You will make an excellent Belle, Claire. So kind of you to step in at the last minute and help out after Danielle broke her leg."

Claire smiled in a way that she thought was gracious, gave a small bow and marched off the stage.

Mrs. Hilton was busy making notes on her script when April approached. "Excuse me, Mrs. Hilton," she began, and her teacher looked up at her. "Have you seen Jamie?"

"She's under the stage, my dear," Mrs. Hilton said dramatically "...getting into character! Have you come over to tell me you'll join the choir?"

"Um, yes," April confirmed distractedly. She needed to find Jamie and tell her about Claire being in the play.

She quickly thanked Mrs. Hilton, then ran through the small door cut into the side of the stage where the lights and props were stored. Jamie was sitting on a box and Claire was towering over her.

From where she stood, April couldn't quite make out what was being said, but it looked like they were arguing. She wasn't surprised; she hadn't exactly expected them to be making friends.

April crept nearer, hiding behind the night-sky backdrop she and Tom had been working on, wishing he was there with her, moving quietly along the canvas until she could hear every word.

"Drop out of the play, Jamie," Claire demanded. "Now!"

"No!" Jamie refused. "You know how much I want to act!"

"Yes, well I've decided I want to act too, and I don't want you anywhere near me. So, get up there and tell Mrs. Hilton you're dropping out."

"Why are you doing this to me, Claire?" Jamie asked,

pleading with her. April had never heard her friend sound so desperate. It was horrible.

She wanted to say something, to intervene, but she felt rooted to the spot. Deep down she knew Jamie was hiding something from her about Claire, and she wanted to know what it was.

"You know why, Jamie," Claire seemed to enjoying torturing her. "And you'll drop out of this play, or I'll tell your mother about the gig. I'll also tell her that you're wasting your time doing silly little plays, instead of concentrating on your mocks. You know she won't approve... Jemima." She drew out the last word, knowing exactly how much Jamie hated it.

"You can't make me," Jamie said, bunching her fists at her sides.

"But I can. All it'll take is one phone call to my mummy, and you'll be out of this play and out of this school before you have time to wash that ridiculous make-up off."

"And what if *I* tell, Claire?" Jamie said, her voice suddenly cold. "What if I tell everyone *your* little secret?"

"Who'd believe you?" Claire sneered back. "You? With your pathetic life and pathetic friends, who'd believe anything you said, ever?" Her face was so close to Jamie's, that Jamie had to move her own head back to hold her gaze, which she did admirably.

That's more like the Jamie I know, April thought proudly.

"I know you don't really want Tom," Jamie said, changing tactics and attitude swiftly. Claire had dared to attack her friends – April knew it was a bad move. "You're just trying to hurt April. Why?" She straightened up and gained some of her personal space back. "She's done nothing to you."

"I don't like her," Claire sniffed. "I don't like the way she follows you around. I don't like the way she sucks up to the teachers. I don't like her mother, who seems to think she's something special. And I don't like the way she thinks she's good enough for Tom. Tom belongs with Alex and the football boys. April belongs on her own and you…"

She looked Jamie up and down as if she were a piece of rubbish, something she did so well to anybody she considered beneath her. "You don't belong anywhere."

She leaned in close again as she said: "You're a freak," emphasising the last word.

For a second neither of them spoke, just glared at one another instead.

"And what does that make you then?" Jamie said at last, and April saw there were tears on her face. She continued despite them. "If I don't belong anywhere, then neither do you. If I'm a freak, then so are you. Why are you making this all about me? You're the one who…."

"I did *nothing*!" Claire practically screamed at Jamie, then looked around quickly to see if anyone was listening.

When she saw April, she laughed. "I might have guessed you'd be creeping around in the shadows, April. How's Tom? Have you put-out for him yet…?" She turned away from Jamie and made her way towards April.

April forced herself not to take a step back. "… because I did, and he *loved* it."

She looked back over her shoulder at Jamie. "Drop out, *now*. Or you know what I'll do…"

The stage door slammed behind her and April rushed to Jamie's side.

"What the hell was that about? What secret? What does she have over you, Jamie?"

"Nothing," Jamie said through clenched teeth. "And why were you eavesdropping?"

"I wasn't!" April said hotly, her face going red. "I saw Claire auditioning and I came to warn you."

"Well, you were too bloody late," Jamie said, standing up and kicking the box she'd been sitting on. It collapsed in on one side and black paint fell off in thick clumps.

"Are you going to drop out?" April asked her, moving closer and putting her hand on Jamie's arm.

"What fucking choice do I have, April?" Jamie said, rounding on her and wrenching her arm away roughly. "You heard her. She'll tell my mum and that'll be it."

"She *said* she was going to tell your mum about the gig… but she hasn't," April said carefully.

"She hasn't, *yet*." Jamie's shoulders slumped in defeat. April hated seeing her look so beaten.

"But she has no reason to wait, Jamie – she has nothing to wait *for*. If she really wanted to get you in trouble, she'd have done it by now."

"Maybe…" Jamie admitted, biting her lip.

April took a deep breath and then said. "What secret do you have over her, Jamie? Can't you use that to keep her quiet?"

"I'm not talking about it, April. Not to you, or anyone else."

"Okay," April said, feeling hurt and trying not to show it "Just don't drop out of the play yet, please. I just told Mrs. Hilton I'd join the choir. Don't make me do it alone." She looked at her friend hopefully, knowing that Jamie knew how much she hated being on display.

"Did you?" Jamie blinked in surprise and looked up at her. "But you hate being on stage."

"Yes," April interrupted "But I love you. Come on, we'll have fun, I'll even let you do all my stage make-up," April suggested, linking her arm though Jamie's, who could see was wavering.

Jamie had come alive since joining the play. It was all she talked about and April knew how gutted she'd be to drop-out and go back to lunchtimes doing homework, or avoiding Claire. Not that she could avoid her now they were in the same play...

"Don't hide from her, Jamie," April said fiercely. "Don't let her win."

"Gah! No matter what I do, Claire's won already," Jamie said miserably, but picked up her script again. "Come on, I need to rehearse."

48

TOM

*T*om still hadn't picked up his mum's pills; he hadn't even gone to the chemist.

Instead, he'd walked along the canal with April, kissing her against the lock. He was late to get Em, late to get to school, late to wake up, late going to bed.

When they were alone, April's shyness disappeared completely, and she opened herself to him, kissing him back with as much passion as he kissed her with.

They kissed as if they'd been the ones to discover it. Behind the curtain in the auditorium, in the heating shed at her house (while Em cut out gold stars to hang on the tree), at his house when they snuck away from Jamie and Yuki to 'fetch tapes' – tapes that they invariably forgot to bring back.

Tom was trying hard to go slow, but when she ran her hands through his hair and kissed the side of his neck, it was impossible not to touch her back. Not to reach under the zip-up top of his that she never took off, and run his hands along the skin on her stomach.

She stilled at his touch but never pushed him away. He had to be the one to stop. It took everything inside him to pull away from her.

After they said goodnight on the phone, Tom would lie on his bed with his eyes closed and picture her sleeping next to him. When he was walking home with Em and she was asking him about the wise men in her nativity play at school (and if the donkey got tired), he just blithely thought of April.

Tom was starting to believe things might be on the up. His mum had started to get up before him in the morning and made an effort to cook them breakfast. Halfway through, she'd often get distracted. He'd walked into the kitchen to find her standing by the sink as the toast burned, or sat in the chair as milk dripped onto the floor. She was never dressed and her eyes were still vacant, but she was up.

Em still avoided her and would stand awkwardly in the kitchen doorway until Tom persuaded her to sit down. He would end up pouring cereal for the three of them. His mum would spoon cereal into her mouth on autopilot, smiling weakly when one of them said something, but rarely responding with any words of her own.

Until one morning, just as they were about to leave for school. She waited until Emily was out of earshot then touched his arm and whispered to him: "Please Tom, it's been two weeks. I need my tablets. I *need* them, love."

He could tell she was trying to hide it, but he hated the urgency he sensed in her voice. "Do you?" Tom asked her carefully. "Are you sure? You seem to be better without them, Mum. You're getting up and getting dressed..." he trailed off and looked at her, willing her to agree with him.

She just smiled sadly at him. "You don't understand, pet. You're too young. They help me sleep and they stop me thinking too much about, you know..."

"No, Mum!" Tom said, louder than he'd meant to. Em had been watching the exchange from the door and run up to her room, slamming the door behind her. Tom turned back to his mum, anger rising. "I can't be too young to understand, but old enough to do all this!"

He stopped and waved his hand around at the kitchen, the washing up, the bills on the table. "And I *can't* keep doing it alone. Em needs you, Mum…" He dropped his hands to his sides as the anger towards his mother subsided into heavy sadness, and finished in a quieter voice "I need you Mum. It's time to move on. It's been long enough."

He watched her cry her silent tears and tried to keep his voice steady. "I miss him too, Mum. So does Em. And Nan. We *all* miss him, but we have to get up. We *have* to." He implored her: "Do it for Dad, for Em… please?" He was crying now too, and he hated himself for it.

When she just stood crying, saying nothing, responding to nothing, he lost the cool he'd regained. "I can't do this on my own, Mum. I can't!" He cast his eyes around the kitchen again, seeing the dirty dishes piled in the sink, the burnt toast and spilt milk. The bills and hair ties and piles of washing. "I've been trying to keep everything going, to give you time. But it seems like you'll never have enough."

It was all coming tumbling out now, the damn burst inside him. He'd wonder later if by letting April in, he'd had to let something out. "I want to go to college. I don't want to drop out of school at sixteen and support you. I want to do my A Levels. I want to go to university…" he stopped and swiped at his eyes "And I need you to get better, so I can go! So I can *live* mum. My grades are good enough. My teacher says I can go to the sixth form, maybe even art college…"

He tried to make eye-contact with her, to get through to her, but she wouldn't look at him. "I want to draw like you used to want to dance. Do you remember, Mum? Do you remember when you used to want things? Do you remember when you used to be alive?"

He hadn't realised Em had come back downstairs until he heard her voice. "Please, Tommy, please don't go. Please don't leave me with her."

He felt like he was being torn in half. His mum's face was still expressionless, but he knew she'd heard. She knew because she hadn't taken her pills for over two weeks now. He'd noticed the sluggishness leaving her body over the last few days. Why was she trying to fight it? Why didn't she want to come back to them?

"I'm not leaving you, Em" he said gently, bending down to look her in the eye.

"Promise, Tommy?" she asked, her bottom lip wobbling. Tom couldn't take any more tears today. He sighed and swung her into his arms. "I promise," he said, reaching out with his little finger so they could pinkie swear. "I'll be right here for you."

He turned back to his mum, and in a cold voice he said. "I'll bring your pills home later. But it's the last time I'm doing it, Mum."

She shut her eyes in relief and mouthed a *thank you*.

49

APRIL

*A*pril knew something was wrong the second she saw Tom's face. He looked worried, and angry. She didn't think she'd ever seen him angry before.

For a second, she wondered if she'd done something wrong. *Is it something to do with sex?* she wondered, somewhat bizarrely. She couldn't think of anything else that she could have done.

It wasn't the first time the thought had occurred to her. Had Claire been telling the truth when she said that she and Tom had gone all the way? The thought of it – Tom kissing someone else - made her feel sick. Tom doing those things with Claire, meant that he could never do them for the first time with her. It could never be as special for him.

Maybe he was getting bored with the kisses and wanted to move things on. He hadn't said anything, but he'd pulled away from her a couple of times and asked for a moment to compose himself. She hadn't known what to do. She wanted to tell him not to stop, but the words would get stuck in her throat. She was scared, and she wasn't ready. Not for that, not yet anyway.

253

Had he said that to Claire and been told not to stop? Would he lose interest if she didn't have sex with him soon? How long could a boy be happy with just kissing?

April needed to talk to someone about it, but who? She couldn't ask Jamie. She had no experience either and she'd just be scornful. She was already rolling her eyes whenever April and Tom kissed in front of her. Which they hardly did at all, because of exactly that.

April didn't know if Jamie was jealous that she had a boyfriend (was Tom her boyfriend?) or if she just thought boys were a waste of time. She never talked about them, never looked at them - and other than occasionally chastising them for being sexist pigs - she never spoke to them either. The only boys she spoke to, that April knew of, were Tom and Yuki.

She'd bicker non-stop with Yuki, but never had a bad word to say about him. And no one could dislike Tom; he was kind, funny and he gave Jamie cigarettes and made her mix-tapes of Sleeper and Elastica. April knew that as much as Jamie liked anyone, she liked Tom and Yuki.

April could probably ask Yuki about sex, but she doubted if he was any more experienced than her, despite his bravado. Also, he would tell Tom immediately.

"Hi," April said tentatively "Are you okay?"

Tom looked up and just stared at her. Normally, he'd walk over and kiss her, sometimes even bending her back over the lock dramatically to make her laugh. This morning, for the first time in ages, he was smoking a cigarette, and brooding.

"Yeah, fine," he said with a shrug. "Just family crap." He flicked his cigarette away and came over to kiss her. He went for her cheek, but she gave him her lips; hoping it would be enough for now.

When he pulled away, he was smiling again, and she relaxed slightly. He laced his fingers through hers and they started walking.

"What family stuff?" April asked, relieved it was nothing to do with her (or sex), but feeling guilty for thinking so selfishly.

Tom sighed and kicked a stone into the canal. "My mum, she's run out of pills. You know I told you she's been taking those pills?" April nodded for him to continue. "Well, I haven't collected her latest prescription yet."

"Why not?" April asked, slightly puzzled. "I mean, do you normally get them for her?"

"I collect them once a month from the chemist," Tom said. "She speaks to the doctor on the phone and I pick up the prescription for her. She ran out a couple of weeks ago. The chemist is waiting for me to go get them."

"So, why haven't you?" April asked again. "Has she asked you about it?"

"Repeatedly," Tom replied bluntly, kicking another stone. His tone changed as he went on and April realised it hadn't quite been anger that she'd seen on his face earlier, it was frustration, and when he looked at April, she could see there was hope in his eyes. "But since she's run out, she's been getting out of bed more, she's even been getting dressed."

"I see…" April said, starting to understand "But she *wants* to keep taking the pills?"

Tom's shoulders slumped in a silent yes. "I've asked her not to. I've more-or-less begged her to try staying off them, but she refuses to listen to me. She says they help her sleep." He threw his hands up helplessly. "She's been asleep for almost 18 months! How much sleep does one person need?"

ERICKA WALLER

"Have you told the doctor what the pills do to her?" April asked.

"No, I'm worried he'd get social services involved if he knew how much they knocked her out. I can't risk Em being taken away. She's already lost her dad, and her mum is as good as useless... she's all I have."

April took his hand again and squeezed it. "*I am terrified of this dark thing that sleeps in me,*" she murmured almost too quietly to be heard.

"What?" Tom asked

"Sylvia Plath said it about depression," April explained. "Maybe your mum needs help, like proper help. Maybe there are other pills, or therapy?" she trailed off and shrugged lamely.

"But she won't leave the house, she won't go to the doctor's, she won't talk to anyone. She leaves it all to me and I'm so bloody tired of holding up the universe for her." Neither of them said anything for a moment until Tom said decisively: "Fuck it. I'm not going to get her the pills. If she wants them, she can get them herself."

"Tom..." April began carefully

"April," he cut her off and turned to face her, "For the last 18 months I thought my life was all planned out. I was going to drop out of school and get a job to support my family. But then you came along, and you changed everything. You've made me want a future. You've made me want to do well in my exams. I want to go to art college, April. I want to play football at the weekend. I want to pass my driving test and take you away. I want... god, I want so much. All I do is want, and I can't do anything about any of it unless my mum sorts herself out."

He kicked another stone and they watched it land in the

canal, leaving ripples in the water. April wondered what ripples Tom taking away his mum's tablets would leave.

"Maybe you should speak to the doctor," April suggested "and ask him how to wean her off them?"

"And risk him finding out what's been going on? What if they come 'round to the house? What if they speak to Em?" He shook his head and looked down at his feet. "I can't. It's all down to me."

He pulled another cigarette out of his bag and lit it. April had never seen him so upset before and she had no idea what to do. She found herself almost wishing that he'd been upset about the sex thing instead; that would be easier to cope with than this.

Deep down, April thought that Tom was making a big mistake, but it wasn't her place to say. He'd only just stated really opening up to her. She worried if she pushed him, he'd shut down again.

She slipped her hand into his and said. "I bought ingredients so that me and Em can make Christmas biscuits for her teachers. And I rented *A Midsummer Night's Dream* to watch. It's a pretty naff version but it might help us remember some lines." Tom tried to smile but it was a poor effort.

April racked her brain for a way to cheer him up "I have black knickers on" she shouted out loudly, then slapped her hand over her mouth and blushed.

Tom almost chocked on the cigarette he was smoking. She could see him turning over the information in his mind, as his gaze dropped down to her waist.

"Can I see them? " He said finally, quirking his eyebrow at her.

"Okay" she said in a small voice, too embarrassed to look at him.

"Now?" he said hopefully, tipping his head to indicate a bush by the side of the canal.

"NO!" April said horrified, but then saw he was only joking and laughed. " I'll show you them later."

"I'll hold you to that" he said, waggling his eyebrows suggestively, and April couldn't help but feel slightly proud of herself.

TOM

om was distracted all day.

He thought about what April had said, but was sure he was right not to get the pills.

His dad dying had been a massive shock to everyone, not just his mum. When the policeman came to the house to tell them about the accident, his head had spun, and he had to be helped to the sofa. A second policeman went and made him some sweet tea, which made him feel sick.

Tom's mum had asked the police to call her mother-in-law and his Nan had appeared half an hour later. She immediately launched into an abusive tirade aimed at the police, stopping every few minutes to moan, "My son, my son…"

Other than that, his mum didn't speak. She just sat on the sofa and turned to stone.

His Nan got a lift back home with the police when they left a few hours later, but he, Em and his mum had remained where they were for a long time. They didn't move to turn on any lights, they didn't even speak until Em finally said, "I'm hungry, Mummy."

Tom didn't know what time it was, but none of them had eaten since breakfast. His mum didn't seem to have heard, so he got up and made Em a cheese sandwich.

He made one for his mum as well, but she didn't even look at it. It sat in the living room for days, the bread dried-up at the edges, the cheese curled and hard.

After her supper, Em had cried herself to sleep on Tom. He covered her with a rug, then helped his mum upstairs. Tom helped her undress. She'd been wearing a yellow dress with blue flowers on, tan tights and ballet shoes - then pulled the covers over her. She fell asleep eventually but he couldn't. Instead he sat in the chair in the corner of the room, still littered with his dad's clothes.

Em woke a couple of hours later and crawled into bed with her mum, curling herself around her legs. "I want Daddy," she said into the dark. "I want my story and my bath and my daddy."

Tom climbed onto the bed next to her and held her until she cried herself back to sleep.

The next day, visitors arrived with flowers and casseroles. The police came back to ask for photos. His Nan went to identify the body. The doorbell rang, and rang and his sister cried.

Upstairs, his mum lay staring at the wall.

The days blurred into one another. He fell asleep in his clothes each night, wedged next to Em on the bed with their ghost of a mother and plates of half-eaten sandwiches piled-up around them.

The doctor called round on the third day. Tom thought the police must have sent him. He spent half an hour with

Tom's mum, then came downstairs with a prescription in his hand for "some pills to help with the shock."

Tom got up the next day to collect them, taking Em along with him. He'd never been out alone with Em before. When she asked for sweets from the newsagents, he said yes. He bought bread, milk and baked beans with the money his mum kept in the blue stripy teapot, then he went to the chemist and collected the pills. When they got home he took them up to her with a glass of water and a cup of tea, then went back downstairs to feed Em.

They'd run out of clean plates the next day, so Tom decided to do something about it. He went around the house opening curtains and collecting cutlery. He threw away the flowers that no one had bothered to put in vases and the casseroles that sat untouched on the kitchen worktop. He knew Em wouldn't eat them, his mum seemed to be living on pills and digestive biscuits to settle her stomach, and Tom lived on the ends of Em's crusts, unable to find the energy, or inclination, to make his own food.

After a week had passed, he told Em it was time for her to go back to school. He dug out her uniform and school bag and was running the bath, when the doorbell rang.

There stood April and her moussaka. Even in his grief and exhaustion, he'd seen how pretty she was and for just a second, he felt like a kid again. Their conversation was the first he'd had with anyone in days. He kept picturing her face long after she'd gone. Maybe because of it, (or hunger had finally kicked in), after Em was asleep, he ate the moussaka, straight out of the dish, sitting at the kitchen table.

It had been over 18 months. It was time for them to move on. It was time for his mum to get up.

If she wouldn't do it herself, then Tom was going to have to make her.

51

APRIL

*A*pril was so distracted worrying about Tom (and whether Claire was going to call Jamie's mum about the gig or not) she hardly thought about the mock exams.

She'd revised thoroughly and felt like she knew everything she needed to know. The exams just didn't seem as important as helping Jamie with her lines, or hanging out with Tom and Em. For once, April had better things to do than bury herself in books. She wasn't even feeling anxious in class anymore. Sometimes she even put her hand up to read or answer questions.

She saved her anxiety for her friends. Tom hadn't mentioned his mum's pills again, but April was sure he hadn't changed his mind. She focussed on trying to make it a good Christmas for Em. April's mum had brought all the decorations down from the loft, so that April, Em and Tom could put the tree up and hang the lights.

While Tom and April made half-hearted attempts at exam revision by asking each other test questions, Em glued cotton wool balls onto snowman shapes that they'd cut out for her and sang songs from her nativity play. Later, Tom lit the fire, April made pasta and Em twirled around in the firelight.

A few days before Christmas, Kate came home early and found them all sat around the fire. Tom immediately stood up to get his things so that he and Em could go home, but Kate insisted they stay. Em stared at her in awe – Kate was still in her work clothes: a sharp pinstripe suit and high heels that she kicked off when she sat down.

"Wow," Em said, her eyes big with admiration. "Are you a teacher?"

Kate laughed and explained that she was a solicitor. Em had no interest in finding out what that meant, but she was very keen to try on the high-heeled shoes.

An hour or so after dinner, they said their goodbyes and April's mum closed the front door with a sigh. "That girl needs a mother," she said, the second they left.

April bristled at this. "Tom is amazing with her, Mum. He couldn't do more and Em doesn't want for anything."

Her mum sighed again and tried to explain. "Yes, but he's not a *woman*, April. What's he going to do when she gets older and starts her period? Or has questions about boys?"

April didn't say anything; she had no answer. Her mum was right.

She thought about Tom's mum's pills again and his decision not to get them for her anymore. She wanted to tell her mum about it, but she couldn't. It wasn't her secret to tell. Her mum would *certainly* get involved and Tom would probably never trust her again. She hated that Tom had given her the secret, but she knew she couldn't bear her life without Tom in it. She had no choice, no choice but to stay quiet.

"She does have a mum…" April said eventually "and she has me and Jamie… and now you." She smiled at her mother and nudged her with her elbow. "You're an awesome mum"

Kate harrumphed but smiled back. "You really care about her, don't you?" she said, putting an arm around April. April nodded in reply. "And Tom too?" she added. April nodded again, a fierce blush rising to her cheeks.

It didn't go unnoticed and April knew what her mum was going to ask her before she even began.

"Are you?" Kate started to say. April shook her head firmly and said "No mum, God No!" before her mum could say anything more.

Kate just nodded and said "Are you planning too?"

April didn't know what to say. She wasn't actively planning to have sex with Tom, but she didn't plan on stopping it from happening either. If Tom pushed her, she knew she'd do whatever he wanted. She was grateful when he pulled away and made the decision for them both.

"Not planning to, no…" she said, with no idea how to finish the sentence.

Her mum nodded again thoughtfully. After a few long (and awkward) moments she said "Well, do you want me to go to the doctor's with you and get you on the pill?" she said it as though she was simply asking if April wanted a cup of tea.

April acknowledged that her mum was being exceptionally cool about the sensitive subject, but the thought of the doctor's and pills only made her think of Tom's mum again. Jamie took a pill and it was horrible. Tom's mum relied on them and it was horrible. She didn't think much good came from them. If and when the time came with Tom, they could just use a condom, right? She didn't say any of this to her mum obviously. Instead she said "No, thanks. Not yet, okay?"

Kate nodded once more, with a smile tugging at the corners of her mouth. "Cool," she said. Then her eyes lit up, as if something had just occurred to her. She grabbed April's arm excitedly. "I have some old clothes of yours from when you were a kid. Let's dig them out for Em."

52

TOM

*H*is mum was up when they got back from April's house.

She was dressed, and her hair was washed. She'd even put on some lipstick.

Em stared at her, mouth agape, until Tom gently poked her on the shoulder, prompting her to close it again.

She'd cooked them jacket potatoes with cheese and even though they'd eaten at April's (and Em was still suspicious about the ethics of eating jacket potatoes), they ate them dutifully, in silence.

Their mum sat watching them, a paper smile pinned to her face. "I did the washing," she said "...and changed the sheets."

"Thanks," Tom said, forcing down the last of his potato and going to wash up his plate.

"Leave that, love. I'll do it. You go and do your homework."

"Are you sure?" Tom asked, surprised how together she

seemed. He didn't want to put too much on her and set her back.

"Of course, you get along. What about you, Emily?" she asked, turning her attention to her daughter. "Have you got reading homework to do?"

"I can read already," Em said, sounding cross.

"Em…" Tom said, his voice a warning.

Em glared at him rebelliously for a moment, but when she spoke to her mum again, she sounded a bit less sulky. "I have to practise my songs for my concert on Friday."

"Oh, well that's nice," her mum said, sounding interested. "Do you need some help?"

"No," Em said shortly. "*Tom* has been helping me."

Tom saw his mum's eyes fill with tears and he instinctively raised his voice at his sister, desperate for her not to ruin whatever progress their mother had made. "*Emily!* Don't be rude!"

But his mum just waved her hand and looked away, wiping at her eyes, trying to compose herself. "It's fine, love," she said to Tom.

Then she tried again with Em. "I'm sorry, Emily. And I'd love to hear your songs, if you'd like to sing them to me." She reached down and took Em's plate to wash it up.

He stared at her back as she walked to the sink, her eyes bright and her voice wavering. The hope that Tom heard in her voice almost broke his heart. A minute passed while his mum carefully washed the plate before Em sighed a sigh far too big for her and said; "If I sing them to you, will you come and see the show?"

Tom held his breath as he saw his mum's shoulders stiffen and tense. He wanted to tell Em not to rush her, but it was too late. If his mum said no, he knew Em would never forgive her.

"When is it?" she asked from her spot by the sink, not looking at them.

"Friday afternoon, at the end of school," Tom replied, not sure how he'd found the breath to speak. This was the biggest breakthrough, the *only* breakthrough he'd had with his mum since the accident.

"And I have to take my costume in tomorrow," Em added, excitement mounting "I have wings, a gold belt and glittery tights…and I have to twirl, and twirl, and Miss Stanton says I'm the best at twirling."

Their mum turned to face them as Em stood up and showed her how good she was at twirling. Tom tried to swallow the lump in his throat as a wave of love for his sister crashed over him. He thought back to what April had said about her: *'Though she be but little, she is fierce'*.

That's it, Em he thought to himself as he saw more and more life come back into his mother's face. *Twirl her back to us…*

"I used to do that with you, Emily," his mum said sadly "I used to hold you in my arms and twirl and twirl."

"Really?" Em asked, stopping to look at her. She was dizzy and her little feet did a random pitter-patter for a few seconds before she regained her balance. "Were you *the best* at twirling, like me?"

"She was amazing," Tom confirmed, clearing his throat.

"Will you show me?" Emily asked, delighted. "Can we twirl like snowflakes?"

Their mum smiled again, but she didn't move and Tom intervened on her behalf. "Maybe another time, Em," he said. "I think Mum's tired." He swooped in and picked Em up, twirling her once more, then slinging her over his shoulder in a fireman's lift. "Time for your bath! Afterwards we can read more of *The Faraway Tree,* okay?"

"Okay," Em accepted. "But only if you do the voices."

After Em was asleep, Tom came back downstairs to a clean kitchen. His mum had even laid the dishtowel over the draining board to dry, like she used to. The table had been wiped and a pile of dried laundry sat on the chair to go upstairs.

Tom found her in the living room in front of the news. He sat down next to her and held her hand.

"I'm trying, Tom," she said, squeezing his hand. "So help me God, I'm trying."

Tom phoned April just before he went to sleep and told her about his evening.

"That's great!" she exclaimed. Tom heard the smile in her voice.

"I wish you were here," he said, he hoped not too longingly.

He didn't like having April round his shabby house with his shabby mum in bed next door. But tonight, with the lamps on and the sheets changed and the kitchen clean, with his mum watching the news downstairs and the Christmas poinsettia he had bought in the window… tonight, it felt like a proper home.

"Me too," April said, a little coyly.

"In my bed…" he went on. He pictured her lying beneath him, her hair fanned out on his pillow and finished by saying "…naked."

"Tom," April said, sounding hesitant.

He sighed, annoyed at himself. "Sorry. Too much, too soon. I'm just so happy tonight, April, and it would be the perfect ending."

"I want it too, Tom." April spoke so quietly that Tom thought he'd misheard. "But I've never..."

"I know," Tom said. April had never said, but he knew she hadn't had sex before, which was exactly why he'd tried not to put any pressure on her. He tried to tell her so. "It doesn't matter."

"Yes, it does," April argued. "*You* have."

"Says who?" Tom asked, confused.

"Claire. She said."

Tom sighed loudly down the phone, realisation setting in. "I don't care what Claire said, April. I have *not* had sex with her, nor do I want to." His voice softened as he said, "But Jesus, April... I want to have sex with you."

"Oh" April said, caught off guard.

"Oh?" Tom asked her. "That's all you have to say?"

"Oh..." April said again, then finished with "... kay" in a quieter voice.

"Okay? You want to?" Tom cringed at how eager (and totally uncool) he sounded.

"Okay... yes," April said, the smile on her face almost audible over the phone.

"Okay then!" Tom said, grinning from ear to ear.

"Okay, but not just yet okay?" April said.

"Okay" Tom replied, deciding it was one of the best words in the world.

Neither of them knew what to say after that. After a minute of grinning down the phone at each other in silence, April finally said, "I'd better go. We have our English mocks tomorrow. We need to prepare."

"*Urgh.* Can't we go back to the other conversation?" Tom said. "We can talk about how to prepare for that?"

April giggled again and he loved the sound. "Let's get the mocks out of the way, okay?"

"Okay." That wonderful word again. Tom didn't think he'd ever stop grinning.

He hadn't been this happy in ages, if ever. His mum was getting better; he'd been right not to get the pills for her. He was ready for his exams, and April was ready for... well, he didn't know exactly what she was ready for, but whatever it was, it was going to be amazing.

He fell asleep imagining himself undressing her, with her saying 'okay' to each piece of clothing he asked to remove.

53

APRIL

The next morning, Tom kissed her with such intensity that her head spun, and she grasped onto him.

"Morning," she said, laughing.

"Morning" he replied, pushing her against the lock and kissing her again. He smiled against her mouth, then kissed down her neck, unzipping her (his) top to get better access to her collarbone. The sound of the zipper opening was the most erotic thing April had ever heard.

"Tom?" she whispered as he pulled the collar of her school shirt aside. She felt him move her bra strap to one side to kiss the skin at the top of her breast. *I should pull away*, she told herself. They were in public, where anyone could see them. She said nothing though. She just *felt*.

The morning breeze hit her skin when his hand came up to undo the button on her shirt and she came back to her senses at last.

"Sorry," Tom said, when she pulled away and readjusted herself.

"How's your mum?" she asked instead of acknowledging his apology – he had nothing to apologise for. "Are you prepared for the exam? Is Em excited about the play?" She was aware that she was babbling and knew Tom was aware of it. He grinned at her, took her hand and stroked his thumb over hers.

"Mum is good. She was up before me, the house was clean, she'd made me and Em packed lunches. And she said she'd collect Em after school today. So, I..." he stopped walking and turned to look at her pointedly "...am all yours this afternoon."

Fear and excitement raced through April, making her pulse race and her face blush hotly.

She couldn't find words to reply and was hugely relieved when Tom smiled and continued. "For homework! Tsk, tsk, April Winters." She blushed even more as he grinned gleefully. "I'm serious about these mocks, which I finally have a chance of passing, thanks to my awesome girlfriend. That's you, by the way," he said in a sideways whisper. "In case you were wondering."

April blushed and grinned and wondered what would happen later that day when they were alone.

Tom took April's school bag and slung it over his shoulder before continuing.

"Em is so excited about the play, she's becoming hard to contain. I was thinking of asking Mum if we should get her a cat for Christmas."

"She'd love it," April said encouragingly, while thinking, *He called me his girlfriend. I am* his *girlfriend. I have a* boyfriend.

"Wanna come to the shelter this weekend and help me pick one?" Tom asked her. "Yuki said he'll drive us, then we can go do some Christmas shopping, maybe?"

"Cool. I need to get something for Jamie, and my brother, and Mum, and Yuki…"

"Are we getting Christmas presents for each other, April?" Tom inquired, looking at her cheekily with one eyebrow raised.

"If you'd like to," she said shyly. She'd been wondering what to get him and was thinking possibly a new zip-up top, as she'd taken his one. Maybe she and Jamie could go up to Camden and do some shopping.

Jamie was always desperate to go to London, but up until now April had been scared of how busy it might be, or about getting lost on the tube. Jamie had never pushed her about her reasons for not going, which she appreciated. But she also suspected that Jamie thought she was too chicken to go, which she didn't appreciate quite as much.

The thought of how happy Jamie would be made her grin again, so April decided to tell her they were going when she saw her at break.

"I'd like to give *you* something," Tom said, bringing her out of her thoughts, and doing his saucy eyebrow waggle.

April laughed but her heart pounded again. Tom and her, alone. No Emily, no Mum. No one to stop them…

She spent the whole morning thinking about it. Lessons had been cancelled so people could do last-minute revision for the exams. Jamie smoked in the bike sheds and practised her lines. April toyed with asking her advice on what to do, but in the end, she decided against it. Jamie could be cruel about that kind of stuff and April couldn't bear the idea of being on the receiving end.

They probably wouldn't go too far today anyway; they hadn't done anything but kiss, and a bit of grinding which made April feel light headed and made Tom mutter swear words.

When the bell went, signalling them to make their way to the hall, April's mind was still on Tom and what underwear she had on.

She took her place at one of the desks, in a daze, and laid down her pencil. She was hardly listening to the teacher as she told them they had three hours to complete the exam, that they weren't allowed to turn the paper over until they were told to, and to sit quietly when they'd finished.

No one was to leave the room, the teacher added, then the bell sounded again, and they were told to start.

She turned over the paper and looked at the title. She went to write her name and the date on the front and the nib of her pencil snapped. She lifted her head up, looking around, not sure what to do. All she could see were people hunched over desks. She could hear their pencils moving over their papers and the squeak of chairs as they shifted in their seats.

The massive clock on the wall ticked, the noise suddenly deafening in April's ears. She shot a look at the doors. An invigilator stood in front of each exit, door closed shut behind them, arms folded in front. April tried to draw in a breath, but her throat had closed. What the hell was happening to her?

Her eyes widened in panic and she pushed her chair back from her desk in alarm. The sound of it screeching across the floor made the people around her stop writing to scowl at her.

She stood up, her chair clattering to the floor behind her, but April still couldn't get a breath in. Her heart began beating so hard and fast, she was sure that everyone in the hall could hear it. Her eyes started to lose focus and her stomach churned as the room swam. She was either going to pass out or throw up. She needed to get out of the room, and she needed to do it fast.

The room was spinning wildly as she made her way to the door. "Excuse me," she panted to the invigilator at the exit nearest her. "I need to get out!"

He didn't move. "If you leave, you can't come back in," he told her sternly.

"I don't care!" April screamed at him. "I need to get out, now! Move!" She pushed him aside and shoved the door open.

She heard Tom call out her name as the door closed behind her, but she didn't stop.

She ran down the corridor, her shoes slapping loudly on the tiles, and raced down to the exit by the dining room. When she was finally outside, she bent at the waist and retched, over and over. When she was finally finished she dropped to her knees and put her head between them.

After a while, her heartbeat slowed down and she managed to draw in a few shaky breaths. Her hands were trembling and her hair was damp with sweat. Hot tears fell down her cheeks and the gravel beneath her dug into her knees.

She had no idea how long she stayed hunched over, trying to breathe, trying to bring the world back into focus. The panic attack had come from nowhere. She'd felt fine going into the exam. Fine until the pencil snapped.

She had just blown her mock exam. She hadn't written a single word. She'd run out, in front of everyone. In front of Tom. God what must he be thinking? April cried until she retched again, hidden outside the exit door, her life unravelling before her.

"'See the darkness is leaking from the cracks, I cannot contain it, I cannot contain my life'."

She whispered the words over and over until her voice

grew hoarse. Then she rested her head on the gravel and moved her body, so that she was curled on her side.

She didn't hear the door open, but she heard Miss Khan when she spoke to her.

"April?"

April opened her eyes and saw her teacher's bare feet on the gravel as she crouched down next to her.

"I'm so sorry it took me so long to find you. I had to get someone to take over from me in the hall." She bent down further and stroked April's hair. "What happened in there, April?"

April couldn't speak. She just cried, and cried.

54

TOM

Tom struggled to concentrate on the rest of his exam.

He saw April run out, called her name and went to follow her, but Miss Khan walked past him before he could even stand up. She whispered, "I'll go, finish your paper Tom" in his ear so quietly he almost didn't hear it.

He spent the next three hours trying his hardest to concentrate, while checking the door to see if she was going to come back. *Maybe she got sick?* he thought. She'd looked awful as she'd run out of the room, she'd looked like she was in pain. Tom was so worried about her, he felt sick himself.

When the bell finally rang at the end of the three hours, he put his pencil down and flipped the paper closed. It seemed like it was taking forever for the invigilator to collect all their papers and watch them all file out of the hall, row by row.

As soon as he was out, he ran through the crowd of bustling chattering pupils to the nurse's office, then to April's locker, then her form room. He went out into the playground, checked the bike-sheds, the English room - everywhere he could think of.

She wasn't there. She was nowhere.

The exam meant that they'd finished school later than usual and it was fully dark already. He spent half an hour looking for April, then decided to go to her house. *They must have taken her home,* he decided.

He thought of the plans they'd made for that evening, his loose suggestion. Was that what had made her freak out? He worried that he'd put too much pressure on her and hated himself for it. Was he the reason she'd screwed up her exam?

He thought back to their conversation on the phone the night before. She's seemed a bit shyer than she'd been in a while, but happy. He'd thought so anyway. Was he crap at reading his girlfriend?

Tom dragged his hands through his hair and tried to think. Thank God his mum was getting Emily from school; it meant he had time to find April.

55

APRIL

"No one will come looking for us in here," Miss Khan said, shutting the door to the staff room and leading April over to a chair in the corner.

April sat down gratefully and leaned back, listening to the sound of Miss Khan putting the kettle on and rinsing cups.

"Here," she said a minute later. "Drink this." She handed April a chipped mug of tea and she took a tiny sip. It was sweeter than she normally had it, but that was fine – she needed the sugar. She felt the heat travel down to her stomach, as if it was thawing her out. She took another sip, her hands still shaking.

"Panic attacks are exhausting," Miss Khan said, looking at April kindly. "There's a lot of adrenaline racing around your system right now. Do you feel sick?"

April nodded.

"Shaky?"

April nodded again.

"Cold?"

April nodded once more, feeling miserable.

But then April's teacher touched her on the arm, making her look up into her kind, understanding face and said, "All *completely* normal."

"Normal?" April asked her. "What is *normal* about this, Miss Khan?"

Miss Khan patted her arm again and said. "A panic attack is your body responding to its sympathetic nervous system." She spoke casually, as if she were telling April not to forget her homework, or they were simply chatting over a book. "It controls the body's unconscious actions, and loves to trigger the fight or flight response."

April was silent for a moment as she took in what her teacher had said. She liked science, understood it even, the way Miss Khan had described her panic attack struck a chord.

Fight *or* flight. She'd certainly felt the need for flight back in the hall.

Swallowing back tears she fixed her eyes on her teacher's face, who nodded at her and continued. "That overwhelming urge you have to either get angry or run away? That's what it's called. It's also known as the Acute Stress Response."

April had put her mug of tea down unconsciously at some point and Miss Khan nodded at her now to take another sip. "Imagine you're walking in the woods and you spot a snake. What do you do?" April sensed that this was a rhetorical question, so said nothing and Miss Khan carried on.

"Do you run away, do you scream to try and scare it off… or do you freeze? Those are the ways that we instinctively react to danger: fight, flee, or freeze." She paused for a moment, letting her words sink in. "It's the same when we feel anxious – we react in one of these ways. Sometimes we run away, sometimes we freeze and our minds go blank. Sometimes we fight."

Miss Khan moved closer to April and said, "Today, the hall was your woods and the exam was your snake. You ran from the snake, and that's perfectly normal. I know it felt horrible and you're probably furious with your body for letting you down. Is that how you see it?"

April nodded in confirmation. It was *exactly* how she felt. She gazed at Miss Khan's face as she spoke, taking in every word. "Your mind was trying to protect you. You were showing signs of danger and it went into survival mode. April, anxiety and panic attacks are very common, and they happen to a *lot* of people."

"I didn't see them happen to anyone else today," April said bitterly. "Just me. Stupid broken me."

She took another sip of her tea, mainly for something to do.

They were both quiet for a moment until Miss Khan spoke again, April could tell that she was choosing her words carefully. " I can assure you, you are not broken in any way at all. Was today the first day you've felt this way?"

April shrugged, trying to look casual. "It's the first day it's been this bad."

"But you've felt this way before, anxious? Light-headed, sweaty palms, shaky legs?"

April nodded. "Yes, tight chest, numb fingers and a horrible kind of dreamy feeling, like the world has gone into slow motion."

Miss Khan nodded again and smiled reassuringly. "April, that feeling is called *depersonalisation*. It's a defence mechanism against extreme anxiety; your brain goes into shutdown mode."

"Like in a bell jar," April said quietly.

"Indeed," Miss Khan said. *"To the person in the bell jar, blank and stopped as a baby, the world itself is the bad dream'.* Is that how you feel, April?"

"Yes!" April said, and it came out as a sob. She'd finally admitted her madness. Although she was petrified about what would come next, she also felt free of her secret and the relief was immense.

Miss Khan's face crumpled in sympathy, as she struggled to maintain her own composure. "How long have you felt this way?"

April shrugged again, her voice thick and wavering. "A while. A long while."

Miss Khan put her hand over April's protectively and said; "I need you to listen to me, April. You're one of the brightest students I've ever had, and I know you can understand what I'm saying to you. But I also need you to *believe* it. It's more important than any text I've ever told you to study, or any exam you'll ever take. There is *nothing* wrong with you, or your brain. You are *not* Sylvia Plath. Anxiety is normal, it's *very* normal. The reason I know so much about it is because I suffered from it too."

April's head shot up in surprise, a thousand questions coming to mind all at once. Before she could ask any, Miss Khan carried on. "Yes, *me*. It started before my final exams at uni."

"Did you run out too?" April asked, amazed by her teacher's revelation. To feel so very alone for such a long time, then have somebody tell you they know how you feel, somebody you *admired*. And that it was okay, in fact, it was *normal.* April couldn't take it in.

"No, I didn't." Miss Khan said and April's heart sank again. Scrap that, Miss Khan didn't understand at all. She looked up at her teacher, who smiled and said "I didn't turn up at all. I couldn't even face walking into the hall. You're braver than I was April."

"What happened?" April said.

"Much the same as what's happening now. Someone saw, and someone helped. I got to re-sit my exams and I got help with my anxiety. I was recommended a wonderful book by a woman called Dr. Claire Weeks, who suffered from anxiety herself and it became my bible. It was like someone finally understood what was going on in my head." She smiled as she said, "There's a book for every occasion, you know?"

April tried to smile back, but couldn't. She was too full of questions. "And did it go away, the anxiety? The depersonalisation?"

"Not straight away, no. But just knowing what it was helped me, which is why I wanted you to know what happened to you today. I went to see a therapist, and with their help - along with books and support from my friends and family – I got better. I've not had a panic attack in over ten years."

"I can't tell my mum," April said suddenly. "She won't understand. She can't. She's not scared of anything. And my friends...." she imagined Jamie's reaction. She would probably say something like, *"Panic attack? In the school hall? What the fuck is wrong with you?"*

Then she thought of Tom and the stuff he'd said about his mum being 'a zombie' and how 'she needed to snap out of it'. How fed up he was of her weakness. What would he think of April's weakness? She didn't even have anything to blame it on. She thought of the pills Tom refused to get his mum.

"Will I need to take tablets?" she asked suddenly.

"Not necessarily..." Miss Khan said. "There are things called beta blockers, which slow down your heart rate. They often help people with anxiety in times of stress. Your doctor will talk to you about all this stuff though."

"I can't go and see him; he'll tell my mum."

April went to stand up, but Miss Khan stopped her. "If he didn't tell your mum then I would, April. I have a responsibility to you and I won't let you down."

April felt angry tears spring from her eyes. "You can't. You can't do that! I thought you were my friend." She felt like her entire world was spinning out of control and she was losing everything, all at once. *How could it unravel so fast?* she wondered desperately.

"*Please* April, you need to trust me. I *am* your friend, but I'm also your teacher. I'll talk to your mum with you. She won't be cross, I promise you. We can work this out together."

"What about the other exams?" April replied, hating how her voice sounded. "I can't... I *can't* go back in there."

She thought back to how she'd felt at the gig, of the way she couldn't get breath into her body in the exam hall, the feeling of release as she'd watched blood rushing from her thumb. Everything was getting jumbled up in her head. The panic was coming back, she could feel it.

There was no way she could go back into that room. She wanted to go home and never leave the house again. The entire world felt dangerous.

Miss Khan was still talking, her mind on practical matters at hand. "Don't worry about the exams, I'll sort something out. Right now, I'm going to drive you home."

April went to protest but her teacher held up her hand to stop her. "And I'm going to call your mother's office number and ask her to meet us there."

April knew from Miss Khan's no-nonsense tone that there was no point in arguing. She stood up and followed her teacher out of the staff room, feeling a hundred years old.

The halls were quiet with half the school in lessons and the rest still in exams. She thought of Tom and the plans they'd made for that afternoon. The morning felt as if it had happened a million years ago, and to a different person.

She wondered if she could ever go back to being that girl again. Even if she could, Tom wouldn't want her. As soon as he knew she had something wrong with her, he'd run a mile. His mum's illness had dictated his life for such a long time, there was no way he would tolerate mental illness from anyone else.

Things were just getting better for him. He was finally starting to get his life together. He was even talking about art college and what career it might lead to.

April thought of Tom's mum dragging herself out of bed to go and get Em from school, fighting her demons and anxiety to get to her daughter.

She thought of the gig again and the school hall and wondered how anyone could ever be so brave.

TOM

*a*pril wasn't at home.

He ran all the way there and rang the bell again and again. He threw gravel at her window and went around the back to peer through the patio door. She wasn't in, or wasn't talking to him.

He called her name through the letterbox a few times, then gave up and made his way home slowly, wondering what the hell to do.

When he walked into the house the phone was ringing. He snatched it up thinking it would be April.

"Hello?"

"Tom?" The voice was feminine, but not April's. He recognised it, but couldn't place it immediately.

"It's Miss Henderson, from Em's school. No one has come to collect her yet and I just wondered if everything was okay?" She sounded concerned and perhaps, a little irritated. "Emily told me you had an exam today, so I've stayed as late as I can to look after her, but I have to go home now."

"My mum?" Tom said, confused. "My mum was collecting Em today."

"I'm sorry, Tom," Miss Henderson said "… but she never arrived. Em mentioned it, but I assumed there had been a change of plan?"

"Okay," Tom said, his mind racing. "I'll come and get her as soon as I can. I'll come now."

"Thank you, Tom" his old teacher said kindly. "I'd offer to drop her home, but it's the other way and…"

"It's fine. I'm sorry to make you late" Tom apologised, as a feeling of dread crept up his spine. "Give me ten minutes."

He put the phone down and stared at it dumbly. If his mum hadn't collected Em, where the hell was she?

Tom lifted his head suddenly, realisation hitting him like a slap in the face.

"Mum! MUM?" he shouted as he ran up the stairs, taking them three at a time.

She was lying on her side in bed, facing the door. A bottle of pills were in her hand, and there was a note, with his name on it, on the bedside table next to her. She'd been sick, a crumbly mixture of pills and drool on her chin and down her front.

"Mum!" Tom raced to her side and shook her. She didn't move! He put his head to her chest and heard nothing. He put his fingers to her neck to check for a pulse, but his heart was beating too loudly to hear anything else. He grabbed the phone and dialled 999.

When the operator answered, Tom blurted, "My mum, please, *please*. She's not breathing. She's taken pills and she's not breathing."

The operator calmly asked him his name, his mum's name,

their address and if he was alone. He shouted the answers back to her.

"Tell me what to do!" he screamed to the sound of tapping on the other end of the phone.

The operator responded to his panic by speaking in a firm, clear voice. She told him not to move her. Then asked if she was on her side.

"Yes," Tom said, trying desperately to get himself under control. "She's been sick."

The operator told him gently to check that her airways were clear and assured him an ambulance was on its way. "Have the pill bottle and any remaining pills ready for when they come," she told him.

Tom hung up and carefully prised the bottle from his mum's limp hand. He couldn't bear to look at her face. He just looked at her fingers till he heard a siren and raced down to open the door.

"She's upstairs," he panted to the paramedics when they jumped out of the ambulance. "Please hurry. Please."

The paramedics grabbed their big red bags of supplies and raced towards the house. When they reached the bedroom door they told Tom to stay outside.

"I can't," he said frantically. "I need to help her."

"You have to let *us* help her now, mate," one of them said. "Is there anyone you can call to be with you?"

Em. Tom had forgotten about Emily.

He raced back downstairs and threw open the kitchen door, screaming for Yuki as he raced down the garden path. Yuki popped his head out of the shed door, looking startled.

"Yuki! My mum, she's taken a load of pills... she's... the ambulance is with her." Tom gasped for breath.

"What do you need, man?" Yuki asked him, grabbing his coat and car keys.

"I need you to get Emily from school," Tom said. "And keep her away from the house. I'll call you when I know what's going on."

Yuki zipped up he coat and headed towards his car. "No problem," he said. "I'll look after her. If you need anything else, just let me know." He pulled a twenty-pound note from his wallet and handed it to Tom. "In case you need a cab or food," he explained.

Tom nodded, pocketed the cash and turned to race back up the garden to his mum.

57

APRIL

*M*iss Khan drove along the high street slowly, pulling over once when an ambulance sped-up behind her, blue lights flashing.

April directed her up the road to her house and jumped out of the car as soon as the engine was switched off, desperate to be indoors.

Her mum wasn't home, so she and Miss Khan sat in awkward silence in the kitchen while they waited for her. It was odd to make Miss Khan a cup of tea; to have her teacher here, in her house, as if some unspoken boundary had been crossed.

Everything about the day was wrong.

Miss Khan tried to make conversation, but April was too tired to respond. All she could think about was what her mum was going to say. And Jamie, and Tom...

She wondered if he'd looked for her after school, or come to the house to see her. What would she have said if he'd found her? "*Oh, hi Tom. Turns out I'm mentally unstable, like your mum. Do you still want to have sex with me?*"

She unzipped his jacket and laid it on the arm of the sofa, even though she was still cold.

A car pulled up outside and April shot up out of her chair to open the door. Her mum was on the other side, about to put her key in the lock. She put her arms around April and said, "Thank God. Are you okay?"

April buried her face into her mother's chest, speaking into her hair: " No, I'm not, and I'm so sorry."

TOM

*T*he paramedics didn't want Tom to go in the ambulance with them, but there was no one else to go with her.

When he explained, he'd only be following behind in a taxi if they didn't let him, they stepped aside to make room for him.

His mum was on a stretcher with a tube poking out of her mouth. She had cuffs and wires all over her. "Is she breathing?" he asked the paramedic who'd called him 'mate' earlier.

"With the help of the tube, yes," the man replied carefully.

Tom wanted to ask if she was going to be okay, but he was too scared of the answer. Instead he held his mum's hand and prayed to a god he didn't believe in to keep her safe.

You owe me, you bastard he thought. *You owe me my mum; you've already taken my dad.*

APRIL

*A*pril's mum sat on the sofa and listened while Miss Khan explained what had happened.

She kept one arm firmly around April and had pulled the patchwork cover over both of their laps.

Miss Khan explained about the exam and how she'd found April outside near the playground. Then she relayed the conversation they'd had about anxiety in the staff room. April was grateful. She felt too exhausted to talk.

Her mum waited for Miss Khan to finish speaking, then turned to look at her April. "I feel so bad for not noticing. My own daughter, I should have known."

"It's not your fault, Mum," April said. "It's mine. I'm *so* sorry." She looked down at her hands, not able to look her mother in the eye.

"Hey," Kate said sharply, gently turning April's face to hers with the arm that wasn't squeezing her shoulders tightly. "I don't *ever* want to hear you apologise again. None of this is your fault. *None* of it." She gave a big sigh and relaxed her grip on April slightly, before continuing. "I should have spotted you were struggling. I've been so selfish. I'm always putting other people's families and problems ahead of my own. Ahead of my own *daughter's*." She put her hand over her mouth and made a chocked sobbing noise.

"Mrs. Winters…" Miss Khan interrupted quietly.

"Kate. Call me Kate, please. My mother in law was Mrs Winters and she was a bitch" The joke broke then tension and they both smiled.

"Okay, Kate," Miss Khan said. "I, too, feel guilty that I hadn't noticed April was struggling."

She turned to April with a smile, full of admiration. "You've always come across as so capable, April. So cool and in control. You often reminded me of myself and now I see why. It's not just our love of books and literature - it's our bravery."

"Bravery?" April said, shock making her laugh. "I'm not brave, I'm a coward."

"People battling anxiety are not cowards," Miss Khan said with absolute certainty. "They're incredibly strong. You walked into school every day, even though you knew it was going to be hard. You faced your fears *every single day*. Never, *ever* call yourself weak or a coward, because I know better."

"So do I, April," her mum agreed. "And we'll do whatever we need to do to help you with this."

Miss Khan mentioned the book by Dr Weeks, that had helped her so much, and April's mum wrote down the title. She also recommended they make an appointment with April's doctor as soon as possible.

"Of course," said April's mum, who'd regained her usual composure; "What about her exams?"

"Let me worry about them," Miss Khan said confidently.

She left soon after with assurances that she'd get in touch soon and NOT to worry about the exams.

Once she'd gone, Kate called the doctor's and asked for an emergency appointment for her daughter. April could hear her mum in the kitchen, arguing with the receptionist in her 'solicitor voice' while she waited in the living room. After a few minutes of bickering, she heard her mum slam down the phone.

"Bloody doctor's receptionists!" she said as she blustered through the door. "They should be defence lawyers; lord knows they make up enough excuses not to get you an appointment."

She looked at April and smiled. "I managed to persuade her to have the doctor call me at the end of surgery." She sat down and took hold of April's hand. "Would you like me to make you some food, love?"

April shook her head, her stomach was still in knots.

"How about I go and run you a nice bath?" she tried again. "I'll bring you up a cup of tea and a book?" She raised an eyebrow at her, knowing that she'd said the magic word – 'book'.

April nodded this time, smiling weakly. "Not *The Bell Jar*, though."

Kate grimaced and agreed, "No, not *The Bell Jar*. Not today." She stood up, saying she was off to find the 'fluffy guest towels' and the bottle of Radox a client had bought her for Christmas, which was apparently 'just the thing'.

The phone rang as April was making her way upstairs. "I'm on the loo!" her mum called down. "That'll be the doctor. You can talk to him, or tell him I'll be there in a second." Her voice echoed down the stairs and April smiled slightly as she added, "Don't tell him I'm weeing!"

"I think doctors know that we wee, Mum," April replied as she picked up the phone nervously. She really didn't want to talk to the doctor right now.

"Hello?"

"April?" Tom said. "Fuck April, are you there?"

"Tom? Are you okay?" April gripped the phone tighter.

"No, it's Mum... she went and got the pills herself, April. She got them and she... she took them all." He broke down in tears on the phone. April reached out to hold on to the bannister for support, her mind reeling with what to do, what to say.

She tried to get him to calm down so she could help, but she couldn't understand what he was saying. He was almost hysterical, babbling about how it was all his fault.

She heard a *click* as her mum picked up the extension in her bedroom and said "Hello?" When all Kate could hear was crying, she asked: "Who is this? What's going on?"

"April," Tom said finally "I think she's going to die. I need you. I *need you*."

April went to say something - that she would go to him wherever he was - but her mum got there first.

"Tom? It's Kate, April's mum. Where are you?" Her voice was calm but firm. April had heard her use it on the phone to clients a million times.

"Watford hospital, A&E," Tom said.

"Who has Em?" her mum asked.

"Yuki," he paused before adding in a quieter voice, "She doesn't know."

"Is Yuki okay with her?" she asked. "Is there anyone else she can stay with?"

"My Nan," Tom said automatically then "Fuck, my Nan is going to go mad!"

"Don't worry about what your Nan will do, Tom. Just give me her number and I'll sort it out."

Tom recited her number and April wrote it down on the pad next to the phone.

"Stay where you are, Tom. We're on our way," Kate said as reassuringly.

Tom put the phone down before April could say anything else.

"Did you know how bad things were?" April's mum asked her as she made her way downstairs to her.

April shook her head. "I knew she spent a lot of time in bed and I knew she'd run out of pills. Tom wanted her to stop taking them, as he thought they were making her worse. He told me he wasn't going to get them for her anymore…"

"So, she went and got them herself," Kate finished for her. "Christ, what a bloody mess." She ran her hand through her hair and said, "I need to phone his grandmother and tell her to get Emily, and then I need to go and be with Tom. I don't want to leave you on your own, but I can't leave him to deal with this alone either. Will you be okay?"

"I'm coming with you," April said quickly, baffled at the question; it had never even entered her mind that she'd stay home when Tom and Em needed her. She gathered up Tom's zip-up top while rushing to the kitchen to fill a bag with snacks, in case he was hungry.

"Are you sure you'll be okay?" her mum asked her, following her into the kitchen. "You've been through a lot today."

"I've been through nothing compared to Tom, and his

mum," April said firmly. "And I feel fine now." She meant it too.

As soon as she'd heard Tom's desperate voice on the phone, all she'd wanted to do was get to him. She needed to be with him, because he needed her.

"Okay," her mum said, nodding. "You pack Tom some stuff. Grab some of James' clothes from his cupboard, I'll call his Nan."

She wasn't on the phone for long and when she came back in, she didn't look very happy.

"You okay?" April asked, stuffing a Tupperware box of food into the bag she'd been packing.

"Yes, I suppose," Kate said with a sigh, looking sad and a bit angry at the same time. "Those poor kids. Their grandmother wasn't exactly warm on the phone, and she didn't ask a single thing about their mum."

"Is she going to get Em?" April asked.

"Yes. And take her back to hers. She said something about a cat?"

"Em loves animals," April said, feeling her eyes fill with tears. She wondered how they were still able to produce any. "Tom was going to get her a cat of her own for Christmas. He was so excited about it."

"Well, it may well still happen; we don't know anything yet," her mum said as they got into the car. "I'm sure it'll be okay," she added as she pulled out of the driveway.

April thought she sounded very sure, but she drove through three red lights on the way to the hospital.

TOM

*N*o one was telling him anything.

His mum had been taken into a room and he wasn't allowed in. Doctors and nurses rushed in and out. He heard machines beep and shoes squeak. Blood tests were ordered, charcoal was administered.

The whole corridor buzzed with noise - and people full of purpose - while he had none. Tom sat with his head in his hands and silently begged his mum not to die.

Time seemed to slow down, he had no idea how long he'd been sitting there before a doctor finally opened the door and made his way over to him.

"Your mum is going to be okay," he said and Tom felt himself crumble. He slid down the wall he had been leaning on and rested his head on the cool tiles.

A nurse rushed over and helped him back up, another went to get him some water.

The doctor sat down next to him, speaking kindly. "You got to her in time, Tom. She's going to be fine. We've given her some medication to help reverse the drugs she took, and something called activated charcoal, which will help bind the tablets she swallowed and allow them to pass through her system quicker. She's conscious, but disorientated, dehydrated and exhausted."

Tom said nothing, he couldn't. His hands shook as he took a sip of the water the nurse passed to him. He wanted to thank the doctor, but couldn't get any words out.

The doctor put his hand on Tom's arm and said, "When you're ready, we can take you in to see her. Don't mind all the machines and wires; they're monitoring her, that's all. They're helping her body do what it needs to do to heal."

Tom was scared to walk into the room, scared to see his mum again. She'd looked utterly lifeless on the bed when he'd found her. When the paramedics had carried her out, her arm had flopped uselessly over the side of the stretcher. The hand that used to hold his. The hand that had made his breakfast that morning - limp by her side.

Sitting in the corridor with the doctor's hand still on his arm, he cried huge racking sobs that hurt his ribs. When they finally died down to hiccups, the doctor said, "Ready son?"

Tom nodded weakly, and stood.

His mum was asleep. Her lips still looked blue and her skin was white, but he could see her chest rising and falling, and her heartbeat spiking and dipping on the monitor.

He approached the bed quietly and picked up her hand. It was still cold, but not as cold, not as dead as the last time he'd seen it. He pressed his lips to her skin and said, "Mum. Mum, I'm here."

She didn't stir, but her eyelids fluttered.

"She won't be able to talk yet," the doctor explained. "The

tube we had to put in her throat will have made it very sore. She can probably hear you though."

Tom looked back at his mum again, no idea what else to say' "Mum, I'm so sorry." His voice was thin and reedy, "I'm so sorry I didn't do what you asked me to do."

He sat with her and stroked her hand, while nurses checked on her and made notes on clipboards.

After a while Tom knew he needed to find a phone and call Yuki. He needed to know how Em was, if April and her mum had collected her and taken her to his Nan's. He wondered what they had told her.

"I need to phone my sister," he said to the nurse who was taking her blood pressure. "You will stay with her, won't you?" he asked

"Yes, love." Her face was full of sympathy. "I won't leave her. Go and get some food, some sleep. I'll be right here."

He walked out of the room and pulled the door closed gently behind him, looking back at his mum one last time, and her heartbeat on the machine.

The doctor was behind the nurse's desk. He stopped Tom as he went past. "Tom, your mum has been unwell for a long time. The pills she took weren't the right ones for her and they weren't helping. This isn't your fault, not at all. You didn't collect her prescription because you were trying to *help* her get better, and you *did*. I know it doesn't seem like it right now, but your mum is where she needs to be, and she's going to get the help she needs. She's been struggling for a long time, but she won't struggle anymore, I promise you. You did a brave thing, son. Everything is going to be alright." He smiled at Tom.

Tom nodded, but he didn't agree. As far as he was concerned, he'd almost killed his mum, and nothing would ever be alright again.

He pushed open the door to exit the ward and saw April and her mum stalking towards him.

"Tom!" April shouted, running to throw her arms around him and burying her head in his neck. He let himself relax in her arms briefly, before pulling away.

Kate put her arm around him as he stepped back; "Are you okay?" she asked him. Any news?"

"She's going to be okay. The doctor said she's going to be okay." He tried to remember what he'd been told about charcoal and blood tests, but he couldn't.

Kate nodded at him in silent understanding. "Thank God. I'll go and speak to the doctor. We have food and clothes for you. Stay with April and I'll be right back."

"I need to phone Em," Tom said suddenly. "Yuki's with her, I need to tell her..."

"I spoke to your Nan," Kate explained. "She went to collect her from Yuki's and took her back to her house. She's fine, Tom. You don't need to worry about her."

She took his hand and squeezed it while April held the other. "You're not on your own anymore."

APRIL

They found a spot outside and Tom lit a cigarette.

April had no words to help him so she just stood holding his hand and resting her head on his shoulder.

Once he'd smoked two cigarettes in a row, he straightened up and said, "I should have listened to you, April. You told me not to keep her pills from her."

"No, Tom, you were right to do something," she said. "You were trying to make her better."

"Look at what *that* did for her," he said angrily, kicking the kerb.

"It brought her here, where she needs to be," April unknowingly echoed the doctor's words to Tom from just a few minutes before.

"I thought she was dead, April," he whispered, his voice hoarse. "When I found her, I thought I was too late."

April turned to him and took his face in her hands. "She isn't dead, Tom. She's going to be fine, you got there in time and you saved her." She lifted his chin and found his eyes with hers. "You saved her."

His eyes filled with tears as he said, "It's going to take me a long time to believe that."

"Then I'll just keep on telling you," she whispered.

April's mum was talking to the doctor when they went back into the ward. She was in work mode and had that familiar intense, but efficient, look on her face. She heard them approaching and stopped talking for a moment to study Tom. The doctor said something to Kate, which April didn't catch, then walked off down the hall.

Kate's attention was still focused on Tom. "She's awake now, love. The doctor has done some more tests and he says the drugs won't have had any long-term effects. She's going to be fine. She needs a lot of rest, but she'll recover."

She put her hand on his shoulder in a comforting gesture as she continued. "Tom, the doctor has spoken with your mum and she knows she's not well. They asked her if she'd agree to being moved to the psychiatric ward, and she said yes."

Tom looked up at that, but Kate wasn't finished. "Even if she'd said no, they still would have admitted her. I need you to understand that. You've done an amazing job looking after her, but she needs a different kind of help now. Help only experts can give her. She wants to go, Tom; she understands she needs to, and she *wants* to go. I think maybe today was her cry for help and it has been heard."

"That's good, Tom," April said softly, while squeezing his hand.

He nodded tightly and said "How long will she be in there for? What about Em? Will they let me look after her still?"

"No, Tom," said a voice from behind them. "I'll be looking

after Em… and you too. I should have been doing it for the last two years."

"Nan?" Tom said looking shocked to see her there.

Em ran out from behind her and launched herself into his arms. "Tommy! Yuki says you are a hero and saved Mummy. Is that right, Tommy?" Tom didn't reply, he just hugged his little sister tightly.

April's mum answered for him. "Yes, Emily," she said, smiling at her. "That's exactly right."

Yuki appeared a moment later. He looked completely out of place in his leather trousers and his open shirt. His voice was calm though, as always. "Hey, man," he greeted Tom with a look of concern. He kept any questions to a minimum, however, "You okay?"

Tom nodded and tried to smile and failed. He just went over to Yuki who slapped him on the back and said "Yeah, I think I might be."

TOM

*N*an sat with his mum in her room for a long time.

Tom went with Em, Yuki and April to find a vending machine. He was amazed at how hungry he was. They sat on the Lino floor and ate crisps and Kit Kats in silence. April sat inside Tom's open legs, Em sat on Yuki's knee. Though no one said anything, Tom couldn't remember having a better conversation.

Once they'd all eaten enough salt and sugar to refuel, they went back to the ward.

Em yawned on the way and Yuki hoisted her onto his shoulders. "I can take her, dude," he said, then. "Let me, okay? You've been taking on enough." Before Tom could argue.

Tom was so used to looking after Em, it had become second nature to him. It took effort to let go and let Yuki take over, but he agreed. His world suddenly felt like a mixed-up jigsaw. His Nan talking to his mum, it didn't fit right. April here with her mum, who was talking to the doctors - it was all wrong. He'd tried so hard to keep his life in neat little sections, but now they were blurring into one another and there was nothing he could do to stop it.

It felt strange to have all this support – to be told that he was brave, that he wasn't alone anymore. It was a relief too, but would take a while to get used to. He worried the police would arrive and take him and Em away. He worried his Nan was going to make them all move into her house. He worried about how long his mum would be in the hospital and if he'd be allowed to look after her when she got home.

When his Nan finally came out of his mum's room, her eyes were red, and she looked all of her sixty-two years.

"Go and say goodnight to your mum, and then we're going home."

"I can't go," Tom protested. "Someone needs to stay with her."

"The nurses will do that, love. They're going to give her some medicine in a minute to help her settle. Go and say goodnight now while she's awake, and then Yuko will drive us home."

"That's me," Yuki said proudly, not even slightly perturbed that she still couldn't get his name right.

Tom pushed the door to his mum's room open gently. It was almost dark inside, the only light coming from blinking LEDs on the machines around her, which buzzed softly. She turned her face at the sound of the door opening and as his eyes adjusted to the gloom, he saw her offer him a brave attempt at a smile. He gave her a wobbly one in return and went to sit by the bed.

"Mum," he said, taking her hand, which was warm again now.

"Hello, love," she said quietly. Her voice was croaky.

"Don't try and talk," he said gently. "It's okay."

She smiled at him again. "I need to, Tom. I've needed to talk for a long time now."

His tears dripped onto their hands.

"I'm so sorry," she rasped, her voice small but determined. "Sorry for… for everything."

"It's okay, Mum," Tom tried again, but she squeezed his hand and shook her head.

"It's not. I've been selfish, and I've been weak. I've left you with too much." She was exhausting herself, but refused to stop when Tom shushed her. "Your Nan is going to look after you for a while and I'm going to try and get better. Properly better."

"I can look after you, Mum," he said, crying freely now.

"You can't, love. I can't look after *myself* right now, and I can't look after you two either. You've got to let me do this while you concentrate on school, and those exams."

"I don't care about them, Mum! I'll stay here with you."

She shook her head again firmly. "No, son." Then she added in a quieter voice, "You *will* go to school, sit the exams. Make your dad proud." Her voice broke on the last word.

Tom could tell it hurt her to cry. "Okay, Mum, okay," he relented. "I'll go to school and we'll stay with Nan. For you, I'll do it for you. And I'll come here to see you every day, I promise."

She smiled, and her eyes drooped sleepily. "Not every day, love," she said. "Have a break."

Tom kissed her hand and stroked her hair back from her face, just like she'd done for him a million times in another life, and he'd done for Em.

The door opened behind him and his Nan popped her head

in. "Come on, pet. Time to go. Yuku's coming back for tea. He's demanded his erotic dinner."

APRIL

*A*pril didn't go back to Tom's Nan's house with the others, although she'd been invited.

She was tired after her eventful day and she knew her mum wouldn't let her anyway.

She said goodbye to Tom by Yuki's car, kissing him softly on the lips and telling him to call her later.

When they got home, her mum made a dinner that neither of them really wanted, then April went upstairs to have her bath. The water was still in it from earlier, but it was cold, so she drained it halfway and topped it up with water from the hot tap. She shivered as she lowered herself in, watching bubbles emerge in the water, hiding her pale skin from herself.

There was too much to think about. Her mind flitted from Tom, to his mum, to the exam, to Miss Khan's words and her mum's face as she'd said them. Today had been the worst day of her life, but it was kind of the best day too. Sometimes, she thought, as the bubbles grew up around her, life had to fall apart, for it to be put back together again.

Just like Tom, April had tried her hardest to control her environment, but it had been impossible. The more she had fought to keep herself safe, the more dangerous it had become.

She felt something shift and lift inside her and realised the weight she'd been carrying was gone.

April lay in the bath until the water cooled again and her skin pruned. When she got out, she found her mum had put a hot water bottle in her bed. She climbed under the sheets, clutched an old teddy and fell asleep in seconds.

Her mum woke her the next morning with a cup of tea. "What's the time?" April asked groggily, sitting up and reaching for her watch. "Oh my god, I'm going to be so late. It's 11am! Why didn't you wake me up? Why aren't you at work?"

Kate smiled and took a sip of her tea. "Good morning, darling," she said. "I didn't wake you up, because you didn't need to get up." She perched on the edge of April's bed as she explained. "Miss Khan phoned me this morning. She's spoken to your teachers and the headmaster, who have all agreed that you don't need to sit your mocks. You have been predicted A grades in all your subjects. You need to focus on resting and getting better for when the real exams come up."

April went to argue, but her mum held up a finger to stop her. "Getting better starts *today*. We have an appointment at the doctors in half an hour and I've taken the week off work to be with you. And Tom," she added.

At the sound of his name, April stiffened. "I didn't call him last night," she said guiltily. "I need to call him now."

"No, you need to get dressed. Tom's Nan called me this morning. He isn't at school either, nor will he be taking his mocks." Kate stood up and started opening drawers, finding clothes for her. "They won't go on his predicted grades, as they've done with you, but he won't lose any marks for not doing them either. He was still asleep when I spoke to June and I said you'd call him later." She pulled the cover off April and handed her a random outfit, with mismatched socks. "Now get up and get dressed."

The doctor said much the same as Miss Khan had. He said anxiety was more common than people thought and she wasn't the first, nor would she be the last teenager, to suffer from it.

"Will I have to take pills?" April asked nervously.

"Do you want to?" the doctor asked, and April shook her head fiercely.

"Then I see no reason why you need to. There's an excellent type of counselling called Cognitive Behaviour Therapy. It's had remarkable success in helping people with anxiety, panic attacks and the like. Would you like to give it a go?"

"What is it?" April asked him. "What do I have to do?"

"CBT addresses negative patterns and distortions in the way we look at the world and ourselves." April nodded, but didn't really understand. He smiled and explained more: "The 'cognitive' part looks at how negative thoughts - like fear or anger - contribute to anxiety. And the 'behaviour' part looks at how you behave and react in situations that *trigger* anxiety."

"So, it's therapy to retrain your brain?" April deduced and the doctor's smile widened into a grin.

"Exactly. People who suffer from anxiety often begin to fear the fear. If you imagine going back into the exam hall, how do you feel? What is your body saying to you?"

"It says it doesn't want to go," April said, beginning to understand. "I don't ever want to go through that again."

"Your mind is telling you to avoid all situations that may present you with anxiety. Would you believe me if I said to you that you could go into that exam hall and sit your exams today, without any anxiety and without having a panic attack?"

"No!" April almost scoffed at him. "That's impossible."

"It *is* possible, when you realise that the negative thoughts you're having, are just thoughts. Thoughts cannot hurt you, not if you don't let them. Think of the old rhyme about 'sticks and stones'."

... may break my bones, but words can never hurt me, April automatically finished the rhyme in her head.

The doctor was still explaining. "Your brain thinks it's looking after you by telling you to avoid situations that may make you panic. It also thinks it's helping you when it floods your system with adrenaline, so you can run away fast." He paused, letting what he'd told her sink in. "When you learn to see your thoughts as just thoughts - not orders you need to act upon - the panic will stop."

April's mind whirred with this new information, but her doctor wasn't finished. "Winston Churchill called his depression his 'black dog'. " April wrinkled her nose at that; she'd never considered herself depressed. The doctor laughed and he cut in before she could argue. "I don't think you have depression, but it presents a wonderful image, doesn't it? Your anxiety is a black dog on your shoulder, April. It tries to tell you what to do, and what *not* to do. You can't get it to stop yapping, but you don't have to listen to it. CBT will teach you how to ignore it. You'll get past this. You're a bright girl with a *very* bright future ahead."

He made a couple of notes on his pad and cut in in conclusion: "I'll put the referral in for you today. It may take a few weeks for you to be seen, but in the meantime I suggest exercise and sleep. Take some Rescue Remedy if you feel worried or stressed. Look after your body, April, and teach it how to look after you."

"Are you okay, sweetheart?" her mum asked her after a few minutes of silence; "Is there something else you'd like to ask?"

She shifted in her seat, as she struggled to reply. "No. It's just, um, did Sylvia Plath have anxiety? Did she have treatment which didn't work and is that why...?"

"Ah, I see where you're going with this, April," her doctor said astutely. "No, Sylvia Plath didn't have anxiety. Well, not just anxiety. I believe she also had manic depression and quite possibly slight schizophrenia too. Far more complicated than anxiety, and far harder to treat."

April nodded and sat back in her seat, relieved. All these years she'd thought that she was just like Sylvia, and part of her had thought she would end up the same way.

"Have you had any suicidal thoughts, April?" the doctor asked her carefully.

"No," April said without much hesitation. She thought back to the day she'd deliberately cut her thumb over the kitchen sink and realised she hadn't she'd got it in her to self-harm, let alone commit suicide.

"I'm too much of a coward," she said. "Even if I wanted to - and I don't, Mum," she said turning to look her in the eye to assured her. "I want the opposite. I want to live without fearing everything. I want to be strong."

"April, I see a lot of people with anxiety," the doctor said. "They're some of the bravest people I know."

Miss Khan had said the same thing, so maybe it was time for April to start believing it.

They stopped at Boots and got some Rescue Remedy, then went into WHSmith to order the book by Claire Weeks, which Miss Khan had recommended. Her mum wandered off while April looked at colouring stuff in stationery, deciding she'd get some for Tom. She picked up some soft pencils, a huge artist's sketchpad, some watercolour paints and a pack of brushes.

Then she went to the kid's section and picked up *The Jolly Christmas Postman,* for Em, which had been April's favourite book as a kid.

Her mum came back as she was looking at music tapes for Yuki and Jamie and pushed a book into her hands.

"Here, this is for you."

"Helen Keller?" April asked, then flipped the back over and read aloud: "When she was nineteen months old, Helen Keller suffered a severe illness that left her blind and deaf. Not long after, she also became mute. Her tenacious struggle to overcome these handicaps - with the help of her inspired teacher, Anne Sullivan - is one of the great stories of human courage and dedication."

April looked at her mum quizzically, so Kate explained. "Not everyone who struggles goes down the Sylvia Plath route, April. People can overcome challenges and be stronger for it. As Helen Keller herself said: 'Character cannot be achieved in ease and quiet. Only through trial and suffering can the soul be strengthened'."

April murmured the quote to herself, already liking it almost as much as some of her favourite Plath quotes even though the sentiment was almost the exact opposite.

"I like it. Thanks, Mum - for being so great about all this. I'm sorry I didn't talk to you sooner, I didn't think you'd understand. I mean, nothing ever seems to faze you."

"You'd be surprised, April," her mum said; "Besides, if I didn't understand how even the most brilliant people can struggle and suffer, I wouldn't be the solicitor I am." She put her arm around April's shoulders. "Us women, us *strong* women," she emphasised, pointing to herself and then April "Aren't made this way; we *grow* to be that way."

When they got home, April called Tom at home, and then at his Nan's, but there was no answer. With nothing else to do, she went and sat by the fire to pore over Helen Keller. "I think we're going to be good friends," she whispered to the stern-looking woman on the front of the book.

When the phone rang at 5pm, April jumped up thinking it might be Tom and was surprised when she heard Jamie on the end of the line.

"April?" she said before April even had time to say hello. She sounded more pissed off than April had ever heard her; "Where the *fuck* have you been?"

"Jamie?"

"Yes, April - it's me, Jamie. Your so-called best friend, who you haven't spoken to in three-fucking-days. Jamie, who doesn't know what the hell has been going on. First, you run out of the English exam, then Tom goes missing, meanwhile no one fucking calls me, or answers my calls. Where have you been?"

"Jamie," April said sheepishly "I'm so sorry."

"Sorry?" Jamie said angrily. "*Screw* your sorry, April! I needed you and you just dropped off the face of the fucking earth." She started sobbing loudly down the phone and April had to shout to be heard over the noise

"Please, Jamie listen, just listen."

After some huffing and puffing and more swear words, Jamie finally calmed down enough to listen and April told her about her panic attack, as quickly and succinctly as she could, not wanting to get into a big discussion about it.

When Jamie tried question her further, April interrupted her: "That's not all, Jamie."

Then she told her about Tom's mum.

"Fuck!" Jamie said once she'd finished. "I had no idea... about any of this stuff. Why doesn't anyone tell me anything?" She let out a breath that *whooshed* down the phone audibly then said "Is Tom okay? Is Em okay?"

April explained that they were with Tom's Nan and that neither she nor Tom would be doing their mock exams.

"I need to see you," Jamie said decisively. "When?"

"I don't know. I'm going to the hospital to see Tom in a bit with Mum. It's Em's play at school tomorrow and I'm going along to watch. I'll call you when I get back and maybe you can come over? Will your mum let you out in exam week?"

"I'll worry about my mum," Jamie said grimly. Then she asked April some more questions about her doctor's appointment. "Why didn't you tell me?" Jamie asked her quietly. "I could have helped."

"I don't know," April said honestly. "I didn't know how... I didn't know what to say. I thought you'd think I was a coward."

"You? A coward? No way, I'm the bloody coward, April."

April was about to ask why, but her mum, who'd just walked into the room, interrupted her and said "We need to go now, love. Visiting hours end soon."

"Go," Jamie said. "But bloody well call me later, okay?"

"Promise," April said.

"Hey, April," Jamie said before she could hang up the phone "I love you."

"I love you too, Jamie."

64

TOM

*A*pril, her mum and Yuki all arrived to the hospital together.

April's mum gave Tom a bag of clothes and when he looked at her questioningly, she explained "Just some stuff I gathered for your mum."

She had packed soft flannel pyjamas (which looked brand new), slippers and a dressing down. There was also a hairbrush and body wash, even face cream and a small bag of make-up. Tom hadn't thought of doing any of it and felt ashamed.

Kate must have noticed his face fall, because she tapped him on the head lightly and said, "Hey, you're not on your own anymore, remember? Let people help."

"Thanks," he said finally and grinned at her.

"Well, I can see why my daughter likes you so much when you grin like that," she said, and he grinned wider.

April was catching up with Yuki. When Tom approached them, Yuki stood up and excused himself. "I need to, um, have a wee." He sauntered off, leaving them alone.

319

"Discreet as ever," Tom said, which made April smile.

"You okay?" Tom asked her. "You never told me what happened in the exam."

April nodded at him, her smile fading just a touch. "I'm fine, I promise. And I'll tell you all about it, but not right now, okay?"

"Okay," he said reluctantly. "But you're not doing your exams? You're not missing them for me, are you?"

"No, I'm not," she said. "But I would, if it came to that."

He smiled at her again, not knowing what to say, not quite able to believe that she was here with him. He thought she'd run a mile when everything about his mum came out. Who'd choose to take all this crap on if they didn't have to? *But then*, he thought, *I'd do the same for her*. Even with his own crap to deal with, he'd gladly take on anything that April needed help with. And be honoured to be the one she trusted.

He took her hand and led her outside. "I know my mum is really ill and I should be with her and I will be. I'll go back in a minute. I'll sit with her all day happily, I just need to do this first" and then he kissed her and told her without words what she meant to him.

He was still kissing her when April's mum interrupted them. "*Ahem*… Tom? Your mum wants to see you."

They sprang apart, Tom blushed and let go of April's hair, which he'd wound around his fingers. "Okay, erm, thanks," he said, looking anywhere but April's mum's face.

He was still smiling when he walked into his mum's room. She was looking better each day. They didn't talk much - she slept a lot - but her hand felt strong in his and her eyes looked clearer as she told him she was being moved to the psychiatric ward the next day.

"I'll come visit you," Tom promised, "*every* day."

"If you want to, love," his mum said. "But don't spend all your time sitting watching me. You've done enough of that. They'll be trying me on different drugs and it won't be easy." She smiled at him thinly and carried on, "I'm so sorry I'm going to miss Christmas and Em's concert."

Their Nan had done her best to explain what was going on to Em. She'd told her that their mum was sick from being so sad about Daddy, and she was going to go somewhere to help her get happy again.

Em was young, but not stupid, and was still suspicious she wasn't being told the whole story. Tom knew she had questions about what had happened the night Yuki had fetched her from school, but she didn't say anything. Tom thought that maybe she didn't want to know.

There'd be time to tell her, when she was ready, but right now he just wanted her to be a kid at Christmas.

Tom showed his mum all the stuff that April's mum had brought her. She stroked the soft flannel pyjama trousers and said, "She's so kind. I should have phoned her before. Maybe she could have helped us."

"She did, without knowing it," Tom said "She sent me April."

His mum smiled at him knowingly and bit-by-bit, he told her everything - about April, and the camp, and Yuki and Jamie. He talked long after she'd fallen asleep. He talked until the nurse knocked on the door and kicked him out.

As he walked down the hall, a shaft of light fell in his path. It looked a lot like hope.

65

APRIL

"Jamie, what are you doing here?" April asked loudly when she saw Jamie barging her way past parents to find a seat next to her in Em's school hall.

"You're missing your science exam!"

"So what?" Jamie replied just as loudly. She pushed past a mum holding a small crying child. "You'd better take him outside if he's going to squawk the whole way through," she said as she stole the woman's seat and threw herself down next to April, ignoring all protests. "It's only bloody science. I have no plans to be a scientist. Plus, you and Tom aren't doing any of the fucking exams..." She clamped her hand over her mouth briefly as she remembered where she was. "Whoops!" she chuckled to the man on the other side of her, who was holding a massive video recorder. "I do hope you weren't filming." She gave him a 'don't mess with me' smile then turned back to April. "So, it's no big deal if I miss one, is it?"

April grinned and squeezed her hand. "I'm so pleased you're here."

"Me too," Jamie said as a teacher walked on stage. She squeezed April's hand back and said "*Shush*, it's starting."

April thought the play was above average for primary school kids, but she allowed that she was probably a bit biased. Nobody (except perhaps old Ebenezer himself) could deny that it was adorable.

When the children came on to do a bow, Em twirled and waved and bowed, while April, Jamie, Yuki and Tom cheered and clapped louder than everyone else there.

When it was over, Em ran over to them all and shouted: "FAMILY!" which made them all go a bit misty-eyed, especially Yuki, who lost his trademark cool for a few minutes.

"Wasn't I brilliant?" she asked rhetorically, Em wasn't the type to need anybody's affirmation. "Wasn't I the best?"

They all told her she was the star of the show, even though the star of the show was a boy named Angus, who'd forgotten his lines and wet himself.

"Where are we going?" she asked, when they got to the car.

"To my house," April said, bending down to whisper in her ear, "we have a surprise for you."

All the lights in the house were dark when they pulled up. Em got out of the car pouting. "This is a rubbish surprise," she said, sniffing. "No one's here."

The front door opened and Em saw balloons then ran in to find her Nan and April's mum hiding in the kitchen.

"Surprise!" they shouted when Tom turned on the lights. The table was covered in glitter, mince pies and tiny sandwiches cut into angels and stars.

"But, it's not my birthday," Em said looking surprised, then shoving a sandwich in her mouth before they could be taken away.

"I know that, love," her Nan said. "But we wanted to do something a bit special for you. To say well done on your play."

Tom's Nan hadn't gone to see the play; she'd been busy collecting her son's things from their house: his clothes, shoes, watch and wallet. She'd emptied wardrobes and packed boxes ready for Yuki to take to the charity shop.

Tom had told April about it when they'd met just before the play.

"Do you mind?" April had asked him. "All his stuff being taken away?"

"No," he said, and he meant it. "It's time to move on. It'll be good for us. Nan is going to move in, which is great because I didn't want to live at hers. But bad, because now we'll have a responsible adult around..." he trailed off and stared at her suggestively, waggling that eyebrow of his.

She smiled back, catching on. "I'm sure we'll manage to find some time to be alone."

Em spent her surprise party twirling, occasionally making herself dizzy and wobbling about. They all ate and drank and sang naff Christmas songs.

When Em finally stopped dancing with Yuki (who she'd declared was the best at twirling) and sat down, April's mum slipped out and re-appeared with a big box.

"Happy Christmas, Em" she said, handing it over.

Em opened the box and a small furry nose poked out.

Em didn't speak, but her eyes grew to the size of wagon wheels. She opened and closed her mouth, but no words came out.

"Like him?" April's mum asked her. Em nodded slowly as a fat tear rolled down her face, which the dog tried to lick off.

"He's a rescue puppy," Kate explained. "Can you believe no one wanted him?" Em shook her head.

The puppy wriggled out of the box and began yapping happily as Emily stroked him.

"Now, I know your Nan has a cat, who probably doesn't want this little chap about. We can give it a go, but if the cat isn't happy, he can live here, okay? April is going to walk him." She looked at April and smiled. *That must be the exercise part of the therapy,* she thought wryly.

Her mum looked back at Em, who was scratching her new puppy behind the ears. "But you can come and see him every single day."

"Can't you have the old cat?" Em asked her suddenly.

"I thought you loved Brian!" her Nan said from across the room.

"Well, I do but he's old and boring." The puppy crawled into her lap and April could see that he'd never be accused of being boring, like poor Brian.

"Nonsense," Emily's Nan said. "And he'll be fine with the dog, so we can take him home tonight, okay?"

"Okay," Em replied in an uncharacteristically tiny voice. April had never seen her so quiet and realised how overwhelmed she must be.

"Mrs. Winters…" Tom began.

"My name is Kate!" April's mum replied, smiling from ear-to-ear.

"Kate," he tried again, looking awkward "you didn't have to do that." April could see her mum was about to tell him to stop trying to control everything and let her help, when he said, "But I'm so glad you did. Thank you."

They were trying to think of a name for the dog when the doorbell rang.

"Shit, Jamie," Yuki said, peering out the window. "Is that your mum? She's hot. I'd ride that snake."

Before Jamie could punch him, Kate quickly said: "I'll go!" and made her way to the door.

"Is Jemima in there?" they heard Jamie's mum screech from the doorway in her upper middle-class voice.

"Even the dog looks scared," Yuki said, sounding impressed. "Don't you, *Morrison*?"

"Felicity," they heard Kate say to her "please calm down, let me explain."

"Explain?" she screeched again. "Explain what? That you encouraged my daughter to miss her mock exam. I knew your April was a bad influence on her. She has a shifty look about her."

April blushed. Tom and Yuki giggled, stupidly, and April realised that they must have taken a trip to the heating shed.

"And you! Well, my husband was right about you."

"Was he?" Kate asked, her tone changing instantly. "What did he say about me, then?" April knew that tone (it had teeth) and she hoped for Jamie's mum's sake that she knew a warning when she heard one.

She didn't get the chance to reply. Jamie stood up and marched to the door. "Mum, stop it! Just bloody stop it!"

"Don't you dare swear at me, or use that tone of voice, Jemima," Mrs. Fenton-Jones said, sounding horrified.

"You were brought up better than that. Not dragged up, like these."

She stopped and sniffed, not finishing what April knew she was going to say: *like those friends of yours*. She may as well have, however – it wasn't hard to figure out.

Tom's Nan stood up to say something and Kate hastily grabbed her arm to stop her.

"I will talk how I *fucking well like*, mother darling," Jamie said in her faux-posh voice, then dropped into the voice she used when her mother wasn't around – her real voice. "I swear, and I smoke."

Felicity held a hand up to her pearls and gasped.

"And I get drunk, and I shoplift," she was counting the things off on her fingers now. "I take drugs, and I wear shit-loads of make-up. Yes, SHIT-LOADS!" She hollered in her mum's face, then said over her shoulder, "Sorry Em, Nan."

She turned back to her mother, who was looking a little faint, "And I decided to skip my science exam to be with my *friends*." She looked around at April, Yuki and Tom quickly, giving them a wink.

"I'm not going to need an A in science, Mum, because I'm not going to be a doctor. I…" she said dramatically, before jumping onto the table in the living room. "I'm going to be an actress. A *brilliant* fucking actress," she added.

"I am going to take drama for my GCSE and my A-levels and I am going to go to drama school. I'm in the school play and I'm BLOODY GOOD IN IT, TOO!" she roared triumphantly. Slipping into the voice she used for her character, she sang, "I have been going to rehearsals, not lessons!"

Felicity had fallen back into a chair but found her voice at last. "You are *not* going to drama school. No, no, *no*," she said, trying to sound authoritative.

"Oh, but I am, Mother," Jamie said gleefully, jumping off the table. "I am, and you are going to support me. Because if you don't, when I turn sixteen next month, I *will* leave home and I promise to God, you'll never see me again. Not that I think God exists," she added superfluously.

Her mother was too stunned to speak. She just stared at her daughter as if she'd never seen her before.

"Have you finished?" Yuki interjected.

"No," Jamie said with a determined look on her face. "I am also a lesbian."

Everyone looked at her.

"I knew it!" Yuki declared. "I knew it was the only reason a woman wouldn't want me."

"You tried it on with Jamie?" Tom asked him, looking surprised and a little appalled.

"All the bloody time," Jamie said, sighing. "And I threw him a bone once, just to check. But I'm definitely a lesbian. Sorry, Yuki," she said, patting him on the arm indulgently.

"A lesbian?" April asked softly, the news taking her completely by surprise.

"Yes. A lesbian," Jamie said proudly. "I'm gay. That secret Claire has over me? We spent the summer before I met you, kissing." She turned to her mum, throwing the words at her like weapons. "KISSING A *GIRL*, MOTHER! And I really liked it."

"I really liked it," she repeated in a softer voice, but this time to April. "But when school started, I guess Claire had a change of heart. She dumped me – just as a friend, of course - in front of everyone. She told me if I ever said anything, she'd deny it and claim I'd hit on her. Said my life would be over, no one would believe me."

She stopped for a moment, looking at Tom. "But I don't care if no one believes me. Because I know it's the truth. This is *my* life and I have to make *my* choices. "Tom, your mum made a bad choice."

Tom immediately looked at Em to make sure she wasn't listening, and saw she was busy playing with the puppy, so he turned his attention back to Jamie.

"But she still made a choice. She chose to change her life. It made me realise no one else can take responsibility for your life. You have to take responsibility for yourself."

Tom nodded as if he understood and Jamie made her way over to her mum.

"Mum, I know you love me and you only want the best for me, but I can't be the person you want me to be. I can't."

Tom's Nan stood up and said, "I don't mind you being a lesbian, love. I love Whoopi Goldberg."

"Thank you," Jamie said sincerely.

"Me neither," said Tom easily.

"Nor me," April said, fiercely proud of her friend.

Jamie smiled at them all, then said, "Come on then Mum. I think I've shocked you enough. Let's go home."

APRIL

*S*ix months later...

It was the first warm day of the year and April couldn't wait to get to the camp. Tom and Yuki had left early to get stuff ready. Em wanted to come along too, but Tom said dogs weren't allowed, so she soon changed her mind.

Jamie was meeting her there. She said she was bringing along 'a friend' she'd met at Drama Club and already told them all that they were *not* to make a big deal out of it. "If you dare tell me to ride the snake...." she'd warned Yuki, "I'll kill you."

Yuki had laughed, but looked nervous at the same time. April was excited to see how Jamie would act, trying to impress a girl. She'd changed a lot since Christmas. She didn't wear as much make-up and (*thank goodness*, April thought) blithely stopped shoplifting.

Jamie and April got A grades in her exams. In contrast, Claire had failed almost all of them and her parents had sent her to a private school instead.

Jamie's mum was still shocked by her daughters revelations, but having been told by her husband that if she didn't stop calling him at work eighteen times a day, he'd leave her for his secretary, was clinging onto Jamie with all she had. She even *called* her Jamie now. When they went shopping, Jamie picked the clothes, for both herself and her mother.

Maybe that was why Jamie had stopped shoplifting, but April thought it was more likely that the theft and make up was all part of Jamie being angry at having to suppress herself. Now Jamie was living life as herself, she didn't seem to need war paint to leave the house.

April had gone back to school after Christmas. Walking in on the first day had been a bit scary, but she'd had Jamie on one side of her, Tom on the other - and Helen Keller in her bag.

She'd been going to her CBT sessions for five months and her therapist was talking about winding down the sessions, as they were no longer needed.

Tom had also been seeing a counsellor to help him deal with the loss of his dad and what had happened with his mum. The hospital arranged it for him. Em didn't need any counselling at all, the doctor said, after a social worker went to see her. Tom may have let his homework slide, but Em was exactly where she needed to be on all the charts.

Neither of them spoke much about what they did in their sessions, but Tom wondered why April went to hers.

"You could have told me," he'd said, when she explained about her anxiety.

"I didn't know how to," she said. "I didn't know what was happening to me and I thought I was going mad."

"I would never have thought you were mad" he said fiercely, then "Well, actually, you must be slightly mad to be with me" April had nudged him in the ribs at that they'd grinned at one another.

"So this is 16, with no secrets" she'd mused, as they sat round the fire, thinking about the year before and how much life had changed. Her mum knew where she was, *she* knew where she was in her head and who she was in Tom's arms. Jamie wasn't going to dictate the night drinking and spewing. When they got home they'd all be welcomed by their loved ones.

April wondered if she'd ever have appreciated it so much, without the work it took them to get there.

TOM

*T*he camp looked great.

Jamie had dropped a load of gear off earlier in the week. Candles, rugs and sheets.

"Very seductive," Yuki had said to her as she was setting them up. Jamie warned him, again, not to say or do anything to embarrass her.

It was strange to see the new, nice Jamie. Well, nic*er* anyway. Tom thought she looked much better with less make-up on, beautiful even. Her hair was light without the dye, and her brown eyes were more striking without make-up all over them. She even had a cheeky dimple when she smiled. If April wasn't in his life, and she wasn't gay, he'd probably tried to have pull Jamie. He told her as much as she blushed and then cackled.

"You were always April's" she'd said, ruffling his hair, "And there is no better man for the job."

"I'm proud of you" Tom had told her, feeling like his dad, and feeling the lump in his throat.

He could just *miss* his dad these days, without the

resentment , and it felt like he'd just lost him all over again. His counsellor said he'd not even started to grieve for his own loss. He hadn't been able to, he'd had to hold everyone else while they gone through theirs. "You will miss him Tom" she'd told him "But you have to learn to live with that grief, put it in your pocket. By all means pull it out sometimes, but don't let it stop you living."

Tom had thought about her words nonstop after that session. Later, when dinner was done and Em was in bed, he'd pulled out his football boots and traced a line over the studs on the bottom. Before he could talk himself out of it, he'd called Alex and asked him for a kick around after school the next day. When he put the phone down he went into his mum's room to tell her.

"Tom, that's wonderful!" she said, her eyes lighting up. She wasn't in bed anymore. She worked from her bedroom now, sewing and making alterations on dance costumes. Tom still had to steel himself before he knocked each time, scared she'd be back facing the wall with her lifeless hands, but she never was.

Her hands were always busy, stroking fabrics, stitching and folding. Sometimes she made Tom wear the costumes so she could pin them. Her and Em would cry with laughter at Tom in sequins and neon taffeta. It was the best sound, Tom had decided, the best sound in the world (apart from April when she said his name as a sort of prayer).

"I will be there watching, with Em, and I'll make your favourite sandwiches" she'd said, stroking his hair "*If* your nan will let me in the bloody kitchen." His nan had decided to carry on living with them, although their mum was fine almost all the time. She had the odd low day still but instead of going to bed, she'd go out walking and she helped out at Em's dance classes which got her out the house and making friends for the first time in years.

"Your dad was my only friend, my best friend," she'd told him one night, when she was still in hospital, "I moved here, knowing no one and never needing too, because I had him. I thought I'd always have him," she'd said, squeezing his hand "I was wrong. Life doesn't always do what you want. You need more than one person in your life. You need friends, because you can't put all your life into one person. I did that and I let you down and I'll never stop being sorry. You reminded me so much of your dad, somedays I could barely look at you, and yet I still let you pretend to be him and look after us all. You were not him, and you never will be, you have the best of him but you are my Tom, my boy, my son, my responsibility. Not my nurse or a ghost of my husband."

She'd told Tom one day she might even run her own dance studio, but not yet. His Nan and his mum had found a way to live together that didn't always work, but worked well enough to continue. Em loved having all of her family under one roof.

Em fell back in love with her mum within seconds of her putting on her ballet shoes and showing Em her twirl. It was probably because of a whole lot of other things too, but Tom would never forget Em's saucer eyes the first time she saw her mum pirouette in the kitchen. "Is that *our* mum?" she'd whispered in his ear *"really?"*

They'd become inseperable after that, and for every costume his mum sewed a customer, Em was made three more. Tom was slightly envious of the relationship they had as mother and daughter and the loss of closeness he and Em shared now she had her mum back, but that was life, he'd decided. Not easy, not fair, but full of colour and noise and friends and hope.

He'd passed his exams with B's in all subjects apart from art, which he got an A*. In the end, for his final piece, he'd taken photos of all the artwork on his walls, and photos of the pictures he drew on his friends.

When the photos were developed he mixed them between old polaroid's of his dad, him and his dad playing football, his mum and dad on their wedding day. He'd even braved the train station to make a sketch of the empty platform.

Among the photos and sketches were football boots cut from magazines, still life drawings of rotting plates of uneaten food, an empty bench and a bleeding heart. Lines from 'Daddy' by Sylvia Plath were scrawled here and there. He'd even stuck parts of hospital gowns and dried flowers between some of the photos.

Overlaying it all was a ballerina, twirling across the page. It was a huge piece. The biggest he'd ever made. *"Encounters, experiences and meetings"* was the topic, Tom had named the piece 'My dad, a journey in grief'.

APRIL

*J*amie was late and when she finally appeared, she was walking hand in hand with a girl who had short red hair and glasses.

"This is Harry," she said, grinning.

"Hello, Harry," they all chorused at her as if they'd met her a hundred times (which they hadn't, but had been forced to practise the *greeting* a hundred times till Jamie was satisfied with it) . They must have got it right became Jamie nodded and did a thumbs up then went to get a drink for Harry, while Yuki quizzed the poor girl about music, particularly Jim Morrison.

When they were all settled round the fire, April made a toast; "To the first camping trip of the summer!" she said smiling.

"And the last... for me, anyway," Yuki said, putting his drink down and picking up his guitar.

"What?" Tom looked up from the joint he was rolling, and Jamie stopped whispering in Harry's ear.

"I'm off to India tomorrow," Yuki explained. "I'm going on a Shamanic Yoga retreat for a while."

"But, you can't leave us," April said. "Nothing will be the same!"

"The future is uncertain, but the end is always near," he said, in his best Jim Morrison voice. "Time for me to go and join my spiritual family."

Yuki told them his plans as the sun slid down in the sky and the field glowed gold in the last of the day's light. Jamie and Harry were giggling and holding hands. April lay with her head on Tom's knee.

"We'll miss you man" Tom said "When do you get back?"

"July 1st" he said, readjusting his open shirt

"Yuki, that's in about three weeks' time, you made it sound like years" April said, sitting up to glare at him.

"Yes, well, I can't afford to go for any longer, and I can't leave you clowns for too long can I?" Yuki said, rolling his eyes, but grinning.

Tom got up to clap him on the back and share the joint he'd rolled. Jamie rolled her eyes and led Harry off to the spare tent.

Later, when Yuki had fallen asleep cuddling his guitar, April shyly pulled at Tom's hand and led him to his tent.

"Are you sure?" he asked her as April wiggled out her skirt. "You want to do it here? In a tent?"

"Yes please," she'd said simply.

TOM

"*D*ad, I did it" Tom told his Headstone.

The Headstone said nothing back. It was possibly in a mood with Tom because he'd only just started to come and visit.

"It was awesome" Tom said, plucking away a weed, "better than a goal, a hat trick even."

He finished picking weeds, then lay on the grave with his arms behind his head, looking up at the sky. He imagined his Dad frozen in time, forever 45, six inches below him. The urge to dig away at the earth between them faded more each time he visited, but never left him completely.

"I hope I did it right, Dad," he confided "I think I did, the second time anyway"

The headstone still said nothing, as Tom told it about April and football, but Tom felt something as he left his words there with him.

"See you Saturday, Dad" he said, patting the headstone softly before walking away, headphones in his ears.

AFTERWORD

So, they all lived happily ever after.

Sort of.

I wanted to give all my characters a happy ending in this book, but I know in real-life it doesn't always happen that way.

As someone who's struggled with some of the issues in this book, I know how scary life can be. I didn't get help for my anxiety for a very long time. It ate up an awful lot of my years and opportunities before I found Doctor Claire Weeks and CBT. I still got better in the end, and my god, am I stronger for it. I've tried hard to put all my pearls of wisdom in this book for you. I sat my GCSE's outside the main hall, on my own and I felt like failure, even though I passed.

Not everyone will make it in life. Some people will choose to find a way out, and some people will always try their hardest to hurt others that they know need help. #Ihateclaire

But I also know this; there is help out there. Whether it's

for anxiety, depression, self-harming, sexuality, or suicidal thoughts, there is help. This book is set back when I was fifteen and we had no internet or mobile phones (GASP!). Now there is help online for all these issues and more.

I would not be who I am without the Smashing Pumpkins, or the Stone Roses. To those of you who have never heard of them, check them out.

I wanted an awful lot from this book. I wanted to write about my experience with anxiety. I wanted to create strong female characters. We need them now more than ever (can you imagine what Kate and Jamie would make of Donald Trump?!) and I wanted to be fifteen again. I wanted to write a love story, because there's nothing quite like falling in love for the first time, whether it's with a boy or a girl or both at once.

We all deserve a Tom or April in our lives.

ABOUT THE AUTHOR

Ericka Waller is a wife and mum to three small children (age not size; she is a wife to her husband, not the kids).

Once, BC (before children, not Christ), she worked in PR and currently has a weekly column in The Argus, 'A Fresh View'. Her blog, Mum In The South, describes her life as a mother and occasional person in her own right. Her blog won the Brits Mum's Brilliance in Blogging Award in 2013.

When not writing or wrestling with her children and/or husband, she can be found walking the dog, bidding for retro furniture on eBay or hiding in the bath with a book.

Supernova is Ericka's second book, the first 'Confessions of a Mother Inferior' released in 2015, was an instant hit with readers and was compared by Amazon as the spiritual follow-up to Bridget Jones.

ALSO BY ERICKA WALLER

Confessions of a Mother Inferior

Printed in Great Britain
by Amazon